NO LIGHT BUT THE STARS

OTHER TITLES BY LINDSAY JAYNE ASHFORD

Through the Mist

A Feather on the Water

The House at Mermaid's Cove

The Snow Gypsy

Whisper of the Moon Moth

The Woman on the Orient Express

The Color of Secrets

The Mysterious Death of Miss Jane Austen

Frozen

Strange Blood

Where Death Lies

The Killer Inside

The Rubber Woman

NO LIGHT BUT THE STARS

A Novel

LINDSAY JAYNE ASHFORD

LAKE UNION
PUBLISHING

This is a work of fiction. Names, characters, organizations, places, events, and incidents are either products of the author's imagination or are used fictitiously.

Published by Lake Union Publishing, Seattle
www.apub.com

EU product safety contact:
Amazon Media EU S. à r.l.
38, avenue John F. Kennedy, L-1855 Luxembourg
amazonpublishing-gpsr@amazon.com

ISBN-13: 9781662536083 (paperback)
ISBN-13: 9781662536090 (digital)

Cover design by Kimberly Glyder
Cover image: © Melome / Shutterstock; © Aron Filep, © Anna Gorin / Getty

Printed in the United States of America

To Ivy

Prologue

Cornwall, England, 1606

The field at the edge of the woods is feathery white on this bitter morning. A Shrovetide frost crept across the grass in the hours after midnight. But there is no trace of it on the body lying beneath the rowan tree. The flesh is still warm. The blood pools in a cleft at the roots, clotting on rotten leaves and withered berries.

It will be an hour or more before the discovery is made. By dusk the whole village will know. Well in advance of the announcement at the Sunday service, the whispering will begin. The irony will not be lost on these countryfolk—the body was found beneath the same tree people plant beside their cottages to keep witches away.

There are some who cross their fingers behind their backs when they enter the church. The angels and demons who once crowded the walls have been whitewashed out, making the place feel cold and unwelcoming. Those who cling to the Catholic ways believe that coming here now puts their very souls in peril.

After the service, gossip flies around the churchyard. Murder or accident? No one can be certain. One member of the congregation holds her tongue. She is the only one who knows what really happened. No doubt it was wrong to kneel at the altar, giving silent thanks that a life has been snuffed out. But for her it feels like a deliverance.

People are saying that the bishop is demanding an investigation, that such a death will cast a long shadow. She fears that it will point toward the farmhouse that lies within sight of the bloodstained tree.

If they come asking questions, she must make sure they never find what links her to the marks on the corpse, nor discover what she did in the days before that fateful encounter in the woods.

It will mean saying goodbye to the best friend she has ever had. And hiding a secret that has nothing to do with the body under the tree—but would just as surely send her to the gallows.

Chapter 1

1941

In London nowhere felt safe. When darkness fell, you were too scared to close your eyes. And in the morning, you dreaded what the daylight would reveal. I remember the smell of charred wood and powdered brickwork, the crunch of broken glass underfoot, the bleak gardens and naked trees—as if winter had arrived too early.

We took to bedding down on one of the platforms at King's Cross because it was too dangerous to spend the nights aboveground. Crammed in with hundreds of others, we'd be woken by the first train hurtling in through the tunnel, sending a wave of fuggy air over the slumbering bodies.

One morning we made our way back from the station to find that the roof and most of one wall of our place had been demolished. The door of the safe was hanging open, and the cash had been looted. Whoever had stolen the money had also taken the van we used to pick up stock from Covent Garden.

We were the lucky ones, though. People on our street had been killed. An old couple who couldn't face spending nights underground had died when the rafters fell onto their bed. We knew them. They used to come into the shop to buy apples. I think that upset Mum more than anything. It took the shock of what had happened to a different level. That night she decided we should move to Cornwall.

I had no idea how far it was from London, nor that it was the farthest west you could go in England without falling into the sea. But I knew that Lowartha Farmhouse was old—older than America, Mum's sister had written. Ancient but sturdy. And the only place the Germans had targeted in that part of Cornwall was an airfield more than seven miles away.

"I hope there won't be any ghosts." Mum looked up from Aunt Ruby's letter with a brittle smile.

I shrugged. Said nothing. Because I'd been talking to a ghost every day for the past year of my life. I knew what it felt like to be haunted. If we moved to Cornwall, I would be taking my ghost with me.

We left London on a chilly afternoon in the first week of November. There was a man selling roasted chestnuts at the entrance to Paddington Station, and we bought some just to warm our hands.

"I don't know what your father's going to say." Mum turned to me as the guard slammed the carriage door shut. We were breaking our promise. Closing the business and running away. When Dad was captured at Dunkirk the summer before last, he'd written from the prison camp in Germany, urging us to keep the shop open, reminding us that the Rookwoods had been selling fruit and vegetables for three generations.

"We can't tell him. You know the rules, Mum—we can't say anything about how bad things are."

"He'll know something's happened, though, won't he?"

I nodded. We couldn't avoid telling him we were moving to Cornwall. Otherwise, his letters would never reach us.

"I hate having to keep things from him." Her eyes searched my face. "We always promised each other: no secrets." Sometimes, when she looked at me like that, I was convinced she knew. *No secrets.* How many times had I echoed those words with my fingers crossed behind my back? It still hurt to remember. Not the deceit, but the aching loss of what had made me tell all those lies.

"We'll have to say we've moved to Cornwall because they need help on the farm," Mum went on. "That's not a lie, with all the young men going to fight. I expect you'll be digging up turnips and potatoes instead of taking your pick of them at Covent Garden. It's going to be rough, dirty work: not the kind of future your dad and me ever imagined for you."

"I won't mind that," I said. "If I'd been born a boy, I'd be on a battlefield by now."

Mum sucked in a breath. "You're a good girl, Violet. God knows what I'd do without you."

A good girl. The words mocked me. I dreaded to think what she'd call me if she knew what I'd kept from her. And as for the future, it was something I never thought about. All my plans and dreams were snuffed out that first night of the Blitz.

Twilight closed in as the train headed west. Out of the window there was nothing but darkness. In the old days, we might have seen the flicker of distant bonfires: On this night, all over Britain, people would have been gathering around towering piles of wood, eating burnt sausages and cinder toffee, cheering as the effigy of Guy Fawkes caught alight. But those days had passed. Now, fire was what you dreaded, what you ran away from.

The image of that ritual burning stayed with me as the train chugged on through the night. As a child, I'd loved sewing Dad's old clothes together and stuffing them with straw to make the Guy. It had been fun, going from door to door with the other kids, pushing the masked mannequin in a wheelbarrow, collecting pennies to buy toffee. And when the lumpy body was hurled onto the bonfire, we would dance with glee. Remembering that part made me shudder. That silhouette, so like a real man, against a wall of flames. What a gruesome thing to celebrate.

Just six months ago, the Houses of Parliament had burned. With bombs and incendiaries, the Germans had succeeded in doing what Guy Fawkes had tried and failed to do with gunpowder three centuries earlier. Mum said that if, by some miracle, we won this war, it should be Hitler's effigy we burned on Bonfire Night.

I must have dozed off as the train rolled through the West Country. At one point we had to change to another one with only two carriages, but I was too tired to notice the name of the station. It was very quiet when we finally stepped off the train. Like that eerie silence before a bomb hits. I tensed up, listening for the crackle of antiaircraft guns or the death wail of a siren. But all I heard was the chug of the engine as the train pulled away.

It wasn't easy in the dark, but Mum found us a taxi. The farm was only a couple of miles from the station, but it was slow going along twisty roads. I remember the taxi inching along a bumpy track before stopping, the hoot of an owl as we climbed out, and the black fingers of enormous trees silhouetted against an inky sky. Then the disturbing smell of woodsmoke as the door of the farmhouse creaked open.

I recognized Aunt Ruby, Mum's sister, even though I hadn't seen her since I was twelve years old. She told me to go and get warm while she showed Mum around. I didn't move. The thought of going near a fire made my heart race. But she took me by the arm and propelled me into the sitting room.

He was standing there by the hearth—the man I'd been told to call Uncle Felix. He was older than I'd expected—much older than Aunt Ruby, with thinning hair and pouches under his eyes.

"Miss Violet Rookwood!" The way he greeted me made me sound like a member of the royal family. He beckoned me over to the fireplace. I took a step forward, trying not to look at the flames.

His eyes ran over my body as he asked me if I'd ever been inside a house as ancient as Lowartha.

"I . . . I don't think so."

"The foundations were laid in 1420. I don't suppose you know which king was on the throne then?"

"Er . . . Henry the Fifth?"

His mouth turned down at the corners. "So, they do still teach history in those London schools."

I could have told him that I'd learned it from English lessons, not history. From reading Shakespeare. But the way he was looking at me put me off.

He launched into a speech about the number of oak trees it would have taken to construct the place, and the method by which the massive flagstones that lined the floor would have been transported from a nearby quarry. I couldn't take it in. All I could hear was the hiss of the burning logs.

I tried to quell the sick feeling in my stomach by fixing my eyes on the wooden beam above the fireplace. There was a mesh of angry scratches gouged into it, as if a mischievous child had been let loose with a penknife.

"Ah! You've spotted them!" He reached out, rapping his knuckles on the wood. "I don't suppose you know what they are?" He tapped the side of his nose, as if letting me in on a great secret. "Witch marks. Carved into the wood by Catholics to stop evil spirits coming down the chimney."

He said I should touch them. *For luck.* When I hesitated, he took my hand and rubbed my fingertips across the puzzle of lines. His skin was clammy, and he pressed down hard. He must have felt me shiver as I pulled away. He laughed. Thought he'd spooked me. I let him think that, if he wanted to. Evil spirits? How could anything that came *down* the chimney be more frightening than what went up it?

The logs flared and spat, pitching me back fourteen months in time to the night people in London call Black Saturday. It was the night the Thames ran red with rivers of fiery sugar from the blazing warehouses, and rum barrels exploded in the Royal Docks, shooting flames high into the sky.

It had been my idea to go to the wharf. We were lying there, among the sacks of tea and rubber and spices, when the first bombs fell. It was the place where he bought supplies for his family's shop: cloves, turmeric, cumin, coriander, ginger, and saffron. I used to love the sound of the names as he reeled them off. And the scent of them on his skin.

That Saturday afternoon we'd hidden in the wharf until everyone had gone home. We'd made a bed among the sacks, not knowing the docks were one of the most dangerous places in Britain, about to come under attack for the first time. The newspapers didn't report how many were killed that night. The Germans were not supposed to know. I should have been one of those who died. Me, not him.

Taslim's name was not on the lists stuck on the lampposts on Brick Lane. Because he wasn't born in this country, he didn't seem to count—as if he were invisible, as if he had never existed. But to me, he was everywhere. In the birds, the wind, the trees. I talked to him—and sometimes I heard his voice.

If Mum suspected there was someone, she never asked. If she caught me glancing across the street to the Taj Stores, she never remarked on it. Perhaps it simply never occurred to her that I could fall in love with someone as different to us as mangoes and guavas are to apples and pears.

Mum had warned me that we were going to have to work hard at the farm to earn our keep, that I'd be digging up vegetables instead of haggling for them at Covent Garden Market. If she thought I was too soft for that, she was wrong. I was willing to dig until my hands were raw if it would make the nightmares stop.

Chapter 2

We had a late supper in the farmhouse kitchen. Bread and cheese—which was far better than it sounded, because everything was homemade and there was plenty of it. The tub of cream cheese Aunt Ruby brought out of the larder was an object of wonder to Mum and me. We hadn't seen anything like it since rationing came in. There was even jelly to spread on top of the cream cheese. It was unlike any I'd ever tasted. Mum asked what it was.

"Rowan berry. From the trees at the edge of the woods. They were bursting with fruit this year." My aunt smiled. "You know I'm not much of a cook, but I could see them across the field—red as blood—and it seemed wicked to waste them. I got the recipe from a woman at church."

She pushed the bread toward me and asked if I'd like the last slice. I hesitated. "What about Uncle Felix?" He hadn't followed us to the kitchen.

"Oh, he's gone to bed—he's got to be up at six to do the milking," she said. "That's one of the jobs he could do with some help with." She looked from Mum to me. "We had a cowman up until last month, but he's gone to fight now, like the two farmhands we had working here. I've been trying to help, but it's not easy, with Billy to see to. I can generally manage the evening milking, but the mornings are impossible."

I'd only ever seen photographs of Billy. He was a little over two years old, born just after the war started. We'd longed to see him, but with Dad away, we couldn't leave the shop.

"I'll help." I glanced at Mum, who shot me a grateful look. I didn't mind getting up at the crack of dawn. I was used to it. Covent Garden Market opened at 5 a.m.—and if you wanted the best produce, you had to get there early.

"Thank you, Violet." Aunt Ruby smiled. "It'll be a long day for you, I know, working in the fields on top of that. But at least you'll have plenty to eat."

My eyes roved around the kitchen as I helped myself to the bread. There was a range cooker against one wall, fed with wood stacked in a huge basket in the corner of the room. A large sink with a single tap above it was on the opposite wall. Blue-and-white cups and plates were arranged on an old wooden dresser. But something else caught my eye—something I had never seen in a kitchen: a gun, resting on two hooks on the wall, just above head height. I didn't know much about firearms, but it looked like a double-barreled shotgun.

Aunt Ruby caught me looking at it. "Best give it a wide berth," she said. "He keeps it loaded—in case of foxes. We used to have a dog that kept them away, but it went lame, and Felix had to shoot it."

I couldn't look at Mum. We'd had a dog when I was a child, and it had been run over by a milk wagon in the street outside the shop. We were all devastated, but it hit Mum hardest. She said we could never have another one because she couldn't bear the pain of losing another pet.

"Do you get a lot of foxes here?" I could hear the tremor in Mum's voice.

My aunt misinterpreted it for fear. "Don't worry, Pearl—I doubt you'll see one. But they can come prowling around the farmyard at this time of year. They're after the chickens—they won't hurt you."

I'd seen the odd fox slinking around the alleyways of Covent Garden in the gray predawn light. To me, they were magical creatures;

shy, inquisitive, but never threatening. The idea of Uncle Felix blasting them with a shotgun was as horrible as the thought of him executing the dog. It was a salutary reminder that we were in Cornwall now, not London. And life was going to be very different.

~

It was close to midnight when we went to bed. My room was at one end of the house and Mum's at the other. There were two staircases in the farmhouse. To get to my room, you had to walk through the dairy, where the cheese and butter were made.

There was no electricity, so I had to take a lighted candle up to the bedroom. I must have flinched when Aunt Ruby passed it to me because she asked me what was wrong.

"Oh, just tired," I said. "I think my arm's gone to sleep—I've got pins and needles."

I held it at arm's length as I made my way through the farmhouse. I hated candles. Anything with a flame made panic surge in my belly.

The dairy felt chilly after the warmth of the kitchen. In the flickering light, the great rounds of cheese stacked on the shelves glowed like Halloween lanterns.

The candle guttered and almost went out as I opened the door at the foot of the staircase. I'd brought a flashlight with me to Cornwall, but it was still in my suitcase. I hadn't realized just how much I was going to need it.

I couldn't remember living in a house without electricity. From what Aunt Ruby had told us, most people in this part of the country lit their homes with lamps and candles and cooked on wood-fired stoves. She said they were luckier than most people in the village because they had a tap in the kitchen. The majority had to draw their water from a well. There was no bathroom in the farmhouse, though—just an outdoor privy next to the pigsty in the yard. She'd smiled at the look on my face when I heard that. She told me I wouldn't have to go down there at night, as there was a chamber pot under my bed. And for washing, she'd left a bowl and a jug of water on the dressing table.

When I entered the bedroom, I almost lost my balance. The wooden floorboards sloped away from the door. Walking across them felt like stepping onto a boat. I grasped the metal rails of the bed and stood still for a moment, afraid of dropping the candle. Then I spotted my suitcase lying in a corner of the room. I crouched down and set the candlestick on the floor, then crawled across the boards. Rummaging through the clothes in my case, I found the flashlight. I felt a wave of relief as I switched it on. Moving back toward the bed, I blew the candle out. The smell of it lingered as I shone a beam of light around the room.

It was unlike any place I'd ever slept in. A sloping ceiling rose above the foot of the bed, with a great wooden beam running across its whole length. Other beams formed a series of rectangles in the wall beside the bed. Touching one, I could feel the rough grain of the ancient tree from which it was hewn. There were cracks in the wood here and there. Not surprising, I thought, that the effort of holding up these walls for so many hundreds of years had taken its toll.

A single window was screened by curtains with a pattern of rosebuds. There was a slight gap between the panels of fabric. Instinctively I reached out to pull them together. In London, it had become second nature to block out any light that might escape from a window at night. We'd painted the glass black as a backup to drawing the curtains. They hadn't done that at the farmhouse. Probably they weren't so worried about enemy planes in this part of the country. That should have made me feel safer; should have helped me to settle down and get a good night's rest. But it didn't.

Lying in bed, I could feel a cold draft coming through the window. When I shone my flashlight on it, I spotted a place on the wall where the plaster had crumbled away, leaving a crevice where it met the frame of the window. I rummaged in my suitcase for a stocking and stuffed it into the hole.

It stopped the draft, but I still couldn't settle. I thought of Mum, sleeping on the other side of the house. It seemed so strange, going to bed alone, because we'd slept alongside each other every night for months and months on the underground platform at King's Cross. It had been uncomfortable, noisy, and claustrophobic, but there had been so much comfort in having her beside me.

I wished I had something to read. All my books had been destroyed by the bomb that had fallen on our building. I could have bought a magazine at Paddington Station, but I'd been too worried about getting safely out of London to think about it.

I closed my eyes and willed myself to drift off. Instead of counting imaginary sheep, I tried working out how many generations of people had lived under this roof since the house was built. Five hundred years, roughly, with, say, four generations per century. That made twenty generations altogether. Impossible to imagine. Some of them might have been born in this room—and, very likely, several had died in here.

A sudden noise made my eyes snap open. I could hear a scratching sound. It sounded like a twig brushing against the window, but it wasn't coming from that direction—it came from somewhere behind my head. I sat up in bed and twisted around, half afraid that something was about to drop onto me. I fumbled for my flashlight. As I shone the beam onto the wall, the noise stopped.

It had to be some creature, I decided. A mouse, perhaps. I lay down again and closed my eyes. We'd had an invasion of mice in the shop once. I'd set traps for them, baited with cheese, but the cunning little creatures often managed to dislodge the lumps and eat them without getting caught. Taslim had given me a slab of *barfi*, the sweetmeat they sold in his family's shop. He showed me how to mold it into sticky balls that wouldn't come off the traps. Mum was thrilled with the result and wanted to know where I'd got the bait from. I'd had to make up a story about it being something they used at Covent Garden to keep vermin away from the fruit.

As I turned over in bed, the scratching noise started up again. I felt my skin prickle. What if it wasn't a mouse?

I hope there won't be any ghosts. Mum's words came back to me in the darkness.

"Taslim." I whispered his name; tried to imagine him lying beside me, telling me not to worry. His face appeared on the backs of my eyelids. We had a silent conversation, in which he told me that there were bound to be mousetraps at the farm and tomorrow I could work out the best place to set one.

I must have dozed off for a while, because I had a dream about him. Whenever he came into my dreams, they turned into nightmares. In this one he was trapped inside the wall of the bedroom, trying to claw his way out. I woke up, my heart pounding against my ribs. For a moment the scratching behind my head made me believe he really was there, frantic to get out.

Breathe in. Count to four. Breathe out. Repeat. I let his voice fill my head, willing it to drown out the scratching. But I couldn't see his face. My mind's eye was filled with an image of the fireplace in the room downstairs, of the strange marks scratched into the wooden mantel. *"Witch marks . . . To guard against evil spirits."* Was that what I could hear? Evil spirits trying to invade this house?

Telling myself I was letting my imagination run away with me didn't help. I tossed and turned until the luminous fingers of my watch told me it was time to get up for the milking.

~

The stairs creaked as I made my way down. Opening the door at the bottom, I almost tripped over a large black cat. It hissed at me before jumping onto a shelf and settling itself between two rounds of cheese. Presumably it was kept in the dairy to deal with any mice that ventured in. That probably explained the noise I'd heard last night: A mouse might well climb upward to escape the cat.

I shivered as I made my way through the dairy. It was much colder than the rest of the farmhouse—like an enormous larder. I could hear the lowing of cattle and the clatter of hooves outside. I switched off my flashlight and pushed open a door that gave on to a cobbled yard. It was before sunrise, and the sky was gray. I could just about make out the figure of Uncle Felix, who was herding the animals into the milking shed. He had a long, whiplike stick in his hand, which he flicked at the bony flanks of any cow that strayed out of line. When he caught sight of me, he beckoned me over. I stepped gingerly across the yard. I could smell what the cows had left in their wake, but in the semidarkness it was hard to see where it lay.

"Boots!" he shouted over the noise. "In there! Put them on and roll up your sleeves."

I dodged past one of the cows, narrowly avoiding being squashed against the door as it lumbered through. The inside of the milking shed was illuminated by paraffin lamps hanging from hooks in the low tin roof. There were several pairs of rubber boots lined up against one wall. All of them bore dried-on smears of what I'd already trodden in. I took the smallest pair and kicked off my shoes, afraid to unlace them in case an animal trampled me while I was looking down.

Uncle Felix was guiding each cow into a stall. Wooden barriers divided one animal from another. Once they were inside, he tethered them with a rope. I could hear them munching on the hay stuffed in racks along the wall.

"Fetch me a bucket!"

I looked where he was pointing. He already had a bucket hooked over his arm, and I wondered why he needed another one. But his brusque manner put me off asking questions.

"That one's for the milk," he said as I put the bucket down beside him. "This one's for cleaning the udders before you get started." He scooped a wet rag from the bucket he held and wrung it out. I watched as he sat astride the low wooden stool and reached under the belly of the cow. "Make sure you wipe off any muck and hairs." He grunted as he moved his arm. "Don't want any of that dropping into the milk."

I felt queasy at the thought of it. But I told myself it was not so very different from washing soil off potatoes and carrots before putting them on display in the shop.

He dropped the rag into the bucket of water and got to his feet. "Now you can have a go." He gestured to the stool. "Put the clean bucket underneath, then take the top of the teat between your thumb and your index finger. Make sure you've got a tight grip, then start squeezing with your other fingers."

The smell of the cow's body filled my nostrils as I leaned in. It shifted one of its back legs as I reached for the teat, almost knocking the bucket over. Instinctively I moved backward and nearly fell off the stool.

"Never let them think you're frightened." He sounded cross. "Go on. Try again."

My fingers trembled as I found the teat. I grasped the top, then started pumping away with my other fingers.

"I can't hear anything," he said. "Is it coming out?"

I lowered my head, trying to see if anything had landed in the bucket. "I don't think so," I mumbled. I felt heat rise to my face as I tightened my grip.

"You're doing it wrong!" I heard his boots scuff the ground as he squatted down behind me. Suddenly his arms were around my body, his hands on mine. The shock of him pressing against me made me flinch. I could feel his breath against the back of my neck.

"Calm down, city girl!" He laughed as I ducked my head away from him. "Didn't think you'd be up to the job . . . got to show you how it's done!"

The pressure hurt so much I thought he'd break my fingers. I could hear the spurt of the milk hitting the metal bucket. I wanted to shout, to yell at him to let go. But I clamped my mouth shut. *City girl.* That rankled. I might have been born and bred in London, but I'd been hefting sacks of vegetables since I was nine years old. I wasn't going to let him get the better of me.

After what seemed like an eternity, he released his grip. But he remained behind me, trapping me against the cow's flank. "Just keep going now." His voice sounded gruff, hoarse. "I want to see you fill that bucket."

It took less than ten minutes to extract the milk, once I'd got the hang of it. He didn't stay there the whole time. After a couple of minutes, I felt him move away from me. When I took the bucket out from under the cow, he was standing by the door.

"I'll leave you to it, then." He looked me up and down, as if he were assessing an animal at a cattle market. "Pour the milk into the churn over there." He sloped off across the yard. I emptied the bucket, glad that he was gone. Then I counted the cows munching contentedly on the hay. There were ten of them. It would take at least an hour and a half to milk them all.

My stomach rumbled as I moved the stool to the next animal. But I was damned if I was going to give in before I'd finished the job.

Uncle Felix. He didn't deserve that title. No one should behave that way, let alone a man who was married to your aunt. I was never going to call him that again.

~

I could hear a child's voice as I made my way back through the farmhouse to the kitchen. Tired though I was, I quickened my step at the thought of seeing little Billy.

Never having had a brother or sister, I'd been excited when Mum told me I was going to have a cousin. I understood why we couldn't go and see him, but I'd asked why Aunt Ruby couldn't have brought him to see us. Mum said it was too dangerous. The bombing hadn't started when Billy was born, but babies and children were already being evacuated from London. So, we'd had to make do with the photos Aunt Ruby sent.

Through the open door I glimpsed a chubby face smeared with porridge. Billy was sitting in a high chair, both hands immersed in the bowl in front of him, chuckling as he tried to tip it over. Mum sat beside him, shaking her head as she reached for the bowl. But she was chuckling, too, and it lit up her face. I couldn't remember the last time I'd heard her laugh.

"Oh, isn't he gorgeous!" I pulled up a chair on the other side of him and was greeted by a sticky hand making a grab for my hair.

"Sorry, Violet," Aunt Ruby called across the kitchen. "He's a little monkey!"

"It's okay." *Better than what I've been trying to keep out of my hair all morning.* I didn't say it out loud. It would have sounded as if I were complaining. I wondered if she knew that her husband had left me to do the milking all on my own; wondered if she knew how he behaved when she was out of sight. She was so young. Only eight years older than me. And she was beautiful. As a child, I'd envied her long black hair, wishing mine was that color instead of mousy brown. Why on earth had she married a man like Felix?

"Bacon and eggs all right for you?" I heard the sizzle of fat as she dropped a slice of meat into the frying pan.

"That would be lovely. Thank you." The scent of the frying bacon made my mouth water. I reached to stroke Billy's dark curls.

"You must be starving, love," Mum said. "I didn't realise it would take so long. I should've come to help. Where's Felix? Isn't he coming for his breakfast?"

"He's gone shooting rabbits," Aunt Ruby called over her shoulder.

I glanced at the wall on the opposite side of the room. The gun was gone.

"Rabbits!" Mum lifted Billy out of the high chair and onto her lap. "What does Daddy want *them* for?" She addressed the question to Billy in a high, singsong voice as she wiped his hands. "Going after little bunny rabbits, when he's got all these cows and pigs and chickens . . ."

"It's an excuse to spy on the Italians, really." Aunt Ruby didn't look round. She was cracking eggs into the frying pan.

"I beg your pardon?" Mum and I glanced at one another in blank amazement.

"They come to the farm every day now. Prisoners of war, from a camp up at White Cross. They're helping with the sugar beet harvest."

"Prisoners of war?" Mum echoed. "Aren't you worried they might escape?"

"They're watched all the time." Aunt Ruby flipped the eggs and bacon onto a plate and brought it over. "And they have big red circles on their jackets and trousers. You'd spot them a mile off." She sat down next to me. "I've been working with them, taking Billy out to the fields with me. He loves it—just runs wild. And they're not a bad bunch. They love little kids. Some of them have got children back in Italy. They make such a fuss of Billy." She dug into the pocket of her apron and pulled out a packet of *Woodbine*. She glanced at me as she put a cigarette in her mouth. "You don't mind me smoking while you're eating, do you?"

I didn't dare say yes. It was her house, after all.

"Felix doesn't like it, though." She struck a match and lit her cigarette, inhaling deeply before turning away from me to blow out a plume of smoke. "He's jealous, I think, because they're all younger than him." She turned back to me. "He wants you to take over for me. Wants me to stay at home like a good little farmer's wife." She rolled her eyes.

"But they're enemy soldiers, Ruby!" Mum gaped at her sister. "Violet's barely out of her teens, and they'll soon see there's no ring on her finger. What if . . ."

"Don't worry, they can't do anything." Ruby grunted a laugh. "There's a man with a gun standing over them all day."

"All the same, I'd rather it was me out there than her." Mum huffed out a breath and drew Billy closer as he tried to wriggle off her lap.

"But you can't do that, Mum," I said. "All that bending and lifting—it'd bring on your . . ." I trailed off. We never called it by name because she was embarrassed to talk about it. A prolapsed womb was the medical term. My fault, that. Along with lifting sacks of vegetables when she was expecting me.

"You'll be fine, Violet." Aunt Ruby flicked ash into a chipped saucer. "Honestly, I'd far rather lift sugar beets than be stuck here churning milk and peeling potatoes." She cast a sweet smile at Mum. "But at least I'll have you to keep me company, Pearl. And Billy loves you already!"

Mum glanced at me over the top of Billy's head. "But won't it be too much for you, love, doing the milking and then having to work in the fields?"

"I don't think so." I felt tired enough to drop. The sleepless night and the morning in the milking shed had taken their toll. But hard work was what I'd expected; what I wanted. If I was too exhausted to think, so much the better.

I turned to Aunt Ruby. "Just point me in the right direction when I've finished my breakfast, and I'll get started." I tried to make my voice sound bright. And I told myself that working with a bunch of prisoners couldn't be worse than working with Felix.

Chapter 3

While I waited for Aunt Ruby to find suitable clothes for me to wear for working in the field, Mum took me outside to show me the front of the farmhouse. Arriving in the dark, I hadn't appreciated how enchanting it was. With cream-colored walls and exposed timbers, it looked like something from a fairy tale. Even though it was November, there were still one or two flowers on the climbing rose that framed the front door. The scarlet blooms stood out like drops of blood against the pale walls.

The square windows had a grid pattern of metal between the small panes of glass. I counted nine windows altogether, twinkling like eyes in the early morning sun.

"Have you ever seen anything so beautiful?" Mum turned to me with a dreamy look in her eyes. "Aren't we lucky?"

I tried to smile in lieu of a reply. Of course we were lucky. Coming from London to a place like this was like being pulled out of hell and set down in heaven. But unbeknown to Mum, there was a snake in this paradise.

Aunt Ruby appeared at the front door with an armful of clothes. She handed them over, along with a stout pair of lace-up boots, and I went upstairs to put them on.

The bedroom was still in darkness because I hadn't opened the curtains when I got up to do the milking. The room flooded with light when I drew them back. Climbing onto the bed, I peered out of the window at the farmyard below. I could see chickens, some rusty brown, others speckled black and white, pecking about among the cobblestones. Beyond that was the rough pasture where the cows grazed after being turned out with empty udders.

The pastureland gave way to woodland. As my eyes ranged over the line of trees, I caught a flash of blue. Craning my neck, I saw that it was the sea—just a sliver of it—lying far below the hill on which Lowartha Farm sprawled. I couldn't see much else from my window. The sugar beet fields must lie beyond the trees.

Climbing off the bed, I undressed in the far corner of the room, just in case anyone walking through the farmyard should look up. The idea of Felix catching sight of me in my underwear made me shudder. I hung my clothes up behind a long curtain that concealed a space in the wall. It was the same wall that the scratching noise had come from. When I finished my day's work, I planned to investigate that cupboard for signs of mice.

Looking in the mirror, I made a face. The dungarees were meant to be baggy, but they drowned me. I was going to have to roll up the legs and put a safety pin in the straps to stop them from slipping off my shoulders when I bent down. At least the boots were a good fit, though. Lucky that I had the same size feet as my aunt.

I rummaged in my suitcase for the little tin that contained hair clips, earrings, and safety pins. It was something Taslim had given me, with an image of an elephant in gold and jewel colors painted on the lid. The little compartments inside were intended for spices, and if I held it to my nose, I could detect faint traces of the fragrance they'd left behind. I did that every time I opened it, because it brought the memory of him back so vividly.

I wondered what Taslim would say if he could see me in these clothes. I'd been in my work outfit the first time he'd set eyes on me—but it had been a relatively smart grocer's coat with the insignia of the shop embroidered on it. And he had been wearing an Indian tunic that came down past his knees, with matching trousers. We had smiled shyly at each other across the street before disappearing back inside our shops. The next time we saw one another, he had given me a little wave.

"Stop it!" I hissed the words to myself as I straightened up. Remembering those days was like picking at a scab. It had been pure torture, looking across at his shop day after day, knowing that he wasn't there. That was one thing I no longer had to endure now that we'd moved to Cornwall.

"Are you ready, Violet?" I heard Aunt Ruby calling up the stairs. "I've got the tea brewed for you to take out to the field."

The tea—in two large canisters wrapped in towels—had to be loaded onto a wheelbarrow. Ruby instructed me to push it down the farm track until I passed a barn with a sagging thatched roof. There I would fork right and carry on until I reached a road. I was to cross that, then go through a gate that opened onto the field where the men were working. I hoped I would remember her directions.

It was tricky getting the barrow across the cobbled yard. As I trundled it past the pigsty, the stink of the animals filled my nostrils. Next to that were the stables, where the heavy horses were kept. They snorted as I clattered by. Once I'd opened the gate to the track, the pushing became easier.

Rounding a bend, I lost sight of the farmhouse. I could see nothing but grass and trees and grazing animals around me. I stopped for a moment to rest my arms. All I could hear was the munching of sheep and cows and the distant call of a bird flying over the woods. It felt unreal, this peace, this absence of any loud, harsh noise. I was used to bombs and sirens and antiaircraft guns. I wondered how long it would take for these countryside sounds to seem normal.

Soon I reached the old barn. The thatch was green with decay. It looked as if it might collapse in a strong wind. I remembered to turn right where the track forked, and before long I reached the road. On my right, where it sloped downhill, I could see the village. A square church tower rose above a cluster of roofs—some of slate, some of thatch, like the barn. I would have liked to go and explore the place, but there was no time for that. The tea would go cold if I didn't get on.

Crossing the road, I felt a surge of apprehension. *They're not a bad bunch.* Aunt Ruby's words echoed inside my head. But they were enemy soldiers. Men like them were killing men like Dad. I pictured a gang of wild-eyed monsters who would murder me with their bare hands, given half a chance. But my aunt had said that they loved children, that Billy spent hours out in the fields with them. It was hard to square those two images.

I took a long breath as I went to open the gate. I mustn't show how nervous I felt. The men were at the top end of the field, some bending, some kneeling on the ground. Others held baskets, whose contents they tossed onto the back of a wagon. Even from this distance I could see the circles on their uniforms. They stood out like big red suns on the backs of their jackets.

A single British army officer stood near the wagon, watching over them. Some of the prisoners had tools in their hands—forks or trowels, by the look of it—for prying the vegetables out of the ground. I wondered what would happen if the men turned on the officer. Surely, they could overpower him if they wanted to, even though he had a gun. It occurred to me that there must be a degree of acceptance, that perhaps they found this a better option than fighting Hitler's war.

Dad's face came into my mind's eye. His letters to us were heavily censored, so it was impossible to know how he spent his days. I thought that, given a choice, he would probably be glad to work outdoors like these men, rather than being cooped up in a cell. Thinking of him made the backs of my eyes prickle. I blinked hard and pushed the wheelbarrow forward. It stuck in a muddy rut. I was never going to get it up the field—the men would have to come and get the tea.

I waved, trying to attract the attention of the man in charge. He didn't notice me at first, but one of the prisoners did. He gestured to the guard, who glanced my way. At the sound of a whistle, the prisoners downed their tools and walked in single file across the field. They stopped several feet away, eyeing me curiously.

The guard came up behind them, his rifle slung over his shoulder. He was around my dad's age. Most of the prisoners didn't look much older than me. They weren't the terrifying mob I'd pictured. They could have been barrow boys from Covent Garden Market or stevedores from the London docks.

The guard doffed his cap as he approached me. "Good morning, miss. Is Mrs. Trudgen unwell?"

I shook my head and explained that I was Ruby's niece, come from London to help on the farm. He nodded, asked for my name, and then gestured to the men, who formed a queue beside the wheelbarrow. Each produced a tin mug from the pocket of his jacket, taking it in turn to fill it from the canister.

I felt awkward, standing there watching them, so I set off across the field to where the baskets were stacked. I heard a wolf whistle, followed by a ripple of laughter. I didn't look back. Just carried on walking. But I could feel my cheeks burning.

I heard the guard shout a warning to whichever prisoner had done it: no lunch if it happened again. I hated getting that kind of attention. It felt like a betrayal—as if I were open to attracting someone new into my life. I wasn't. That part of me had shut down.

To my relief, the guard suggested that I should work some distance away from the prisoners. I took two baskets to a different part of the field. It would take a long time to fill them both, so I wouldn't have to go back and forth to the wagon, passing the line of men.

I needn't have worried, though. They seemed to lose interest in me once they were back at work. To my surprise, they started singing as they pulled up the sugar beets. I had no idea what the song was about, but after a while, I found myself humming along to it.

I lost track of time as I knelt on the soft earth, head down, pulling up the pink-tinged globes and tossing them into the baskets. Getting up, I felt slightly dizzy from lack of sleep. I told myself I just had to keep going, that I could have an early night once the work was done—and that, hopefully, I'd be so exhausted that no amount of mouse activity in the wall would keep me awake.

I was supposed to stop at midday to go and collect lunch for the men, but Mum and Aunt Ruby surprised me by bringing it themselves. Billy was riding on his mother's shoulders. She let him down, and he ran across the field toward the Italians. I watched as one prisoner, then another, took him by both hands and whirled him around, making him laugh so much his little face went as pink as the sugar beets.

Mum came over to me when Ruby started giving out the sandwiches. "Cheese and pickle," she said, handing over a waxed cloth parcel tied with string. Then, dropping her voice, she said: "I just wanted to make sure you were all right."

"I'm fine, thanks," I nodded.

"They're not giving you any trouble?" She glanced over her shoulder at the men queuing up in front of her sister.

"Not at all." I took a big bite of the sandwich, surprised by how hungry I felt. No point telling her about the wolf whistle, I thought. It would only make her worry.

"I don't think she likes being cooped up indoors." Mum huffed out a breath. "Look at her! In her element, isn't she?"

Aunt Ruby was smiling at the Italians as she handed out the food. The guard hovered close by, but he was smiling, too. It seemed she had created a rapport with the prisoners, even though she didn't speak their language.

"I can understand your Uncle Felix not wanting her working with them," Mum went on. "It's only natural. No self-respecting man would want his wife mixing with the enemy. She's a lucky girl. He idolizes her—and he wants to keep her safe."

Your Uncle Felix. I took another bite of my sandwich. I was afraid my face would give away how much I disliked the man. I could only imagine what Mum would say if she knew what had happened in the milking shed. There was sure to be a row if I told her. We would have to leave—and we had nowhere else to go.

"I have to admit I was worried when she wrote to say they were getting married," Mum went on. "It was his age that bothered me: There's twenty years between them."

That made him older than both my parents. "A big gap," I said, looking down at my jacket, flicking away an imaginary crumb of cheese.

"It was all so quick. One minute she was out in Singapore, having a high old time. Next thing we knew she was married, with a baby on the way, and moving to Cornwall."

"Is that where they met? In Singapore?" My knowledge of my aunt's life over the past decade was hazy. Mum had told me that she'd gone abroad to work as a children's nanny but hadn't revealed much else.

She nodded. "He was stationed there, in the Royal Navy. From what she said in her letters, life was just one long round of parties. He proposed just a couple of months after they met. Then he got the news that his brother had been killed in an accident on the farm, so they had to come back here."

I glanced over Mum's shoulder at the Italians. Most had finished their food and were sitting on the ground, smoking. One of them offered Aunt Ruby a cigarette. He leaned in close to light it when she put it in her mouth. It was a simple enough gesture—something you saw every day in London—but somehow it seemed overly familiar. I checked myself. Would I have made that judgment if it had been the guard offering my aunt a light?

"She's fallen on her feet, hasn't she?" Mum's words cut across my train of thought. She hadn't seen what I had witnessed. She was staring into the distance, at the top of the church tower, just visible beyond the edge of the field.

"How do you mean?"

"Living in this place," she replied. "That beautiful house. So quiet and peaceful. To think, I was fretting about ghosts! I had the best sleep in ages last night."

Peaceful was not the word I would have chosen to describe my first night at the farmhouse. I muttered something about how quaint the building was, and how pretty the village looked. I was pleased that she felt happy here in Cornwall. I couldn't ruin that by telling her about my sleepless night and the horrible experience with Felix.

"I might come and help with the milking tomorrow." She smiled. "I was too tired last night to offer, but I feel as bright as a button now."

"But what about . . ."

Mum held up her hand. "I'll be fine. So long as I don't lift anything heavy."

"Well, if you're sure . . ."

"We'd get the milking done in half the time."

I nodded. I wasn't thinking about that. I was thinking that Felix wouldn't dare to touch me if she was there.

Chapter 4

At the end of the afternoon, when the wagon was fully laden with beets, the heavy horses came to tow it away. Felix led them up the steep slope. He cast a supercilious look at the prisoners, who were sitting on the ground, smoking and chatting now that they'd finished their work.

"Ought to get those buggers to pull this lot all the way to Bodmin," he muttered as he hitched the horses to the wagon. "Idle bunch of greasy Eye-ties getting . . ."

I didn't hang around to hear the rest of his tirade. I made my way back across the field, but instead of crossing back to the track that led to the farmhouse, I took a right turn. The sea was to the west, where the sun was going down, and I longed to get a proper look at it.

After a few hundred yards, the road gave way to a muddy path bordered by high hedges. I carried on for a few more minutes, wondering if I was going the wrong way, but then the path took me downhill, and I glimpsed a flash of blue between the branches of the bushes. Soon I reached an open stretch of hillside from where I could see the full sweep of the ocean.

The breeze blowing in from the water had a tang of salt mingled with the scent of seaweed. Down below me was a tiny harbor with half a dozen boats moored up. Men were sitting on the stone quayside, some mending fishing nets, others loading baskets onto the boats.

Beyond them was a narrow channel bordered by sand and rocks. It was the kind of place I could imagine spending a lazy summer day, picnicking on the sand and swimming in the sheltered bay. But even if we stayed here long enough for warm weather, there would be no chance of going in the sea. Metal barriers topped with barbed wire barred the way in and out of the water. Even in such a remote spot, no risks were being taken against the feared German invasion.

I glanced at my watch and decided I'd better head back to the farmhouse. I didn't want Mum worrying. She seemed convinced that something awful was going to happen to me, working alongside the Italians.

As I walked the last few yards, I felt bone weary. I longed for a hot bath, but it was a Thursday, and Aunt Ruby had told us that bath night on the farm was Saturday. She'd described the whole ritual: A tin bath that hung from a hook on the wall of the dairy would be brought into the kitchen, while the water was heated in a huge copper cylinder in the sluice room. The bath would be placed in front of the range and buckets used to fill it—a laborious job that meant the water wasn't changed for each person. Mum, Ruby, Billy, and I would all have to take turns when Saturday night came.

Ruby didn't mention Felix when she told us about this weekly routine. Perhaps he didn't bother with a bath—just washed himself at the kitchen sink. I was glad I wouldn't be sharing *his* water.

I popped my head around the door to say hello when I got back, then went up to my room to get changed. Before going down for the evening meal, I had to get rid of the contents of the chamber pot. There hadn't been time in the morning, and I couldn't put it off any longer.

I carried the pot downstairs, holding the lid on tight in case it slipped off. Then I went out, via the dairy, to the privy at the end of the yard. I could hear the pigs grunting as I unlatched the door. A low stone wall separated their enclosure from the outside lavatory. No doubt each time someone came to use it, the pigs hoped food was on its way.

The smell inside the privy was nearly as ripe as the stink of the pigsty. It was clean enough, with whitewashed walls and a neat wad of newspaper squares hanging from a loop of string—but the toilet was just a hole cut into a plank of wood, with nothing to stop the smell from wafting up and filling the tiny room.

I emptied the contents of the pot down the hole, then went to the tap in the yard to rinse it clean. Sooner or later, I would have to use the privy. The smell was something I'd have to get used to—like so much else about life at Lowartha Farm. Things like that I could handle. But what I couldn't cope with was the prospect of being alone anywhere on the farm with Felix. It was a huge relief that Mum had offered to help with the milking.

He came to the table when we gathered for the evening meal but disappeared without a word as soon as he'd eaten.

"Off to the pub," Aunt Ruby said when Mum asked where he'd gone. "The Farmers Arms, in the village." She shrugged. "He goes there on his bicycle most nights."

She didn't sound annoyed. The expression on her face was one of resignation.

"That's men for you," Mum said.

I gave her a quizzical look. Dad had hardly ever gone to the pub. He used to say he much preferred our company to a bunch of rowdy drinkers.

I excused myself a little while later, saying I needed an early night. I refused the offer of a candle—now that I knew the layout of the house, I could find my way upstairs in the dark.

The cat meowed at me as I brushed past the shelves in the dairy. It had an unusual name: Kuching—the word for *cat* in Singapore, Aunt Ruby had told us. She said the cat reminded her of the strays she used to feed when she lived in the Far East. I tried to stroke it, but it darted off into the darkness.

In the bedroom, I groped on the night table for my flashlight. The first thing I did was to lock the door. At first, the big iron key stuck when I tried to turn it. Probably it hadn't been used for some time. I hadn't thought about locking myself in last night, but after the episode in the milking parlor, I couldn't shake the thought of Felix creeping across the landing in the middle of the night.

I undressed quickly and sat on the bed in my nightdress, listening for the scraping sound that had kept me awake. I couldn't hear anything. But before I got into bed, I wanted to check for signs of mice. I knelt on the rag rug that lay alongside the bed, then moved across the room on all fours, searching for gaps between the floorboards and the walls.

When I reached the cupboard where I'd hung up my clothes, I lifted a frayed corner of the curtain that screened it off. Newspaper lined the floor—presumably to protect it from any mud from shoes or boots stored in there. I shone the flashlight beam across it, searching for droppings. I didn't see any—just a few yellow stains on the paper. I slid it out. It was a copy of *The Cornishman*, dated July 21, 1902. The year Mum was born. I wondered who had occupied this room back then and where they were now.

Looking back inside the cupboard, I spotted a slight gap between the floorboards. Could a mouse squeeze through that? I wondered. I reached inside, and as my fingers came to rest on the floorboard, I felt it move. I pressed harder. The other end tipped up, like a seesaw. I leaned in and shone the flashlight into the space beneath, half expecting to find a nest of mice down there. But all I could see was a mesh of thin wooden poles with a rough sort of plaster holding them together.

As I shifted my weight, the beam of light caught something else. It looked like the corner of a box. Gingerly I lowered my hand into the space and felt around. Grasping the object, I slid it toward the gap and attempted to pull it out. It was heavy. I felt something shift inside as I tipped it up.

A spider scuttled out from underneath, and I shrank back, almost dropping the box back into the hole. Its surface was covered in cobwebs. I disliked spiders even more than mice, but I wasn't going to give up now.

I set the flashlight down and got both hands around the box. Lifting it out, I laid it on the newspaper. Even before I'd dusted it with the edge of the curtain, I could see it was very old. About a foot long and a few inches deep, the front was carved with a pattern of Gothic arches on either side of a black metal lock with an ornate key. Beneath the lock was a central panel with something sinuous carved into it, like a sea serpent. The lid was held on by two long metal clasps with curved ends.

To my amazement, the key moved slightly when I tried it. With a little effort, I got it to turn in the lock. Lifting the lid, I ran my fingers over what appeared to be the cover of a book. It felt like old, stiff leather. Very carefully, I picked it up and carried it over to the bed, where I laid it on the eiderdown. It was held shut by a thong wrapped around it, tied in a knot. The thong was shriveled with age. When I touched the knot, it broke away, and something slid out of the book onto the eiderdown.

It was an old playing card. The image, though more ornate than the type I was accustomed to, was instantly recognizable: the ace of hearts. It felt thicker than a conventional card. Flipping it over, I saw that something had been stuck onto the back of it. It was a miniature painting—a head-and-shoulders portrait of a man.

He had spiky black hair, swept up over his forehead, and a goatee beard. His dark eyes were set beneath fine, sweeping brows, like gulls' wings. He wore a white shirt with an intricate lace collar. The style looked Elizabethan. It was open at the neck, revealing the upper part of his chest, on which a gold chain rested. An earring in the shape of a cross hung from his right ear.

He appeared to be standing in front of something yellow and rippled, like a cornfield. As I brought the card closer to the flashlight, I froze. It wasn't corn. It was a wall of flames.

Chapter 5

Sleep overcame me at some point that night, but it was far from peaceful. Memories of Black Saturday invaded my dreams—of bombs falling, sacks exploding, and the terror of being hurled through the air into darkness.

Taslim was there, walking out of the fireball that had engulfed the warehouse, coming toward me with outstretched arms. But when I went to kiss him, his face changed. It wasn't him. I was kissing the man with the goatee beard and the cross hanging from his ear.

I was still asleep when Mum came knocking on the door. I was late for the milking. Scrambling out of bed, I almost trod on the leather-bound book I'd found in the box beneath the floorboards. I'd opened it last night, but the pages were brown with age, and the writing was in an elaborate script. My flashlight wasn't as powerful as it should have been. Probably it needed a new battery. I was going to have to wait until daylight came to examine the book properly.

I pushed the book and the box under the bed and locked the bedroom door as I went out. For now, it was my secret.

Felix was already in the milking shed, wiping down a cow's udder. "Didn't think you were coming," he called out when he caught sight of me. "Thought I'd pinched those pretty hands a bit too hard!" Then he spotted Mum coming in behind me. His head disappeared under the cow's flank.

Mum shot me a questioning look as I showed her where the rubber boots were kept. "I couldn't get the hang of it yesterday," I said. "He was trying to demonstrate, and he ended up squeezing my fingers by mistake."

She nodded, apparently satisfied by this explanation. It wasn't an outright lie—just not the whole truth. The memory of his breath on the back of my neck made me feel sick.

By the time we'd got our boots on, he'd disappeared. I showed Mum what to do, warning her not to attempt to lift the bucket when it was full. It didn't take her long to master the art of milking, and we were back inside the farmhouse before Aunt Ruby and Billy had come down for breakfast.

I left Mum in the kitchen with a cup of tea. I made the excuse of not having had time for a proper wash when she had woken me up. I *did* need a wash—but it was what I'd discovered last night that had me running up to my room. I could have told her the truth. No doubt she would have been as fascinated as I was by the box hidden under the floorboards. I don't really know why I decided to keep it to myself. Perhaps it was because keeping secrets had become second nature.

I knelt on the rug and peered into the space under the bed. In my haste to conceal them, the book had slid further than the box. Reaching to retrieve it, I was careful not to knock over the chamber pot. As I pulled the book toward me, I noticed something else. The lid of the box was open, and something glinted from within it. When I got it out from under the bed, I saw a coil of delicate chain lying in the corner. I picked it out and dangled it from my fingers. A pendant shaped like a tiny whistle hung from the chain. Although blackened and pitted in places, I thought it was probably silver.

Without thinking, I fastened the chain around my neck, then brought the whistle up to my mouth and blew. The shrill sound made me jump. Incredible that it still worked. It could be hundreds of years old if it was from the same era as the man in the painting. Had it belonged to him?

All I'd been able to make out last night was that the book was handwritten. I hadn't managed to decipher much, other than the letters *CON* at the beginning of the word written on the title page. Picking it up, I clambered over the bed to the window.

There was a dark brown smear on that first page, as if something had been spilled on it. But in the bright daylight, I could see traces of the writing beneath. Despite the flourishes, the script wasn't so different that I couldn't recognize the word.

CONFESSIONAL. It was written in capitals. I turned the page. The paper felt as thick and stiff as cardboard. The writing was small and dense. As I brought the book closer to my face, I breathed in its musty scent. The first thing I spotted was a date. The year was 1606. I stared at it in wonder. What I held in my hands had been written more than three hundred years ago. Slowly I began to decipher the words.

> *The Sixteenth Day of January 1606*
> *In this book, given to me by my grandmother for my birthday, I am bid to record my sins. Since I have no priest to confess them to, she says that setting them down on the page is the only way. The Scripture teaches that to harbour an evil thought is as blameworthy as the act itself. By that reckoning, what arose in my mind this morning surely counts as a sin.*
>
> *I did wish ill upon the new rector of St Columba's.*
>
> *He came upon me unawares while I was out hunting with Phantom. We had done well, my bird and me. I came forth from the woods with three fat rabbits for the table, slung in a sack upon my shoulder. Then I spied a man approaching on horseback. Either he lacked skill with the beast or was using it cruelly, for he kicked it, making it rear up and toss its head. When he drew near, I knew him for Robert Archer, who took up the rectory at Michaelmas.*

Like me, he bore a bird on his wrist. His was but a sparrowhawk, fit for taking pigeons, not for chasing rabbit and hare through woodland, as my goshawk will. Mayhap he took offence that I, a woman, should hold a falcon superior to his own, for his eyes narrowed even as he gave me greeting.

He doffed his hat, revealing brown hair thinned and plastered unto his shining pate, as though painted thereon. His gaze fell from the sack on my shoulder to my girdle. Then his small green eyes slid slowly upward till they did fasten on my bosom. I clutched my cloak about me, shamed at such immodest regard.

The look in his eyes bred unease in me. No Mistress Archer attends him in church of a Sunday. Folk whisper that he seeks a wife to keep his handsome new home in order and minister unto the sick and the poor of the parish, that he is casting about amongst the maids to take his pick.

I wonder what he knows of me. Surely he has heard the tale: how my father, for holding to the old religion and refusing to attend church, was thrust out of the manor house and I, his daughter, with him. Aye, there is no soul in this village ignorant of that story.

I misliked his eyes on me and bade him good morrow, saying I must hasten home. He called after me, warning in tone, that he looked to see me and my grandmother in church come Sunday.

In the pulpit, he makes it plain that he is not the kind to turn a blind eye to those who cling to the old ways. In his sermons, Catholics are superstitious fools, mired in witchcraft. The pope he portrays as the very prince of fiends.

Since the late plot by Guy Fawkes and his fellows to blow up King James, hatred and suspicion of Catholics has increased a hundredfold. I believe he has me down as a soul in peril, the daughter of one in league with the devil.

If that is so, mayhap he deems it his duty to save me. Would that duty stretch unto making me his wife?

The thought of his hands upon me makes my flesh creep. I pray that his gaze will alight upon some other maid who hungers for marriage. But if his will is bent upon me . . .

As I walked away from him, visions did spring within my head: I saw the horse unseat him, casting him headlong upon the stony ground. He lay there, quite still, those green eyes staring lifeless toward heaven.

Was it wicked to conjure such an image? More wicked than the lecherous glances he bestowed upon me?

I crave no husband, least of all him. I would not be ruled by any man's words, nor peril my life in childbirth, as did my mother when she bore me.

Phantom is the only male companion I need or want. He was my father's last gift to me before the king's men stormed our house and dragged him forth in chains, bound for prison. I recall full well his words as he took me to the stable, where my goshawk awaited:

"He's fierce and bold and he shall never lie to thee."

Phantom might fly off across the ocean if he so desired, yet he never strays far from me. He finds food for the table, and when he is lost from my eyes in the wood, the hawking whistle brings him swift back to my side.

What man is so loyal?

The words blurred on the page as an image of the woman who had written them filled my head. My fingers went to the tiny silver pendant.

Could it have been hers? Held to her lips more than three centuries ago? The thought of it made the hairs on the back of my neck stand on end.

And who was the man whose image had been tucked inside this book? From her description of the rector, it was not Robert Archer. Mounting the painting on the back of the ace of hearts hinted at a lover. And yet she had made it very clear that she didn't want a man in her life.

I turned the page, longing to know more about the mystery woman who had lived in this house—and had likely slept in this very room—all those years ago. But a shout from downstairs cut me short. It was Aunt Ruby. The tea was ready to take across to the field. I put the book back into its hiding place under the bed. But I kept the whistle, tucking the chain under my sweater.

~

A strange thing happened as I pushed the wheelbarrow along the farm track. I felt as though something was following me. I thought it might be a rabbit—I'd seen one or two darting out of the hedgerows—but when I glanced around, I saw nothing.

Then I heard a noise that spooked me. It was a long, shrill whistle—identical to the sound I'd produced from the little silver pendant. Looking up, I saw a big bird with a long, forked tail gliding right above my head. The sun lit up its feathers—reddish brown with a flash of white—as it angled away from me to swoop low over the pastureland.

It looked like a hawk, but I didn't know what kind. You didn't see birds like that in London. I watched until it disappeared. Then I remembered the tea. Grasping the handles of the barrow, I trundled on. But the bird appeared again, letting out a piercing cry as I passed the old barn. It seemed incredible that anyone could train something so wild. But *she* had done it. I wished I knew her name.

Suddenly a shot rang out. Instinctively I hit the ground, bringing my arms up to protect my head. Then I heard laughter somewhere behind me.

"No need to panic!" It was Felix.

I scrambled to my feet. He came around the side of the barn, the shotgun tucked under his arm and a sack slung over his shoulder.

"Bloody bird!" he huffed out a breath. "Taking my rabbits!"

"You didn't kill it?" I glanced up at the sky.

"No—worst luck. But I'll get it next time." He patted the sack. "Lucky I was out early—a couple of fat ones in here." He came closer. I saw blood drip from the bottom of the sack. "Have a feel inside. They're still warm."

He went to grab my hand, but I dodged away. "No thanks. I'm already late with the tea for the men. I'd better get on."

"We'll have you skinning them later," he called after me. "I'll show you how."

"No, you won't." I muttered the words under my breath. I would have to speak to Mum before he had the chance to inflict that on me. I probably *could* skin a rabbit if I had to—but I couldn't stomach the thought of him breathing down my neck as he demonstrated what to do. Mum was already worried about how much work I was doing. She would surely take on that task if I asked her to.

I looked over my shoulder when I reached the fork in the path. Felix was a small figure in the distance, walking in the direction of the farmhouse. It occurred to me that he might know the identity of the woman who had written the journal hidden beneath my bed. He'd reeled off facts about the history of Lowartha the night I'd arrived—but I'd been too worked up about the blazing fire to take anything in.

If only he wasn't so creepy. I couldn't possibly reveal what I'd found. No doubt he would insist on me showing him exactly where it had been hidden. It would be the perfect excuse to invade my bedroom.

I shook him from my mind as I concentrated on getting the wheelbarrow across the road and through the gate. The men must have been looking out for me. Some of them waved. This time I didn't march off across the field when they lined up with their tin mugs. I poured the tea for them and nodded a greeting at each prisoner. I didn't smile at them—although some of them did smile at me. I was trying to be civil, that was all. I felt they deserved some respect for their work, whatever the reason they were doing it.

At lunchtime, Aunt Ruby came on her own with the food. She said that Mum had stayed behind to look after Billy, whose latest game was chasing chickens around the farmyard.

We sat together on the edge of the sugar beet wagon while I ate my sandwiches. "What do you make of them?" She was looking at the Italians, who were sitting in a circle on the ground some distance away.

"They're all right, aren't they?" I shrugged.

"Well, more than all right, some of them?" She arched her eyebrows as she took a drag on her cigarette. "Quite fanciable—if fancying them was allowed!"

There were rules about fraternizing with prisoners of war. I'd read a story in the newspaper about a woman in the north of England being fined for simply giving a POW a packet of cigarettes. But something in Aunt Ruby's voice made me wonder if it was her husband, not the government, she was referring to. Felix had stopped my aunt from working alongside these men out of jealousy, according to her. In view of the way he'd behaved toward me, he had no right to lay down the law about her simply helping the prisoners with the harvest. Clearly it was one rule for him and another for her. But had she done something to arouse his suspicions?

I watched her as she went to gather up the wax paper wrappers that had covered the sandwiches. She was casting the odd glance at the prisoners. I noticed one man purse his lips when she looked at him, blowing a ring of cigarette smoke in her direction. From the look on his face, he might have been blowing her a kiss.

Was I witnessing an illicit flirtation? I couldn't say. But what I'd seen triggered a painful memory. Taslim would sometimes blow me kisses from behind the window of the Taj Stores when he thought no one was looking. I would be outside our shop, arranging apples and tomatoes in baskets, or inside, looking out across the street, and the sight of him would set off a surge of desire in my belly.

For the rest of the afternoon, as I pulled up beets, his face floated in front of me. I couldn't help comparing how it had been for us with how it might be for a woman who fell for a prisoner of war. There was no law against what we had meant to each other—but there may as well have been.

~

The setting sun cast an orange glow across the sky as I made my way back from the field. When I reached the farm, I sneaked into the milking shed and unhooked one of the paraffin lamps. I planned to read more of the confessions of the woman with the hawk when I went to bed—and for that, I would need extra light. I felt less nervous about taking a lamp into my room than a candle. The flame was behind glass, and I could control it by turning the wick up or down.

There was no time to linger upstairs before darkness fell. Mum needed my help to prepare the supper while Aunt Ruby got Billy into bed. I stepped out of the dungarees and put on my own clothes before heading down to the kitchen.

As I mashed potatoes to go with the sausages and onions Mum was frying, I found myself wondering how my aunt and uncle had coped before we arrived. I said as much as I reached for butter to mix into the mash.

"They've had girls from the village working here," Mum said. "But they don't seem to stay long. There are better-paid jobs to be had nowadays, I suppose. The last one went to work in a munitions factory in Falmouth, apparently."

I dug a knife into the butter. If Felix had given those girls the same treatment I'd had, it was no wonder they'd all quit.

He didn't appear at the table that evening. Mum put a plate of food in the range to keep warm for when he returned from the pub. Aunt Ruby didn't seem to mind his absence. She laughed as she told us what had happened to the rabbits he'd killed that morning. He'd accidentally left the door to the game larder open, and Kuching had crept in and dragged them off. I laughed with her, glad that I no longer needed to worry about the business of skinning them.

The noise we made must have woken Billy. He wouldn't stop crying, so Aunt Ruby brought him down to the kitchen. I held him while Mum and my aunt did the washing up. I'd never held a child before. I didn't know what to do to stop him from whimpering. In the end I tried bouncing him on my knee, reciting a rhyme Mum had taught me when I was little. It seemed to work. He beamed at me as I repeated the verse, his eyes shining.

The color of those eyes reminded me of Taslim's. They were as dark and shiny as the Egyptian dates that adorned the window of our shop every Christmas before the war. And they had a gentleness that seemed to flow from somewhere inside him. When you looked at him, it was as if you could see his soul.

I wondered fleetingly what a child of ours might have looked like. But I batted the thought away the moment it entered my head. To dwell on it would be pure agony.

It was nine o'clock when I went up to my room. Despite my efforts to banish thoughts of what might have been, grief weighed heavy on me as I climbed the stairs.

My hand trembled as I struck a match to light the paraffin lamp. To my relief, the wick quickly caught alight. I closed the glass door and turned up the flame. Then I stepped back, watching it from a distance, half afraid it would explode and set the room on fire. I had to tell myself that it was safe, that otherwise such a lamp would never be used in a wooden shed full of cows.

When I had convinced myself, I felt under the bed for the box that contained the journal, desperate to escape from my own life into somebody else's. I ran my fingers over the intricate carving on the lid. If it had been created around the same time as the book it contained, it would be Jacobean. The Jacobean box. I liked the sound of that.

I undressed and slid between the sheets, pulling up the eiderdown and propping the book on my knees. With the dim beam of the flashlight augmented by the lamp, it was just possible to read the next entry:

The Twentieth Day of January 1606
I have tried to atone for the sin I committed on Monday. This day I ventured to the rectory with a remedy for Robert Archer's horse, whose leg was sorely strained.

The potion, a strong brew of comfrey, I learned of from a groom who once served my father. He told me he heard of it from the Gypsies who made camp in the wood on the edge of our land. The potion must be massaged into the animal's leg, then a flannel soaked in the same mixture be bound to it.

The rector quailed, fearful the beast would kick him, so I put my own hands to the task. It seemed the poor creature was afraid of him. Once he left the stable, the horse was pacified and I dressed his hurt limb.

When I had done, Master Archer pressed me to take a draught of ale within his house. But I made an excuse to leave, unwilling to be shut up with him. Though a rector he be, I do not believe that the love of God abides in his heart.

The living at St Columba's is his by right of inheritance, my grandmother says. It sits ill with me that a man who has responsibility for the souls of others should hold such office by accident of birth.

He grew peevish when I bade him give the beast seven days' rest for the cure to work, for he had conceived a plan to go hawking with me before the week was out. God grant, for my own sake and for that of his horse, his impatience does not get the better of him.

My flashlight began to flicker. Moments later, it went out. I wanted to read the next entry in the journal, but it wasn't possible with just the paraffin lamp. Reluctantly, I extinguished the light and lay down. I listened for the scratching sound that had kept me awake on my first night. But no sound came from the wall behind me. Perhaps, in moving the box from its hiding place, I had frightened away whatever creature had taken up residence there.

I didn't dream of Taslim that night. It was the woman in the journal who appeared while I slept. She stood by the side of the bed, with the hawk on her wrist. Its eyes were mesmerizing—fiery red with streaks of gold, like twin fires in its enormous head. She said that I was welcome to her bed, that she didn't need it anymore. I started to explain why I'd come to live at the farmhouse, but when I mentioned London, she grasped the whistle on the chain around her neck. Putting it to her lips, she blew a piercing blast, loud enough to wake everyone in the house.

The hawk rose from her wrist, and the sound of its beating wings terrified me. I cried out for help. The bedroom door opened. But the person who came running to my bed was Felix.

I woke up in a cold sweat. Groping for my watch, I saw that it was only just past midnight. Somehow, I had to try to get back to sleep. But my mind was reeling with the images from the dream. I couldn't shake the idea that, in opening the box, I had unleashed the restless spirits trapped inside. On successive nights, both had invaded my dreams. Who were they, the man standing in front of a wall of flames, and the woman whose best friend was a bird of prey?

I tried telling myself that whoever they were, they had died long ago, that they weren't real. But it didn't work. As I turned over in bed, I felt something dig into my skin. I had forgotten to take off the whistle pendant when I got undressed. Was that why she had appeared in my dream? Because I was wearing what had once belonged to her?

I could see her face behind my eyelids; her gaze fixed on me as I lay in bed. And the man, looking out from the painting, his face gentle but determined. It was as if they were hovering around me in the darkness, waiting for the chance to creep inside my sleeping brain.

I went to take the necklace off, but as my fingers found the chain, Taslim's voice came through, like a balm to my troubled soul: *Keep it on. They only want to tell you how it felt to be alive.*

A wave of relief washed over me as I lay back down. And yet it was a strange thing that he had said. Why would they want to tell me that?

I must have drifted off as I puzzled over his message. And, mercifully, I fell into a dreamless sleep.

Chapter 6

It was daylight when I opened my eyes. For a while, I forgot where I was. Then I sat bolt upright, horrified that I'd overslept, missed the milking. I pulled on my clothes and raced downstairs.

Mum was just coming out of the shed when I got there.

"I'm so sorry—I overslept," I gasped. "You didn't do it all on your own, did you? Those heavy buckets . . ." A wave of guilt engulfed me.

"Don't worry—Felix shifted them." She smiled. "I told him he had to stay and help, that he couldn't go off shooting rabbits this morning."

"But why didn't you come and wake me?"

"You looked so tired yesterday, love. I thought you deserved an extra hour in bed."

A shout from inside the shed had us both dodging out of the way of the cows, who were coming out into the farmyard. Felix followed behind, urging them toward the gate. He glanced at me as he passed by. His expression was one of disdain verging on disgust.

Mum didn't see it. She was examining her sweater, which had a smear of cow dung on the right arm. She blew out a breath. "It absolutely stinks! I'd better go and get changed."

Aunt Ruby was in the kitchen with Billy on her hip when we went inside. She asked me to hold him while she got on with making breakfast. "They'll be finishing up in the sugar beet field this morning," she said as she handed him over. "When you're done, I'll take you and your mum down to the village. It's a bit old-fashioned compared to London—not the kind of cafés and shops you're used to—but it'll be a change, at least."

"I'd like that," I said. I wanted to see what St Columb Minor was like—and hopefully I could buy a new battery for my flashlight. I winced as Billy grabbed a stray lock of my hair. I tried to pull it from his grasp, but he let out a wail at being deprived of this new plaything.

"Billy!" Aunt Ruby bellowed over her shoulder as a dollop of lard spat in the frying pan. "Leave poor Violet alone!"

But his little fingers were already burrowing under the neck of my sweater. They closed over the chain that held the silver hawking whistle.

"No, Billy . . ." I turned away as I tried to pry his hand off it. If my aunt caught sight of it, she'd be bound to ask what it was. I was afraid that if I had to explain, she would think me deceitful, taking something that could be valuable for myself.

It wasn't that I intended to keep it forever, but Taslim had said I should keep it on. Now it felt like a lucky charm—something that had summoned him when I needed him most.

I'd managed to free the necklace from Billy's grip by the time Mum came back into the kitchen. She held out her arms to take him, drawing him close and kissing his dark curls.

"You don't mind me stealing him, do you?" She beamed at me as she looked up.

I shook my head. It was good to see her so happy. I knew that Mum would have liked to have had another child. But the damage caused by my birth had ruled that out.

I thought of the woman whose words lay hidden beneath my bed. One of the reasons she had given for not wanting to marry was the fear of dying in childbirth, as her own mother had. I wondered how it must feel, knowing that your own life had come at the cost of another's.

I watched Billy pat Mum's head, his face screwed up in a frown as he puzzled over the absence of hair, which she'd tucked away beneath a scarf. How could anyone blame a child for living when its mother had died? There should be no burden of guilt about that—unlike my own guilt about Taslim. Because that had been my fault. I could have prevented it. If only I hadn't arranged that secret date at the wharf.

~

I went back upstairs to get changed before heading off to the sugar beet field. When I drew back the curtain to get my boots out of the closet, I saw something lying on the newspaper that covered the floor. At first, I thought it was a leaf I'd brought in on my boots, but when I crouched down, I saw that it was a feather.

It wasn't soft and downy, like one from a pillow or an eiderdown—it was long and rigid, like the quills people used to write with centuries ago. When I held it in the palm of my hand, it was several inches longer than the space between my wrist and my fingertips. Much too long to have come from one of the chickens in the farmyard.

I took it over to the window and held it up to the light. The color was reddish brown with a white bar halfway along the shaft. Just like the bird that had soared over my head yesterday. Could it have shed one of its feathers when Felix tried to shoot it? If so, I wondered how it could have stuck to one of my boots, and how I had failed to notice something that size when I'd taken them off.

The dream image of the goshawk with outstretched wings flashed across my mind's eye. How weird that the very next day I should find this feather in my room—one that, quite possibly, belonged to a bird of prey.

I wished I knew more about such birds. I had no idea what a goshawk looked like, nor how it differed in appearance from a sparrowhawk—the other falcon mentioned in the journal. The author had said that the rector's bird was smaller than hers and incapable of catching rabbits. Felix believed that the bird I had seen was taking rabbits—so was it a goshawk? Or something else?

I laid the feather on the night table, wondering if Aunt Ruby might be able to enlighten me. I certainly wasn't going to broach the subject with her husband.

Crossing the farmyard a few minutes later, I heard an axe chopping wood. I caught a glimpse of Felix as I went out through the gate. He had his back to me with his arm raised, ready to strike. The way he brought down the axe was ferocious. I had a horrible feeling it was me he was thinking of as the split log flew across the yard.

I turned up the collar of my jacket as I made my way along the track. It felt colder today than the last couple of days. Mum had said that the winters were milder in Cornwall, but it didn't feel much different from London. Not cold enough for a frost yet, but I suspected that might not be far off. A good thing that the beets were nearly all gathered in. I couldn't imagine what it would be like trying to pry them out of frozen earth.

I'd been working hard for an hour or so when I took my first basket over to the wagon. One of the prisoners was emptying his at the same time. I stretched out my arms and tipped back my head, trying to ease the ache in my neck and shoulders. As I did so, I caught sight of the hawk gliding above me. It might not have been the same bird, but it looked identical. It let out that long, piercing whistle.

Then I heard a thud. The man on the other side of the wagon had dropped his basket. He was standing to attention, arms by his sides, looking across to where the guard stood.

"It's okay," I called across to him. "It's just a bird!" Thinking he wouldn't understand, I pointed to the sky.

"Ah!" A smile spread across his face as he spotted the hawk flying toward the church tower. "*Un falco.* We have this bird in my country."

"Oh—you speak English."

"A little," he nodded. "Before the war, I am a waiter in a hotel. Many English people come to . . ."

Another shrill whistle interrupted him. This time it *was* the guard. He motioned to the prisoner to move away from the wagon.

As I watched him go back to where the others were working, I thought it was a shame that I wasn't allowed to talk to the Italians. The man had given me a small glimpse of what his life had been like before the world turned upside down. One day he had been chatting to British people as he served them drinks and food, and the next he was ordered to kill them.

I wondered whom he'd left behind in Italy. A wife, perhaps? And children? I remembered the delight on the faces of the men who had scooped Billy up and swung him around when his mother brought them their lunch. It must be bittersweet, I thought, to hold a child in your arms when your own son or daughter was far away, and you had no idea when or if you would see them again.

My thoughts turned to Dad then. We hadn't heard from him since before the shop was bombed. Mum never talked about the strain of waiting for a letter. The initial relief that he had not died at Dunkirk had given way to unspoken fears about what his German captors might do to him. I hoped and prayed that, like these men, hard work and homesickness were the worst things he had to contend with.

As I went back to digging up beets, the sound of singing drifted across the field. The men were singing a different tune from the one I'd hummed along to on the first day. I wished I could understand the words. But it didn't seem to matter. Somehow, just the sound of it lifted my spirits.

~

Mum, Aunt Ruby, and Billy came to meet me when the beet harvest was finished.

"No point you having to walk all the way back to the farmhouse," Mum said. "We're going to have lunch in the village."

I would have liked to change out of my work clothes for this afternoon off. I thought I looked like a scarecrow in the baggy dungarees and mud-smeared boots. But Aunt Ruby said I looked fine. "No one bothers much about what you're wearing in the countryside, Violet. And the war's made it even less important."

I noticed that she was wearing a smart coat—camel-colored, with a velvet collar. As we set off down the road, she turned to wave at the Italians, who were waiting for the truck that brought them to and from the prison camp.

"They'll be sowing the winter wheat next week," she said. "Goodness knows where we'd be without them."

"I heard one of them speaking English," I said.

"To *you*?" Was it incredulity I saw in her eyes—that any man would bother to make conversation with a ragamuffin like me—or was it something else?

"No—he was speaking to the guard." Lying to her was the only way to sidestep the interrogation I sensed I was about to receive.

"One or two of them do speak English," she nodded. "It's best not to encourage them if they try to speak to you, though."

"I know about the rules," I said. I couldn't help remembering what I'd seen in the field when she'd come with the sandwiches. No words had been exchanged, but the looks some of the men had given her needed no words. Had she encouraged them? She certainly hadn't seemed to mind the attention she received.

Billy started whimpering as we walked down the road. His mother had him by the hand, but he broke away and tried to run off. I caught him as he made for a gap in the hedge. I hoisted him onto my shoulders, which seemed to pacify him.

"Thanks." Aunt Ruby smiled. "I couldn't have his dirty boots anywhere near this coat."

A short distance down the road, we passed a large house that stood beyond a low stone wall. The sign on the gate set off a frisson of curiosity. *The Rectory.* The building wasn't old, like Lowartha, but there was a tumbledown outhouse beside it that looked ancient. I wondered if this could be the place I'd read about in the journal—the house rebuilt since the time the man with the leering green eyes had lived there. Was that outbuilding where the woman with the hawk had come when she brought the remedy for his injured horse?

I longed to get back to the book, to find out how she was going to shake off his unwanted advances. I noticed a cross made of green-and-blue stained glass hanging in one of the front windows. I hoped that whoever lived there now was a better person than Robert Archer.

"That's where we'll be going in the morning." Aunt Ruby pointed farther down the road, to the entrance to the church, whose tower could be seen from the beet field. "St Columba's." She lowered her voice to a whisper. "The rector's a bit of a bore, but his wife's very nice."

The entrance to St Columba's was a Gothic stone arch with steps curving up through the churchyard. I wondered what it must have been like for the writer of the journal, having to climb those steps every Sunday. She had gone to the services out of fear, not because she wanted to. Her life had changed completely because of her father's refusal to come to this place. They had lost their home, and he had gone to prison.

"Felix says that tower is the second tallest in Cornwall." Aunt Ruby had stopped in front of the arch. "There's a lovely set of bells, but they can't ring them now, of course."

"Such a shame, isn't it?" Mum said. "You'd be terrified if you heard the sound of church bells now."

It seemed impossible to imagine the Germans invading this quiet corner of Cornwall. But the sea was within sight of the farmhouse. Any place near the ocean was vulnerable to an enemy landing. And if that happened here, the bells of this ancient church would sound the alarm.

"Let's not think about that, Pearl." Aunt Ruby took Mum's arm and steered her across the road. "Look—there's Felix's favourite place!"

A painted image of a cow hung from a metal bracket on the side of a thatched building. The Farmers Arms looked as if it had been a fixture of the village for centuries, like the church. It stood on the corner of the main street. I could smell beer and tobacco smoke as we walked past, even though the door was closed.

On the way to the café, I spotted a butcher's, a bakery, a fish-monger's, and a post office. The chances of getting a battery for my flashlight looked slim. The thought of not being able to read at night set off an irrational wave of panic. I sent up a silent prayer that I'd find some other shop tucked out of sight down an alley. I *needed* that distraction from the thoughts that overwhelmed me when I tried to sleep.

Billy patted my head as we walked along. It was almost as if he sensed my anxiety and was trying to soothe me. A sudden blast on a horn made me jump. Luckily, I had hold of Billy's legs, or he might have fallen off my shoulders. It was the truck taking the Italians back to their camp. It was stuck behind a delivery van that had pulled up outside the butcher's, blocking the street.

The men waved when they saw us, and we waved back. Eventually the driver of the delivery van appeared and moved it out of the way—but not before letting out a string of expletives. Clearly, he resented having to shift his vehicle for the benefit of a bunch of prisoners of war.

As the truck began to move, I caught sight of the man I'd spoken to earlier. He was looking at Billy and me, and his eyes remained on us as the truck rolled by. It might have been my imagination, but there seemed to be something wistful in that look. I wondered if the sight of Billy on my shoulders had triggered a memory from before the war.

Something flew past my ear as I stood watching. It was a pack of cigarettes, tossed toward the truck by Aunt Ruby. One of the men caught it and the others let out a cheer.

"I owe them." She gave me a wry look. "I've had umpteen ciggies from them since they started working on the farm."

Across the street I could see the driver of the delivery van walking back toward the butcher's shop. I hoped he hadn't seen what my aunt had done. In a small place like this, word was sure to get around. And the story would get twisted in the telling. If Felix heard it, there would probably be repercussions. And knowing what pleasure he seemed to take in inflicting pain, I dreaded to think what he might do to Aunt Ruby.

Chapter 7

The café in the village was crowded when we walked in. There were a lot more women than men, and the tiled walls amplified the volume of their voices. It looked as though Saturday lunchtime was when the farmers' wives got their own back for all the nights their menfolk spent in the pub.

The menu was chalked up on a board above the till. I saw that all but one of the dishes had been crossed out.

"Mushrooms on toast!" Aunt Ruby groaned. "Sorry—we should have got here sooner."

As we waited to be served, I caught one or two of the women eyeing Mum and me. I supposed that in such a small place, strangers were bound to attract attention.

After lunch, I bought a battery in an ironmongery shop hidden away behind The Farmers Arms. I wouldn't have found it if Aunt Ruby hadn't shown me the way. I was tempted to tell her why I was so desperate to get my flashlight working again, but I thought better of it. She would want to see the book and the box that had contained it. And she would be sure to show it to Felix. If that happened, I doubted I would ever get my hands on it again.

There was the whistle pendant, too. I hadn't taken it off since I'd found it. It was beginning to feel like part of me. I didn't like the idea of handing it over. And I told myself that Taslim wouldn't want me to.

I would have liked to get the journal out when we got back from the village, but I needed to help get everything ready for bath night at the farmhouse. First, we had to fill buckets at the pump in the sluice room off the kitchen. I tipped them into the wood-fired copper, the huge cylinder where the water would be heated up. It took dozens of bucketfuls to fill it.

When I'd finished doing that, I went to get the tin bath from the dairy. As I unhooked it, the cat brushed past my legs and meowed to be let out. Through the open door, I spotted Felix in the farmyard. He had an axe in his hand. I guessed that he'd been chopping more wood to feed the fire that heated the bathwater.

I wondered where he would be when we were bathing. I had a horrible vision of him peeping through the kitchen window when I was sitting naked in the water. I would make sure that the curtains were shut tight before I got undressed.

When I carried the bath into the kitchen, Mum and Aunt Ruby were talking about Felix. There was to be a meeting at The Farmers Arms that evening to discuss fire watch duties in the village. The men would compile a list of volunteers who would be on patrol each night in case a bomb fell, and any building caught fire.

"Do you think that could happen here?" Mum's face creased with worry. I looked away as I set the bath down on the floor, fear welling up in my stomach.

"You wouldn't think so," my aunt replied. "We're not close to anything important. But there's no harm in being prepared, is there? That's what Felix says." She grunted a laugh. "If you ask me, it's just another excuse for a long session at the pub."

She and I got started on filling the bath after that. Mum couldn't help with the lifting, so she got Billy undressed and held him on her lap until the water was ready. I said I'd help her bathe him while Aunt Ruby went to do the milking.

Billy took great delight in splashing me when I leaned in to soap his little body. I didn't mind getting wet, and his loud chuckles were infectious. Mum's worry lines had disappeared by the time we got him out.

She asked me to take him into the sitting room and get him dressed in front of the fire while she had her bath. "You'll be all right in there, won't you?" She held my gaze as she passed me Billy's pajamas.

I nodded. It hadn't escaped her notice that I'd avoided that room in the evenings since the first night at the farmhouse. She knew how fearful I was of fire. But now I had no choice. Billy needed to keep warm, and Mum needed her privacy in the kitchen.

The logs crackled as I pushed the door open. There were two armchairs in the room with a low table between them. I sat down on one of them with Billy, still wrapped in a towel, on my lap. I turned sideways so that I wouldn't see the flames as I tried to dress him. But he wriggled so much it was an impossible task. The only way to get his pajamas on would be to lay him down on the hearthrug.

I could feel the heat from the fire as I went closer. Billy rolled over when I put him on the rug, reaching out, clearly captivated by the flickering colors. He kicked out when I pulled him back, fighting me all the way. There was no guard in front of the fire. The thought of him burning himself made my hands shake. It took forever to guide one foot and then the other into the legs of his pajamas. What a useless mother I would have made.

Would have. The voice inside my head spoke in the past tense. I'd never contemplated motherhood when I was with Taslim. We'd never taken any risks because the consequences would have been catastrophic.

Now, I was six months older than Mum had been when she gave birth to me. She mentioned it sometimes, in a not-very-subtle dig at my lack of interest in the opposite sex. I couldn't tell her that it was never going to happen, that there would be no grandchild to cuddle and push about in a pram. That would break her heart. And she would want to know the reason why.

When, at last, Billy was ready for bed, I scooped him up and retreated to the armchair. But he fretted when I sat down. So, I did what I'd seen Mum and Aunt Ruby do, cradling him against my shoulder and walking around the room. I've never had much of a singing voice, so instead of a lullaby, I hummed one of the tunes I'd picked up from the Italians.

After a while I felt his head loll against my neck. I thought he must be asleep, but I was afraid to sit down in case he woke up again. Instead of walking, I rocked gently back and forth on the spot. I felt trapped. But I couldn't escape this room with its terrifying flames until Mum or Aunt Ruby came to take Billy from me.

In the light coming from the oil lamp that hung from the ceiling, I could see the marks on the beam above the fireplace. When I'd first spotted them, they'd looked like a meaningless series of scratches. But as I gazed at them, I began to see patterns. On the left side was what appeared to be the letter *W*—although it looked more like two *V*s, linked to form an *X* in the middle. Further along was the letter *A*, close to another that resembled a capital *M*.

Felix had told me that the marks had been made by Catholics. He'd called them witch marks. But he'd said that they were meant to stop evil spirits from coming down the chimney. That explanation put witches and evil spirits in the same category—as something to be feared and kept away at all costs.

The writer of the book beneath my bed had mentioned witches. She'd had to sit in church each Sunday and listen to the rector bad-mouthing Catholics. *Mired in witchcraft.* That phrase sprang from my memory. That made no sense. Why would they go to the trouble of carving those symbols to keep witches at bay if they had leanings toward witchcraft?

I puzzled over the letters as I stood rocking Billy. The *W*—or the twin *V*s—and the letters *A* and *M*. What did they mean? As I stared at them, I felt him nuzzle my neck. I shifted my position so that I could see his face. His eyes were wide open. He was looking, not at me, but at the space above the fireplace. His gaze traveled up the wall to the ceiling, as if he could see something up there. And then he smiled. It gave me the strangest feeling. It was almost as though he was looking at someone I couldn't see.

Was it possible that Billy was seeing the spirit of a person who had once lived in this house? Could a small child possess the ability to sense something that an adult couldn't perceive? I watched him intently. I saw no hint of any fear in his expression. I found myself wondering if it was something or someone he'd seen before. Could it be the spirit of the woman with the hawk?

Just as suddenly as Billy had woken up, he closed his eyes and lolled back onto my shoulder. A moment later, I heard the door swing open behind me.

"Oh, well done, you've got him to sleep!" It was Aunt Ruby, her voice lowered to a whisper. "We milked those cows in record time. Felix said he was gasping for a beer." She took Billy gently from my arms. "You go and have a bath while I put him down. I'll jump in after."

Mum was bundling her hair up in a towel when I returned to the kitchen. She said she'd get it dry by the fire.

I topped up the water with a couple more bucketfuls and dipped my hand in. It was lukewarm rather than hot—but I thought it would overflow if I added much more. I filled a jug and put it on a stool close by so that I could rinse my hair after I washed it.

I must have had my head under the water when the door that led out to the farmyard opened, because I didn't hear it. I was groping for the shampoo, my eyes closed, when his voice boomed across the kitchen.

"Forgot my ciggies!"

The shock took the breath from my lungs as my eyes snapped open. He was standing there, ogling me. I doubled over, arms across my chest, in a frantic attempt to cover myself.

"Don't worry—I've seen it all before!" He sauntered across to where his jacket hung from a hook on the wall. Dipping his hand into one of the pockets, he pulled out a pack of Woodbine and held it aloft. "See you later!"

I stayed where I was, my teeth chattering, until I could no longer hear his footsteps on the cobbled yard. Then I grabbed my towel, clutching it to me as I scrambled out of the bath.

He'd done it on purpose. I was certain of that.

When I was dressed, I stood outside the sitting room door and called good night to Mum, worried that if she saw my face, she would guess I was upset.

"You mustn't go to bed with wet hair," she called back. It was one of her rules. She was convinced it would cause pneumonia.

"I'm going to read for a while—it'll be dry before I go to sleep."

"Well, take a hot water bottle." Her voice followed me as I went down the hallway. "There's sure to be enough in the copper."

I went back to the sluice room and did as she said. It was comforting, hugging something warm as I went up the stairs. I was still reeling from the memory of Felix's leering face.

There was a good, strong beam from my flashlight now that it had a new battery. I slid under the covers, the hot water bottle under my feet, and opened the journal, more desperate than ever to escape into this other woman's life.

> *The Two-and-Twentieth Day of January 1606*
> *The sin I am nigh to commit is greater than any I have ever contemplated. It is contrary to the law of this land. But in my father's view, it is a noble and heroic act.*

I frowned at the letters on the page, thinking I must have misread the words. *Contrary to the law of this land?* Yes, that was what it said. What on earth was she planning to do? I trained the beam of light on the next paragraph.

This morning a letter came hence, conveyed secretly from Papa's prison cell. In the years he has been under lock and key, we have received only half a dozen letters because he must pay a bribe to his jailers for the privilege.

The one I received today contained but a few lines about his health, what he had to eat, and other such paltry intelligence. It is his custom to write trifling news in common ink on one side of the paper, with matters of importance written in juice of orange on the other, visible only when set to flame. The heat brings out the secret message, rendering the letters a faint brown hue.

I thanked God for my grandmother's absence when I read the message. She would be apoplectic with fear if she knew what he bids me do. There is no need to reveal it. Better that she does not know. Safer for her—and for the man who journeys here.

My father bids me conceal a priest who has fled London, fugitive from the king's men. His name is Jago Carlyon. He is a Cornishman by birth, but he cannot hide amongst his kin as that is the first place his pursuers will look. He is to come to Lowartha in the guise of a shepherd, and I am to hire him for the lambing.

I gasped as I read those lines, amazed at the turn the woman's story had taken. One day her only concern was fending off an unwanted suitor, the next she was being asked to hide a man on the run from the law.

There was one last paragraph to that day's entry:

My heart trembles at such hazard. The punishment for concealing a priest is severe. But he is charged with heresy. The penalty for that is death by fire. Can I refuse succour to one pursued for his faith?

I stared at the page in front of me. *Death by fire.* Just three words. But they had triggered the very memories I was desperate to blot out. I felt beneath my nightdress for the silver whistle, rubbing it between my fingers in a bid to summon Taslim.

Read. I heard him whispering in my ear. *Just read some more.*

I had intended to read just one entry each night, telling myself I must try to ration it. I needed to make it last, this distraction from the memories that overwhelmed me when I tried to sleep. I hadn't expected the contents of the journal to echo the very thoughts I was trying to banish. Why would Taslim want me to read on? With a surge of trepidation, I turned the page.

> *The Three-and-Twentieth Day of January 1606*
> *He is come.*
>
> *I discovered him in the woods, sitting beneath a tree, whittling a staff. In his smock he seemed a shepherd indeed. I was surprised when he rose to greet me, for he is much younger than I expected.*
>
> *When I conveyed him to the hut where he is to sleep, he showed me what he wore beneath the rough garments my father's friends had bestowed upon him. It was a white shirt of the finest linen, with a collar of lace. Around his neck was a gold chain which held an* Agnus Dei*—the symbol of the Lamb of God. He told me that the image inside the glass disc was fashioned from a wax candle blessed by the pope.*
>
> *He asked me if I would conceal this token of his faith, along with his own garments, lest they betray him if the hut be searched. I bided without, in the field, while he undressed himself. When I went to collect his chattels, I saw that he had neglected something: An earring, in the shape of a cross, wrought of gold and set with pearls, still hung from his right ear.*

He smiled, his eyes alight with cordiality, when I remarked that no shepherd would have the wherewithal to purchase such an ornament. The parting of his lips revealed a most perfect set of teeth. His mouth is framed by a neat moustache of raven black and a goatee beard. I told him he should not trim it. He must look more unkempt if he is to pass for a shepherd.

He will spend his days and nights in the field, keeping watch on the newborn lambs. That will arouse no suspicion, for we always hire a man for this task betwixt Christmas and Candlemas. He did not say how long he must bide here.

I abhor what men do to one another in the name of religion. Why must he be hunted like a beast for obeying what his conscience tells him? If he is caught, he will be put to the fire to make him recant. How can it benefit a man's soul to be burnt alive?

My hand trembles as I write these words. I must try to go about my daily round as usual; guard my mouth, for one slip of the tongue could betray him. And I must conceal this book where no one will find it.

My eyes darted back up the page to be sure I'd read it right. The man she'd described sounded just like the one in the painting stuck to the back of the playing card. The chain, the earring, and the lace-collared shirt were just the same; the shape and color of the moustache and beard were identical. And the yellow, rippling background that had looked like a wall of flames . . .

I slid the card from between the pages of the book and directed the beam onto it. It had to be him. Jago Carlyon—the runaway priest. Had the writer of the journal painted this chilling image as a way of remembering him after he was captured and executed?

When I'd first set eyes on the painting, I'd thought that he might perhaps be the man she was in love with. But Jago Carlyon was a Roman Catholic priest, forbidden from marrying. So why had she attached his image to the ace of hearts?

I wanted to read on, but my body wouldn't let me. I must have fallen asleep with the book still open, and scenes from its pages drifted into my dreams. I was walking through the woods at the edge of the farm, and I saw a man sitting under a tree. His head was covered by a hood, but I could see an earring in the shape of a cross in the shadow of the fabric. As I drew nearer, I saw that the tree behind him was on fire. I shouted a warning, and the man lifted his head. For a moment I saw Taslim's face. As I ran toward him, his features melted. He turned into a bird of prey with blazing eyes, rising from the flames to fly away.

I don't know what woke me. The room was lit up because I'd fallen asleep without switching off my flashlight. The first thing that I saw was the feather I'd discovered in the cupboard. It wasn't lying on the night table, where I'd left it—it was protruding from the pages of the journal, like a bookmark. I didn't remember moving it. Could I have done it in my sleep? If not, how had it got there?

Once again, I had the frightening feeling that I had unleashed something that I couldn't control.

Chapter 8

I was coming out of the milking shed the next morning when I caught sight of the hawk. It perched on the branch of a tree, just beyond the gate to the track. It was the high-pitched cry that attracted me—I wouldn't have noticed it otherwise. I almost felt that it had been waiting for me.

The sound triggered a flash of memory. The man I'd dreamed about: Taslim disguised as the priest disguised as a shepherd, turning into a bird of prey as the flames from the tree engulfed him. Panic surged in my belly. The realization that I would never see Taslim again, that I would have to go through life without him, hit me with a fresh, raw clarity. I felt as if I couldn't breathe, as though I were drowning in an invisible ocean.

Aunt Ruby was in the farmyard, Billy on her hip, throwing grain to the chickens. The sight of something so ordinary, so down-to-earth, felt like a lifeline. I sucked in a breath, willed my legs to move forward.

"Shall I hold him for you?" My voice came out croaky. I sounded like someone very old. But Aunt Ruby didn't seem to notice. She handed Billy over, and I breathed in the scent of him as he snuggled against my shoulder. I stood there, just watching the chickens pecking around my aunt's feet, and the feeling of panic began to ebb away.

I glanced across to where I'd seen the hawk. It was still there, perched on a high branch.

"What's that bird?" I asked as my aunt tipped out the last of the grain.

"Where?" She shaded her eyes, looking where I was pointing.

"Up in that tree. It's big and it has a cry like a whistle."

"Probably a buzzard or a kite," she said. "I can't really tell from here." She made a face as she turned back toward the farmhouse. "Don't tell Felix—he'll be after it with his gun."

I stayed where I was for a moment, tracking the bird as it rose from its perch and flew toward me. It circled overhead, once, twice. Probably eyeing up the chickens, I thought. I willed it to go away before Felix spotted it. I could hear him in the shed behind me, shooing the cows out of their stalls.

Billy let out a loud wail as the first animal emerged. As I rocked him, I glanced up at the sky again. To my relief, the hawk was gliding off toward the woods.

~

We set off for church soon after breakfast. It felt strange, putting on stockings and a skirt. It seemed like years since I'd worn anything feminine. I stood in front of the mirror as I put on my hat—a green felt cloche with a matching bow. It wasn't my favorite, but it was the only one to have survived the bomb damage.

Mum and Aunt Ruby were waiting in the kitchen when I came down. Felix wasn't there. As we set off down the track, Mum told me that there was a problem with one of the horses, and he was waiting for the vet to come.

I was glad he wasn't going to be sitting alongside us in church. I wouldn't have been able to concentrate. Every time he opened his mouth to sing a hymn or recite a prayer, I'd have been picturing the very un-Christian way he'd behaved toward me since I'd come to live at the farmhouse.

My own relationship with God was complicated. Mum and I had carried on going to our local church even when sleeping in the underground made the journey to the Sunday morning service a long one. But I had a hard time listening to sermons about love and forgiveness. How could a merciful God allow the person I loved most in the world to die? And how could he forgive me for my part in it when I couldn't forgive myself?

I glanced across at the sugar beet field as we reached the road that led down to St Columba's church. It was strange, seeing it deserted. I asked Aunt Ruby what the prisoners did on a Sunday.

"Well, they don't have to work," she replied. "They're allowed to go to church, but they don't come to ours because they're Catholics. The guard told me that they're building their own little chapel at the prison camp."

That surprised me. I would have thought that they'd have welcomed the chance to rest when they weren't laboring in the fields. What was it, I wondered, that drove them to spend their few hours of leisure building a place of worship?

We entered the church through an arched wooden door with a weathered stone sundial above it. There was a musty smell inside: the aroma of age and damp with a hint of wax polish. The walls were whitewashed stone, which gave it a simple, rustic look. The only embellishments were the stained-glass windows.

We sat halfway down the nave, in a pew on the left-hand side. As people filed in, Aunt Ruby whispered their names. "And that's Dorothy, the rector's wife," she said as an older woman in a burgundy turban hat took a seat in the front pew.

Her husband emerged from the vestry a few minutes later. He had white hair and walked with a slight limp. I noticed that he clung to the rail of the pulpit when he went up to deliver the sermon.

My mind drifted during the service. I thought about the writer of the journal, sitting here with her grandmother, forced to listen to the rantings about Catholics being in league with the devil. I thought of the marks above the fireplace at the farmhouse. The strange letter *W*, like two *V*s interlinked to form an *X* in the middle. And the *A* next to the *M*. They must have been made long before the journal was written, at a time when it was acceptable for people to openly display such symbols in their homes, where any visitor might see them. It would be difficult, but probably not impossible, to erase them when the Catholic faith was outlawed. But no such attempt had been made at Lowartha. I sensed defiance in those letters. A refusal to relinquish cherished beliefs in spite of the venom from the pulpit.

But what I had read in the journal last night was much more dangerous. To hide a priest was a far greater crime than to pay lip service to the new religion while holding to the old ways in private. *The punishment for concealing a priest is severe.* What would have happened to her if the priest was discovered?

My train of thought was interrupted as everyone got up to sing the closing hymn. The rector had a few announcements to make before the service ended. After reading out the banns of marriage for two couples from neighboring villages, he asked if there was anyone in the congregation who could drive a truck and had a few hours to spare on Saturday evenings. Someone was needed to drive a mobile shop to the camp where the Italian prisoners were held. The regular driver had broken his ankle and would be out of action for several weeks.

I glanced around. No one raised their hand. The rector cleared his throat. "Well, if anyone knows of someone who could help, please have a word with my wife on the way out."

"I could do it," I whispered to Mum as we stood to leave.

She gave me a look of blank incredulity. "But you're already working all hours at the farm." She glanced over her shoulder at Aunt Ruby, who was chatting to someone in the pew behind. "Why would you want to give up your Saturday evenings as well?" She clicked her tongue against her teeth. "And besides, it's bath night!"

Exactly. I didn't say it out loud. Selfishly, it wasn't the welfare of the POWs that had triggered the impulse to volunteer. It was the thought of avoiding Felix when I was at my most vulnerable, naked and alone in the bathtub. "I could wash my hair in the sink when I get back," I said. "And the bowl in my room is big enough for washing the rest of me. I don't really need a bath."

I made a beeline for the woman in the burgundy turban hat as we neared the back of the church. I explained that I'd just moved to the village and that I'd been driving a vegetable truck around London for the past two years.

"Goodness, you look far too young to have done that!" She cocked her head, scrutinizing me from behind tortoiseshell glasses. "It would be marvelous if you could help us—but do you think you can cope with these narrow country lanes?"

"I don't think it'd be any harder than going through some of the alleys at Covent Garden Market," I replied.

She smiled. "Would you have an hour or so to spare this afternoon? We could do a trial run to the camp in daylight. That would make it easier for when we go there in the dark next Saturday."

We agreed to meet at three o'clock at the shed behind the church, where the truck was stored.

Mum and Aunt Ruby were waiting by the stone arch when I came out. "Sounds like you've saved the day," my aunt chuckled as I repeated the conversation I'd just had. "Shame we can't use a tractor on our steep fields—you could've driven that, too."

"I just hope it won't be too much for her." Mum cast me an anxious look.

"You worry too much, Pearl—she's young and strong."

Her words rang in my ears as we set off up the hill. I didn't *feel* young. The war had robbed me of that carefree sense that life was an adventure stretching far into the future.

I glanced at my aunt, chatting animatedly with Mum about some person in church. There was a vibrancy about her that made her seem more my age than I was. Despite everything she had to contend with, she seemed lighthearted and optimistic. Was it having a young child that did that to a woman? Like an invisible suit of armor that shielded you from life's slings and arrows? The weight I carried in my heart pressed a little harder at that moment. It was a question I would never be able to answer.

Felix was in a foul mood when he came to join us for lunch. The vet's bill for the sick horse had been a lot more than he'd anticipated. He rattled the tin of cash that was kept on the top shelf of the dresser, underlining his annoyance at the amount he'd had to part with. He ate his meal in silence and left the room as soon as he'd finished, pausing only to take down the gun from the kitchen wall.

"He'll take it out on the rabbits, poor things," Aunt Ruby said as she cleared away the plates. "And then he'll drown his sorrows with a couple of pints at The Farmers."

I wondered how she stood it, being married to a man who, to my mind, had not a single redeeming feature. Was it enough for her, having Billy? He was a perfect angel. But could that allow her to see past her husband's awfulness?

I had an hour or so to spare before I was due to meet the rector's wife, so once I finished the dishes, I headed to my room. I retrieved the journal from under the bed and settled down to read the next installment.

> *The Six-and-Twentieth Day of January 1606*
> *Three days since I have written—but I see no profit in recording my smaller sins since my life is now mired in this mighty one.*
>
> *I take him bread and milk each morning and meat in the late afternoon. We talk, and sometimes the minutes turn to hours. I take Phantom with me in the pretence of hawking to cover my absence. I wonder how long my*

grandmother will go on believing that the rabbits have gone to ground.

I was surprised when he bid me give him leave to stroke Phantom. He told me he once possessed a falcon—a peregrine, as fast and deadly as an arrow. He hunted on land belonging to a baronet in the north of England, where he served as priest. But that life ended when the king's searchers came. The story was all too familiar to me. He was concealed in a secret compartment in the chamber where Mass was celebrated, and of all the men in the house, he alone evaded capture.

He resembles no common priest. Even in his shepherd's smock, he has the look and manners of a fine gentleman. Despite the danger of his situation, his countenance is tranquil, and he never fails to greet me with a smile.

I try to picture him in clerical robes, conducting solemn rites—but my imagination fails me. This confusion between what he is and what I perceive him to be is compounded by his refusal of the title of Father. Nor will he permit "Mr. Carlyon" when I address him. He bids me call him Jago. It was awkward at first but feels less so now. Besides, we have broken all the rules of etiquette by biding alone together in the shepherd's hut, so calling him by his given name is the least of the social transgressions I have committed.

This morning, I made so bold as to ask him why he chose the path of priest. He did not reply to me at first. He looked down at his hands, as if the answer to my question was inscribed upon his skin. He confessed that he was born with a rebel's heart, that his grandfather was hanged in the Market Place at Bodmin for his part in the Prayer Book Rebellion of 1549.

My grandmother has tales of that time. She remembers it, even though she was just a child. Thousands of Cornishmen were slaughtered for refusing the new prayer book forced on our people by King Edward VI. She recalls full well the sight of all those dead bodies lying amongst the stalks of wheat.

I bade Jago tell me why we must cleave to the old ways when Catholic and Protestant pray to the same God. His reply was the same my father gave me—that the new style of worship puts a person's very soul in peril. Then he put a question to me. He wanted to know why, if I was not so determined a Catholic as my father, I was willing to put myself in such peril by concealing a priest.

For a moment it felt as though I were back in the confessional, whispering my secrets through a screen. I found myself telling him that I had spent my whole life trying to win my father's blessing, to recompense for not being the boy he had desired; that although I mistrusted his rigid devotion to the faith—which had brought such disaster on our family—I couldn't allow myself to fail him, however perilous the task he charged me with.

He regarded me in silence and I feared my words had offended him. Then he took my hand and raised it to his mouth. I felt the warmth of his lips against my skin. I tremble as I recall it, for it stirred something in my very core. My flesh burned with shame—and joy. I turned my face away from him, mumbling some nonsense about it being the hour when I must go forth to feed the chickens.

It was a feeling that came unbidden. Was it a sin?

I laid the journal on the eiderdown, a vivid image imprinted in my mind's eye. Pulling the silver whistle out from beneath my sweater, I rubbed it between my fingers. It felt warm from lying against my skin. Once it would have held the body heat of the woman with the hawk.

I pictured her coming back across the fields after leaving the priest in the shepherd's hut. Was she falling for him? She'd said that she wanted no man in her life. But the sensation she'd just described was exactly how I'd felt the first time Taslim touched me.

For weeks we'd simply looked at one another across the street. Then, one day, he came into the shop to buy a cauliflower. Mum had left two minutes earlier for a hairdresser's appointment, and he had seized his chance. I remember chatting nervously as I reached into the basket; something about the price of vegetables being affected by the very wet winter we'd just had. And then I handed him the cauliflower, and his fingers brushed mine. It was only for a split second, but it felt like an electric current going up my arm and down into my body.

I think I knew in that moment that I wanted him. No matter what the risk, I longed to repeat that feeling, to intensify it. As I gazed into his eyes, I felt as if he knew impossible things about me. In the weeks that followed, I began to turn into someone I never thought I could be. He made me feel beautiful, desirable. By the end of summer, we were lovers. It was our secret, and no one must ever know.

What would happen to a woman who fell in love with a Catholic priest in the seventeenth century? In this case, she would be heaping danger upon danger. I picked up the journal and turned the page, almost afraid to read on.

Chapter 9

The Seven-and-Twentieth Day of January 1606
Today I chanced upon Robert Archer in the woods. He was hunting on foot with his sparrowhawk. He looked askance when I bade him good morrow, then revealed that his horse reared up when last he rode it out and threw him to the ground. He was not badly hurt, but he accused me of ruining his animal with my remedy.

I reminded him of my advice to rest the horse until the healing of its leg was accomplished. But he waved my words away and stamped off down the path in a fine temper. I regarded him with a sick feeling in my belly. He had been hunting within sight of the field where the shepherd's hut stands. Mayhap he spied me when I took Jago his breakfast. I cannot recall how long I was within the shepherd's hut. It must have been an hour at least.

When I took Jago his meat, I warned him of Robert Archer. He bade me describe him, and as I did so, I told the tale of that first encounter in the woods, and the way the rector had gazed upon me.

"Does it surprise you?" There was a faint smile on his lips as he spoke. "You are very comely. A man would have to be blind not to have his head turned by you."

His words made me blush. I had to remind myself that he was a priest, that he does not think of women in the way other men do. I told him what folk in the village were saying about Master Archer being on the lookout for a wife, and I said that I hoped and prayed that some other maid would catch his eye.

Listening to my own voice, I feared I sounded proud. In my discomfiture, I sought a way to divert his attention from the matter. I bade him explain to me why Protestant ministers were permitted to marry when Catholic priests were not.

"I have often contemplated it," he replied. "It is a man-made rule, not an edict from the Gospels. Saint Paul decreed that it was better for a disciple of Jesus to be unwed—that is the origin of the idea."

What I asked next was impertinent. It came forth from my mouth before I could check myself. "Have you ever had cause to regret that vow?"

He answered that he had found it arduous in the early days, when he was preparing to be a priest. He said he had been in France, at a seminary in Rouen, and there had been a maid residing in a house across the street from his lodgings. He had seen her every day as he went to and from his studies and had become distracted by her. He had confessed this to the abbot, who had counselled him to scourge himself with a flail morning and night, so that the pain might turn his mind from sinful thoughts.

I asked him if that had wrought the desired effect. He shook his head. "It could not quench the feeling in my heart when I looked upon her," he said. "But then, one day, she was lost to my eyes. A week went by without her presence in the street. And then the abbot summoned me to accompany him to a chapel in the parish where I lived.

There was an open casket lying before the altar. He bade me look upon the body within. It was the maid I loved, her flesh green with decay, her face marked by the pustules of pox. 'Would you have her now?' the abbot said to me. 'Remember this when temptation comes.'"

As he spoke, Jago was gazing upon the embers in the little stove that warms the hut. His tale had rendered me speechless with horror. What wickedness men do in the name of religion. Those were the words crying out within my head.

When he turned to me, his eyes glistened, as if he were battling tears. I wanted to reach out to him, to hold him close. For his comfort or my own—I cannot rightly say. Instead, I made myself rise from the stool upon which I sat. I said I was sorry for his suffering, and I begged his pardon for having to leave while there was still light enough to see my way back to the farmhouse.

As I stepped down from the hut, I scoured the edge of the woodland for any sign that I was being observed. I saw nothing but a bird flying unto the trees to roost for the night. It was a crow, not a sparrowhawk, but walking home, I felt a shiver of fear in my belly.

Jago plans to escape by ship to Spain from Porth harbour. The friends who assisted in his flight from London are going to arrange it. Yet there has been no word from them.

I closed the book, the gruesome picture of what the priest had described seared into my mind's eye. To make someone look at a dead loved one in that state was utterly cruel. What terrible times these people had lived in.

I had never seen a dead body. Not even on that awful night when the world exploded around me. I never found out how I came to be lying in the street unconscious but alive, outside the building where

Taslim and I had been hiding. I woke up in the hospital, miraculously unhurt except for a few cuts and bruises. I remember going around all the wards, looking for him. It didn't occur to me that he might not have survived. It was only when Mum took me home, and we saw the shutters down at the Taj Stores, that it hit me. Even then, I refused to believe he was dead. But when I saw his family filing out of the shop, all dressed in white, there was no denying what had happened: Taslim had told me that in Hindu culture, white was the color of mourning.

Don't think of it. I heard his voice inside my head as the familiar, sick feeling curdled my stomach. No, I mustn't think of it. I glanced at my watch. The meeting with the rector's wife was in less than half an hour. I got off the bed and pushed the journal under it. But when I unlocked the door, I found Felix standing there. He held a hammer in his hand.

"I've come to repair the window. Should have done it before you arrived. It must be very drafty in there." He looked past me, into the room. I'd left some of my underwear lying on the chair. I saw his eyes change as he spotted the bra and knickers. It was the same lascivious look as when he'd caught me in the bath. I moved sideways in the doorway, trying to block his view.

"It's okay, thanks—I fixed it myself," I said.

"How?" He frowned.

"Just plugged the gap. It's fine now." I didn't want to tell him that I'd used one of my nylons. I could imagine him going to the window, pulling the stocking out and running it through his fingers.

I turned away from him and pulled the door closed, locking it behind me. "I'm sorry, I have to go now—I'm meeting the rector's wife at three o'clock."

"'I'm meeting the rector's wife at three o'clock.'" He parroted my words. "Miss Lah-di-dah!" He stood there, tapping the hammer against the palm of his hand, blocking my way to the stairs. The look in his eyes now was menacing. My only other means of escape was through the door to the landing, which gave on to his bedroom.

"What are you doing, Felix?" My aunt suddenly appeared from behind the door I was looking at. He spun around, dropping the hand that held the hammer to his side. He muttered something about needing to repair the window, then he disappeared down the stairs.

"Are you all right, Violet?" I saw real concern in Aunt Ruby's eyes. "You mustn't let him rile you—his bark's worse than his bite."

I wanted to tell her then. Wanted her to know how creepy and mean he'd been since that first morning in the milking shed. But how could I? As his wife, she would no doubt take his side. What if she blamed me for what had happened? What if it caused such a row that Mum and I would be thrown out?

"I'm fine, thanks," I replied. "Just a bit late for my meeting with the rector's wife. I was reading and I lost track of time."

She gave me a nod as I made for the stairs. I didn't know if she believed me.

I was worried that Felix might be loitering in the dairy, waiting to corner me again, but there was no sign of him. I made it to the gate without encountering him in the farmyard. I wondered if he had a spare key to my room and if he planned to go in there while I was out. The thought of him touching my things made me shudder. Then I thought of the journal, tucked away beneath the bed. He wouldn't look there, would he? I told myself that the line he'd given me about wanting to repair the window was just an excuse to come into the bedroom while I was in it, that he wouldn't bother trying to fix it if I wasn't there.

I tried to shut it out of my mind as I walked along the track. I heard a whistling sound somewhere above my head. Looking up, I saw the hawk. On an impulse, I pulled the silver pendant out from under my clothes and blew on it. After a moment of silence, the bird answered. It followed me all the way to the church, perching on top of the tower as I made my way to the shed at the back of the building.

I remembered the dream I'd had of the man sitting under the tree. The face had been Taslim's, but it had changed into the head of a hawk.

Was there a message in that dream? Was the bird I kept seeing the spirit of Taslim in a different body?

He'd told me that, as a Hindu, he believed in reincarnation; that when you died, your soul could be transmitted to any living creature. I'd found it intriguing, even though I couldn't fully understand the idea of a person going through an endless cycle of death and rebirth. It certainly seemed a more attractive prospect than burning in the fires of hell—although I wouldn't have fancied coming back as a slug or a wood louse.

He'd laughed when I'd said that. He'd told me that even those creatures had their place in the cycle of life, and that in his religion, all living creatures were respected; that a body, in whatever form it took, was just a vehicle for the soul. I could have listened to him for hours. His voice had the power to soothe whatever troubled me on any given day.

I thought about what I'd heard him say to me since I arrived at the farmhouse. Was he really communicating with me from some other place? Or was my mind just conjuring the words out of wishful thinking?

"Over here, Violet!" The voice that called to me from behind the church belonged to the rector's wife. She was waiting for me outside the shed, which housed the mobile shop, looking very different, minus the turban hat and the smart tweed skirt and jacket. Now she was dressed in baggy corduroy slacks and a woolen sweater, a headscarf knotted under her chin.

"Oh, you're still in your Sunday best!" She smiled. "Please excuse these old rags—I do like to get comfy after church."

Up close, I could see moth holes in both her scarf and her sweater. But she was more appropriately clad than I was for an outing in the antiquated vehicle I could see through the open door of the shed. I should have changed my clothes. If I hadn't sat reading the confessional for so long, I might have remembered.

"Do you have the keys, Mrs. . . ." I hesitated. I hadn't been told the rector's surname.

"It's Frobisher," she said, "but please, call me Dorothy."

I grated the gears as I attempted to ease the mobile shop out of the shed. That was embarrassing, but it didn't take too long to get to grips with the way the vehicle handled. Soon we were driving through the village, past The Farmers Arms, heading for a road that would take us inland.

"You're doing very well, dear," Dorothy said as I followed her instructions to turn right at the junction. "Tell me, how do you like it at the farmhouse?"

I replied that it was very old and full of character, but living without electricity took some getting used to.

"The original rectory was built at the same time as Lowartha," she said, "but sadly it was pulled down after the last war. I would have loved to have lived in the old place. I used to be a history teacher—I'm fascinated by ancient buildings."

I told her about the marks above the fireplace, wondering if she might be able to explain their meaning.

"Oh, those sound like Marian marks," she said.

It was a phrase I hadn't heard. I asked her what it meant.

"It refers to symbols of the Virgin Mary," she replied. "They were a way of showing that the family remained true to the old religion, the Catholic faith, even though outwardly they embraced Protestantism," she said. "The double *V*, made to look like a *W*, stands for 'Virgin of Virgins.' The *A* and the *M* stand for 'Ave Maria.' Both are meant to invoke the mother of Christ as a protector of the house."

"So, they're not witch marks?"

"Who told you that?"

"My aunt's husband."

She grunted a laugh. "I'm afraid that's the sort of twisted story that got passed down over the centuries. It stemmed from a fear of Catholics."

Our conversation was interrupted by the sudden appearance of a bus coming toward us. There was no way it could get past us. I braked hard, then had to reverse until I reached the entrance to a field. There was just enough room then for the bus to get by.

"Golly, that was tight!" Dorothy blew out a breath. "You did wonderfully well."

I felt a glow of pride. I was doing something I was good at. How nice it felt to receive words of praise—and how very different from the spiteful comments I got from Felix.

We drove through a village called Quintrell Downs, and I spotted the railway station where Mum and I had arrived. It had been only days ago, but it felt like an eternity. My life now was utterly different from the one I had led in London.

"Take a left turn here," Dorothy said. "The other way takes you south, toward Falmouth."

"I've heard of that place," I said. "What's it like?"

"It's the biggest port in Cornwall. The Germans dropped bombs on the docks there a few months ago."

My hands tightened on the wheel. "Is it far from here?"

"About thirty miles. I was down there last month with Humphrey. We had a collection of clothes for the refugees. Lots of French and Belgian families fled there when the Germans invaded."

I'd seen refugees in London. I'd often wondered how they felt, discovering that the place they thought would be safe was under constant bombardment from the Germans.

"I do admire them," Dorothy said. "They arrived with nothing, but they're making lives for themselves here. And the local people have been very generous. Of course, the feeling is very different from the attitude toward the Italians. I'd get short shrift if I tried asking for anything for them."

I asked her what sort of things the mobile shop took to the camp.

"Oh, quite a variety," she replied. "Tobacco, chocolate, toiletries—they're the most popular items. And some of the men like to buy books and writing paper, too. Everything we sell is provided by the Red Cross. The men pay us with the tokens they earn from working on the farms. They're not allowed to have real money in case they try to escape."

I thought that they'd be unlikely to get far, with those big red circles on their clothes.

"I feel sorry for the Italians really," Dorothy went on. "They didn't choose this war. They had it imposed on them by Mussolini and his band of Fascists. But not everyone sees it that way. Living in rural Cornwall doesn't tend to bring you in contact with people from other cultures. It's not like London."

I wanted to tell her that Londoners weren't always tolerant of foreigners, either—particularly if their skin was a different color. But I couldn't be sure where a conversation about that might lead. Better to keep silent.

"Have you seen any of the POWs?" she asked. "I know there's a work party going to some of the local farms."

I nodded. "I've been helping them with the sugar beet harvest."

"What do you make of them?"

"Oh, they're fine," I replied. "The guard advised me to work on the other side of the field so that they wouldn't have the chance to bother me. But I don't think they even noticed me after a while."

"Well, I'm glad you've spent some time with them," Dorothy said. "It won't be so strange for you when you go into the camp. One or two might try to get overfamiliar—they're not used to having someone young and pretty bringing them their treats—but I'll be right beside you, and they know I don't stand for any nonsense."

I wondered what Dorothy would say if she knew about my illicit relationship with Taslim—and that our first date had been arranged while I was selling him a cauliflower. But that was then. The last thing I wanted now was any nonsense, as she so quaintly put it.

After about five miles, we came to the prison camp at White Cross, and we drove past a high fence topped with razor wire. We pulled up outside the gates, where an armed guard came out to meet us.

Dorothy wound down the window and explained that I was the new driver of the mobile shop, and we were doing a trial run. Then I had to back into the entrance to turn around. I caught a glimpse of some of the prisoners in the rearview mirror. They must have recognized our vehicle because a couple of them waved.

"Oh dear," Dorothy sighed. She leaned out of the window, looking back at the men, who were coming toward us, calling out. "They're asking us to stop," she said. "The poor things missed out this week because of Albert's accident." She glanced at the guard, who was shooing the prisoners back. "We wouldn't normally do this on a Sunday, but I wonder . . . Could you back up a bit, dear?"

She got out of the van and went to speak to the guard. When she returned, she was smiling. "He says we can have half an hour. Is that all right? You're not expected back at a particular time?"

I shook my head. I had to turn the van around again and drive along the road that wound through the camp until we reached what Dorothy called the mess hall. Word must have spread that we were making an unscheduled visit, because a queue had formed outside.

"We just unlock the back of the van and slide out the shelf," she said. "There's a book to write down what we sell, and the names of the customers. If you can do that, I'll deal with the payments."

The next half hour was a blur. I could barely keep up with recording everything.

"We've run out of chocolate," Dorothy called across to me. "Could you climb in and see if there's another box?"

To access the van's storage area, I had to get back into the driver's seat and scramble over the backrest. It took a while to locate the chocolate among the various cardboard boxes in the cramped space beneath the sliding shelf, but I found it in the end. I emerged from the van to the sound of whoops of delight from the prisoners in the queue.

One of the last men we served was the one who had spoken to me when we were loading our baskets onto the sugar beet wagon. He bought a pad of writing paper and some stamps. As I recorded his purchase, he thanked me.

"My name is Marelli. Francesco Marelli. And your name is Violet, I think."

I looked up, startled.

"I hear Miss Ruby call you that." He smiled. Then he took what he had bought and walked away. When he reached the corner of the mess hall, I saw one of the other prisoners, who was leaning against the wall, step forward and give him a shove, almost knocking him to the ground.

On the way back, I told Dorothy what I'd seen. She clicked her tongue against her teeth. "You get a lot of tension when we're there," she said. "Not all of the prisoners have money to spend—that's the problem."

"Why not?"

"They're given the choice whether to do paid work outside the camp. Some of them refuse on principle—they believe it's wrong to assist British people in any way, because we're the enemy. They say that any Italian who does that is a traitor and will be punished when Mussolini and Hitler win the war."

I shook my head. That certainly explained what I'd seen.

"There have been fights, apparently," Dorothy went on. "It's upsetting. I worry that we're stoking up ill feeling just by being there. But I wouldn't want the men who come to us to miss out. It doesn't seem fair."

It hadn't occurred to me that such hatred could exist among men who all came from the same country. I thought that they would support each other in the distressing circumstances that had overtaken them, all far from home and family. I decided that in the future, when I worked with them, I would try to be as friendly as the guard would allow.

I thought of Aunt Ruby, tossing a pack of cigarettes to the men as they were driven back to the camp. I didn't smoke, but I could buy tobacco for the prisoners if I wanted to. I batted the thought away. I didn't want to end up on the wrong side of the law, like the woman I'd read about in the newspaper.

You don't have to give someone something to make them feel better. Taslim's voice whispered inside my head. Something dawned on me then. I glanced at Dorothy, who was counting the camp tokens as we drove along. She'd given me a feeling I hadn't experienced since arriving in Cornwall. It didn't seem to matter that I was young enough to be her granddaughter. What she gave me was respect.

Chapter 10

It was almost dark when I arrived back at the farmhouse. Luckily, I'd taken my flashlight with me; otherwise I might have lost my footing, coming back along the track.

Mum and Aunt Ruby were toasting bread for supper and wanted to hear all about my trip to the prison camp. I could feel the antipathy coming from Felix as we gathered around the table. He muttered something about me gadding about when I could have spent the time doing something useful on the farm. But my aunt was having none of it.

"Oh, come on, Felix," she said. "Violet works hard enough as it is. And it's hardly going to be a fun Saturday night out, is it, selling ciggies and sweets in a prison camp? You should give her credit for doing something for people less fortunate than us."

"Less fortunate?" He reached across the table for the butter dish and dug his knife into it. "It's their own bloody fault for fighting against us and getting caught."

The rest of the meal was eaten in silence. I got the sense that in defending me, my aunt had stuck her neck out but didn't want to push things too far. I wondered what she'd say if she knew that the only reason I'd volunteered was to avoid her husband ogling me on bath night.

When we'd finished eating, I said I was tired. On my way upstairs, I paused in the living room. There was no fire burning. I guessed that Felix had been too grumpy to lay one. No doubt he would be off to the pub for the evening, leaving Mum and my aunt to keep warm in the kitchen.

I took out my flashlight and shone it over the marks above the fireplace. Marian marks—that's what Dorothy had called them. The letters made sense to me now. It was like a prayer carved into the wood. A prayer for protection that would remain for as long as the house was still standing. It made me feel a bit less uneasy about being in that room, despite the lingering smell of smoke.

When I got upstairs, I ran my flashlight over the underwear I'd left on the chair, and the gap in the wall where I'd stuffed a stocking to stop the draft getting in. There was no sign of anything being disturbed. It was a relief to know that Felix hadn't come creeping in while I was out.

The Jacobean box was exactly where I had left it, pushed far under the bed near the head end. When I'd undressed, I settled down under the covers to read on. The feather, which I'd left in the book, marked the next entry.

> *The Eight-and-Twentieth Day of January 1606*
> *This morning, as I walked through the village on an errand for my grandmother, I spied someone nailing a handbill to the door of the tavern. Folk were gathering to behold it. A man was imparting the message to an unlettered woman standing beside him. The words he spoke are branded in my memory:*
>
> *"A warrant has been issued in the king's name for the arrest of three members of the Society of Jesus, who provided the traitorous advice and counsel upon which every detail of the Gunpowder Plot was decided. They are esteemed no less pernicious to the king and commonwealth than those who have been actors in the main treason itself.*

"Their harbourers will be dealt with severely, without hope of mercy or forgiveness. The names of these men are Oswald Tesimond, Jago Carlyon, and Henry Garnet."

At the sound of his name my heart shifted in my chest. Had I heard right? I edged closer to the door of the inn. Now there came descriptions of the wanted men:

"Tesimond is of mean stature, somewhat gross, his hair and beard bushy and brown. Carlyon is tall and well muscled, with short black hair and a close-trimmed beard and moustache of the same hue. Garnet is . . ."

I did not hearken to what followed. I could scarce draw breath as I traversed the way home.

Is the man I have concealed a would-be assassin? A wolf in sheep's clothing? Did my father deliberately deceive his own child?

My heart tells me not to believe it, that such a man could not be capable of inciting others to such wickedness. But it was there, in black and white. He is named as a traitor. How am I to know the truth?

I stared at the words on the page. *A traitor.* It was the second time I'd encountered that word in a matter of hours.

An odd thing happened as I laid the book down on the bed. I saw them, the woman and the priest, standing beneath the rough wooden beam that supported the ceiling. They seemed to float there, their feet a few inches above the floor. Their arms were outstretched, as if they longed to hold one another, but there was anguish in their eyes.

Just as suddenly as they had appeared, their images vanished. It was as if I had died in that glimmer of time and my soul had joined the ghosts of those who had once lived in this place. I could hear the blood surging in my veins, my heart quickening, as though it were me, not the writer of the journal, who was facing this terrible dilemma.

Turning the page, I read on.

The Nine-and-Twentieth Day of January 1606
I count what happened last night to be no sin. We embraced, that was all, as friends may do in an hour of need.

When I took him his meat, I was inflamed, disposed for an inquisition. I was poised to cast Jago out if I heeded aught to persuade me of his guilt. But he swears innocence of this charge of treason.

He admits that he encountered some of the conspirators, although he disavows acquaintance with the ringleader, Guy Fawkes. His part was to serve Mass when some of them gathered in London, but he heard naught of their plot to plant gunpowder beneath the Houses of Parliament. The other priest present on that day heard confession from the men, but as it is forbidden to repeat what is said, Jago was ignorant of what any of them had on their minds.

The next he heard of them was when the conspiracy was uncovered. London was in uproar then. Folk bayed for the blood of Catholics. He ascertained that he was in great peril when the place where he lodged was searched by the king's men. Had he not fled across the roof of a neighbouring house, he would be in prison now, like the conspirators, awaiting execution.

I bade him tell me how I could be certain that he spoke the truth.

"I have no means of proving it to you," he replied. "But you know that I am Christ's servant. Howsoever I wish for change, for an end to the persecution meted out by this king against Catholics, I could never incite a man to kill him for it."

I yearned to believe him. Words could not recount my perplexity as I weighed his speech. My heart overruled my body at that moment, for I wrapped my arms around him and drew him to me. He did not resist. He clung to me as fast as I held him.

When we parted, he murmured something under his breath. I thought I heard my name. But it must have been a prayer to the Virgin because he crossed himself.

I am very fearful of the consequences of the warrant nailed up in the village. He cannot hide away inside the hut day and night. He must be seen to be watching the newborn lambs; otherwise the farm workers will become suspicious. But anyone walking in the woodland may catch sight of him. Would they recognise him from the description? His beard grows apace, yet his visage is not yet so unkempt as to allay my fears. Tomorrow, I will bring him a leather cap to cover his hair.

Now I must go to church. I will cross my fingers behind my back when I enter, as I always do. This time it will not be for the salving of my conscience, but to summon luck. God alone knows how much I need it.

I closed the book, my mind full of images of armed men roaming the woods around the farm. She could have taken the notice she saw in the village at face value and made the priest leave. He could easily be lying about his role in the Gunpowder Plot. But she saw him through the eyes of her heart.

Was she falling in love with him? Was he wrestling with the vows he had made? What future could she possibly have with a man like that, even if he escaped arrest and execution? Where could they go? Was there anywhere they would be accepted?

These questions swarmed inside my head as I slipped into unconsciousness. Even in sleep, my brain couldn't miss the parallels between what I'd been reading about and the life I'd led with Taslim.

I dreamed of the night we almost split up after a heated discussion about the future. We wanted to get married. But I was too young to do it without my parents' permission. We'd talked about running away to Scotland, where the legal age was lower. We'd both been saving money to fund the trip. But we couldn't agree on what we'd do after that. We couldn't imagine either of our families accepting us as husband and wife. To be together, we faced losing everything.

That row had happened in the summer of 1939. In the weeks that followed, we formed a plan to rent a room in another part of London. Taslim would get work as a waiter at The Dilkush restaurant in Soho, and I would look for shop work. We hoped that, eventually, we would start our own business. But a month later the war started. Dad joined up, and the idea of Taslim and me running away was out of the question. But in my dream, we *did* get married. I wore a white dress, and he wore a golden *sherwani* coat.

I was carrying a bouquet of red roses. But as I threw it over my shoulder, it exploded. Taslim fell to the ground, his wedding clothes covered in blood. As I slipped back into consciousness, grim reality set in. We would never be husband and wife. I had lost him forever.

Over breakfast the next day, Felix barked out my duties for the coming week. The sugar beet field was to be sown with winter wheat. While this was going on, there were fences to be mended. Along with a few of the prisoners, I would be taking out any of the damaged or rotten wooden posts and replacing them with new ones.

"How can you have the POWs doing two different types of work when there's only one guard to watch them?" My aunt frowned as she plopped two fried eggs onto his plate.

"Because *I'll* be doing the ploughing." Felix rolled his eyes. "I wouldn't trust those cowards with the horses. While I'm going up and down the field, I can keep an eye on the ones doing the sowing."

"You'll have to have eyes in the back of your head, then, I should think." She shrugged.

"I'll take the shotgun with me." He grunted as he tucked into the eggs. "Let's just hope they've got some life in them after stuffing their faces with all that chocolate *she* took them yesterday." He glared at me across the table. "Lazy bastards—some of them look as if they'd never done a day's hard work in their lives."

I scraped my chair against the flagstone floor as I got up from the table. That earned me another black look.

"Don't go straight to the field," he called after me as I reached the door. "I'll need your help with the horses."

I had seen the mighty beasts that pulled the wagon, but I'd never gone near them. They were enormous, more like elephants than horses. My stomach flipped over at the thought of standing next to one of them.

When I crossed the farmyard ten minutes later, I could see that Felix was already in the stables. The idea of being alone with him in there filled me with trepidation.

You have a whistle around your neck. It was Taslim's voice I heard as I stood in the shadows outside the door. My fingers went to the pendant. Yes, I could blow the whistle if Felix tried anything. It would certainly give him a shock. It might even bring my aunt running from the farmhouse. But he would probably snatch it from me. I couldn't bear the thought of losing it. And if Aunt Ruby did come to find out what had happened, Mum and I could lose the roof over our heads as well. I would just have to tough it out.

The stables smelled different from the milking parlor. The sweet scent of bedstraw mingled with the pungent aroma of the animals' manure. There were three horses, but one was temporarily out of action because of a problem with its leg. Luckily Felix seemed more concerned with inspecting the injury than paying attention to me. He pointed to a harness hanging on the wall and told me to put it on a black mare called Betsy.

I turned the leather straps over in my hands, trying to work out how the harness went on. The only way I'd be able to reach the animal's head was by standing on a stool. I spotted one in a corner of the stall. I went to fetch it and set it down gently in front of Betsy's left leg. The earthy, dusty smell of her filled my nostrils as I climbed up. She was munching on hay held in a metal feeder attached to the wall. When I reached for her head, she let out a terrific snort. I almost fell off the stool.

"Easy, girl." My hand shook as I went to pat her neck. Out of the corner of my eye, I could see Felix. He had moved away from the injured horse and was sitting on a straw bale, watching me. I was determined not to give him the satisfaction of seeing me fail.

Somehow, I managed to slide the harness up over Betsy's nose without her shaking her head and knocking me sideways. When I'd fastened the strap, I climbed down, my legs trembling. I could feel the horse's breath on my face as I moved the stool away.

"Saddle next!" Felix pointed to a broad leather belt hanging from a hook. "It goes around the belly."

The thought of getting beneath the horse, between its front and back legs, was even more terrifying than touching its head. I looked at the enormous hooves, as big as dinner plates. A kick from one of those would probably kill me. I wondered if Felix was deliberately putting me in harm's way. Did he take some kind of twisted pleasure in that?

My mouth was dry as I positioned the stool next to Betsy's flank. I stood on it for a while, just stroking her, before attempting to put on the saddle. She shifted her back legs, and I felt the stool shake as one leg brushed it. I wobbled a bit, but thankfully I didn't lose my balance. When she settled down, I laid the saddle gently across her back.

The worst part was having to crouch beneath her belly to fasten the buckle. I prayed that she wouldn't kick me while I fumbled below her. When I emerged, red-faced with effort, Felix was leaning against the wall, arms folded against his chest, his lips curled in a supercilious smile.

He quickly saddled the second horse and led both outside. Then he told me to hold them while he put on the traces that attached to a heavy frame with wheels and a sharp blade at the back. After that he went back inside the farmhouse to fetch his gun. He came out carrying it, broken open, over his arm. Aunt Ruby followed him out with the canisters of tea.

"I'll lead the horses, and you guide the plough." He took the reins with his free hand. "Make sure you keep it straight. If they feel it wobble, it'll spook them, and they'll drag you halfway to Bodmin."

I don't know how I managed to keep from veering off the track. By the time we reached the field, my arms were shaking. I felt as though I'd done a whole day's work already, and it was only half past eight.

The prisoners were already there, waiting for instructions. Felix went to speak to the guard while I held the horses. They tossed their great heads, restless after the trek from the stables. I wondered how on earth I would stop them if they suddenly took off across the field.

Some of the men were looking in my direction. I thought they would probably have liked to get closer to the horses, but they weren't allowed to move. The prisoner who had bought the notepaper was one of those looking my way. He gave me a surreptitious wave. I was about to wave back when the guard blew his whistle.

The men were divided into two groups. One lot followed the guard into the neighboring field, where sheep were grazing. Felix told me to go and join them. On the way I passed the man who had waved to me. He gave me a wry smile and a little shrug, as if to say it was a shame we weren't going to be working together.

I wasn't sure what to make of him. Would it be considered overfamiliar, him calling me by my name at the mobile shop? Was he just lonely, missing his family, longing for a smile and a kind word? I thought it was probably a good thing we weren't in the same working party. If his motive was more than just being friendly, I wouldn't have the problem of trying to keep my distance.

As it turned out, I needn't have worried, because none of the prisoners were allowed to get close enough to speak to me. I was given a pot of paint and instructed to walk all along the fences, inspecting each pole as I went. If I found one that needed replacing, I was to mark it with a red blob. Pairs of POWs would then come and dig those poles out while others dragged new ones across the field to put in place.

At lunchtime, Aunt Ruby arrived with the sandwiches. First, she went to the field where the prisoners were sowing the wheat. I noticed that she didn't linger, as she usually did, when the men came to collect their food. She seemed to have one eye on Felix, who had brought the horses to a halt and was loading his shotgun.

He tucked it under his arm as my aunt approached him. No wonder she hadn't seemed her normal sociable self with the Italians, I thought. He looked ready to use the gun if any prisoner showed an interest in his wife.

As I watched, a flock of crows came down and started pecking at the freshly turned soil. Ruby must have mentioned the birds to Felix, who was facing away from them. Suddenly he wheeled around and fired a volley of shots.

I could hear the screams of the crows across the field. They rose in a black cloud. I couldn't be certain whether he'd killed any. He didn't bother to check—just carried on munching his sandwich, as if it were the most natural thing in the world to shoot at living creatures while eating lunch.

I was thankful that the hawk hadn't come to join the feast of worms and insects in the broken earth. The hawk. *My* hawk. I'd begun to think of the bird in that way. I wondered where it was today. I had seen no sign of it so far.

I saw Aunt Ruby turn away from Felix and head to our field. Once again, she seemed standoffish with the men. When one of them offered her a cigarette, she shook her head. She came to sit with me on a pile of fence posts while I ate my sandwich.

"Do you fancy going to the cinema in Bodmin with me tomorrow night?" she asked. "They're showing *Major Barbara.* Your mum said she'd be happy to babysit."

"Oh . . ." I hesitated. The movie had been showing in London over the summer. I hadn't gone to see it because I'd heard it was a love story—the kind of thing I found too painful to watch.

"It's supposed to be very good," my aunt persisted. "Rex Harrison's in it. We could catch the bus from the village and have a bite to eat when we get to Bodmin."

It sounded as if she'd been planning this trip for a while. I guessed she probably hadn't had a night out in ages. And I couldn't blame her for wanting to escape from Felix for a few hours.

"That sounds lovely," I said. "Something to look forward to." I would just have to close my eyes and pretend to nod off if the movie was too upsetting.

To my relief, I didn't have to help get the horses back to the stables at the end of the day. The contraption they'd been pulling was left in the field overnight, so only one person was needed to lead the animals along the track. When Felix said I could go, I shot off through the gate like a rat up a drainpipe in case he changed his mind.

Aunt Ruby caught me by the stairs as I was on the way to my room.

"Don't mention anything over supper tonight about going to Bodmin, will you? It's just that Felix doesn't really like me going out without him."

But he goes to the pub every night without you. I didn't say what I was thinking. Just nodded and carried on up the stairs. But I wondered how my aunt could endure such an existence.

After supper I was eager to get into bed and lose myself in the story in the journal.

The Thirtieth Day of January 1606
Yesterday in church, Robert Archer thundered from the pulpit against the men named in the warrant.

He called them "this bloody band of elusive gentlemen priests," then further denounced them as a species of men who wear hair shirts under their feathers and fashions, who hunt in public and scourge themselves in private.

His voice shook the very walls as he ranted on, accusing Jago and the others of thirsting for murder and teaching Catholics how to lie.

I quaked at his words. I almost fancied that he looked at me as he delivered that final accusation. But Jago did not teach me how to lie. I learned that from my father when I was barely old enough to converse with my elders. For a Catholic, dissembling is a way of life.

Today my grandmother is gone to Falmouth to visit her sister. She plans to stay for a fortnight and may get word of my uncle William while she is there. He has been away, soldiering in the Low Countries, these past two years. Lowartha is his by right of birth and one day, God willing, he will return to oversee the farm.

I cannot imagine what my uncle would say if he knew that I was harbouring a man like Jago on his land. I am glad that my grandmother will not be here if the king's men come looking for him. While she is in Falmouth, she is out of harm's way. But I also have a selfish reason for being grateful for her absence. No longer must I spin a web of lies to cover up my visits to Jago.

He is never out of my mind. When I wake, my first thought is to be with him. In my haste to reach him, I almost spill the milk I take for his breakfast. I know that this is more than mere concern for his safety and well-being. It is more than any maid should feel for a man who can never take a wife. But try as I might, I cannot quell the fever he stirs in me. It is a kind of madness.

The feeling she described was exactly how I had felt about Taslim. I had become utterly obsessed with him, counting the minutes each morning until I caught that first glimpse of him across the street. But the thrill of falling in love went hand in hand with the fear that our romance was doomed, that I was playing with fire. The appalling irony of that phrase still haunted me.

I took the ace of hearts with the miniature mounted on it from its place at the back of the journal. Jago Carlyon's handsome face gazed out from the flames the artist had painted all around him. Had she painted it? What would have been in her mind as she created such an image? Anguish? Heartbreak? It certainly didn't convey any hope of a happy ending.

Chapter 11

The next day, I didn't help with mending the fences. The truck that brought the men from White Cross Camp had broken down, so they had no way to get to the farm. Felix gave me a list of tasks to do in the farmyard and carried on working in the field on his own.

I spent the day mucking out the stables, cleaning the henhouse, and feeding the pigs. Then I helped Aunt Ruby with the afternoon milking so that we could get to the village in time to catch the five o'clock bus.

"I told Felix you were desperate for a night out," she said as we set off along the track. "I hope you don't mind. He might have made a fuss if he'd known it was my idea."

I shrugged. It couldn't make him dislike me any more than he did already.

The bus picked us up outside The Farmers Arms. For the first few miles, it took the same route I'd followed on my test-drive to White Cross. It was already dark when we passed the prison camp. There was no moon, but I could just about make out the rows of huts beyond the high wire fence. I wondered how the men I worked with would spend their evening.

When I asked my aunt, she said she often wondered about that herself. "They like playing football, but I suppose they can't do that now the nights are drawing in. They love to sing. There's a camp choir, now, I think. And they're allowed to have packs of cards."

I nodded. I'd seen some in the mobile shop.

"Did you have a boyfriend back in London?"

The sudden change of subject took me by surprise. "I . . . er . . . not really," I mumbled. "No one special, I mean." It felt awful, denying Taslim's existence. As if I were betraying his memory.

"Well, I'm glad," she said. "It would be hard for you, coming here, if you'd left someone behind."

"Do you miss London?" I was desperate to steer her away from my love life.

"It's been so long since I left that I barely remember it," she replied. "I do miss Singapore, though. I had a fantastic life out there. It was a bit of a shock, coming to sleepy old Cornwall."

For the remainder of the journey, she regaled me with stories of the parties she used to go to in the Far East, and the string of boyfriends she'd had before she married Felix. Listening to her talk, it was hard to understand why she had settled for a man like him. I couldn't imagine him being part of the sociable, fun-loving crowd she'd described.

"What was it that made him 'the one'?"

She rolled her eyes. "He was very charming in those days. Swept me off my feet with flowers, perfume . . . you name it. And I was down in the dumps when we met. I'd been madly in love with a diplomat, but he left Singapore without even telling me. I got a letter weeks later, explaining that he had a wife and children in London but hadn't had the guts to tell me."

I didn't know what to say. I thought of Mum's description of the whirlwind romance with Felix. Had she married him on the rebound? Jumped in too quickly to find out what he was really like?

"Never mind all that—this is our stop!" She got up and rang the bell.

I don't know what I'd been expecting, but Bodmin wasn't exactly pulsing with life. The shops were all in darkness because of the blackout, and the few cafés that were open were dimly lit inside. The one we went to had only one hot dish on the menu, which was leek and potato pie.

I noticed that Aunt Ruby kept looking at her watch while we were eating. I thought she must be worried about missing the start of the film. When we'd finished, she paid the bill and then handed me two shillings.

"I'm not coming to the cinema," she said. "I've got to go and see a friend. I'll meet you outside when it finishes."

"Oh . . . okay." I searched her face. Why hadn't she told me this before? I hadn't really wanted to see the movie anyway and didn't particularly relish the thought of sitting there in the dark on my own.

Moments later we arrived at the cinema. "See you later." She squeezed my arm. I watched her disappear around a corner of the gloomy street, wondering what on earth she was up to.

I had no choice but to go inside and sit through *Major Barbara*. She'd given me enough money for a drink as well as the ticket, so I sat sipping lemonade while the end of the B movie played out.

When the main feature began, I gripped the arms of my seat, steeling myself for what I expected to be an uncomfortable couple of hours. But *Major Barbara* turned out not to be a love story. It was more about religion than romance.

The lead character was a young woman who was out to win souls rather than a husband. One or two lines reminded me of what I'd read in the journal. The idea that nothing was more important than saving a person from eternal damnation felt uncomfortably close to Robert Archer's rants from the pulpit. But the movie was funny, despite all the talk about God. By the time it ended, I'd almost forgotten that Aunt Ruby had lured me to the cinema under false pretenses.

As I made my way out, I wondered about the friend she said she'd gone to see. Could it be a man? Was that why she'd hoodwinked me into this outing to Bodmin?

And then I caught sight of her. A passing car lit up a couple entwined in a shop doorway. I recognized my aunt's red hat. It was knocked slightly askew. From the way they were kissing, it was a wonder it hadn't fallen off her head.

I stepped back into the shadows of the cinema's entrance. My aunt had a secret lover. For me, that was familiar territory. But this was different. She was already married to someone else. Someone with a violent temper. I dreaded to think what Felix would do if he ever found out.

I felt as though I'd stumbled upon something terribly dangerous, something that threatened to explode and blow life at the farmhouse apart. The only thing to do was to pretend that I hadn't witnessed my aunt in a passionate clinch with another man.

She pulled away, blowing a parting kiss to the man as she left him. Then she came across the street, adjusting her hat, looking for me among the people filing out of the cinema.

"Violet! Is that you?"

It was too dark to get a proper look at her face. I wondered how skillful she would be at hiding her guilt. It was something I'd had to practice in the mirror.

"How did you like the movie? You'll have to tell me all about it on the way home. But we'd better hurry, or we'll be stuck in Bodmin for the night."

On the bus, she took out a powder compact that had little lights around the mirror. I could see her reflection. Her bright lipstick was smudged across the skin above her mouth. She rubbed at it with her handkerchief. Then she turned to me, lowering the compact into her lap, its light shining on my face.

I thought I had mastered concealing what went on inside my head, but she must have detected something in my expression that gave me away.

"Oh, Violet . . . What did you see?" I could hear the panic in her voice.

I felt as though my tongue were glued to the roof of my mouth. For a moment I considered pretending I'd misunderstood the question, that she was asking me about the movie, and I could go off on a long explanation of the story in a bid to defuse the situation. But that wouldn't work. She had already revealed too much of herself, in her voice, in the way she was looking at me.

"I saw you and . . . a man." I whispered the last two words. We weren't the only people on the bus. Very likely some of them lived in our village. "When I came out of the cinema, you were there with him, across the road, and . . ." I couldn't finish the sentence.

She glanced over her shoulder. "It's just a bit of fun," she whispered back. "You mustn't read anything into it."

"Who is he?" If I was going to have to cover up for her, I should at least know that much.

"His name's Carlo. He's Italian."

"What?" I thought I'd heard wrong. "A POW?"

"Yes," she hissed.

"But how . . . ?" I trailed off, baffled by this seemingly impossible scenario. "How did he get out of the camp? What about his clothes?" The man I'd seen in the car headlights had been wearing a dark suit. No sign of the big red suns that adorned the prisoners' uniforms.

"I'll tell you when we get off the bus," she whispered.

The rest of the journey passed in uncomfortable silence. When we got off at The Farmers Arms, she grabbed my arm and steered me quickly past the pub. I guessed that she was trying to avoid Felix catching sight of us through the window and coming to escort us home.

"Okay, it's safe to talk now," she said as we turned onto the road that led up to the church. "Carlo's what they call a billetee. He used to work at our place, but then he was sent to live and work at another farm, in a village called St Lawrence. He gets on very well with the family there—eats with them at mealtimes and makes toys for the children. The farmer likes him so much that he lends him a suit once a week so that he can go and have a pint in Bodmin."

"Is this the first time you've met up with him?" I felt as if I were her mother, asking the sort of questions my mum would have asked me if she'd had any inkling of what was going on with Taslim.

Aunt Ruby shook her head. "He's allowed to borrow a bicycle. Before you and your mum arrived, he used to ride over on his evening off and hide in that old barn halfway along the track. He'd wait until he saw Felix heading off for the pub, and then he'd come to the farmhouse."

Part of me was shocked by their sheer audacity. In all the time we'd been together, I would never have dared to sneak Taslim into the rooms above the shop. But Mum and I had ruined Aunt Ruby's arrangement when we came to live here. Now I understood why she'd had to con me into going to the cinema in Bodmin.

"I suppose you think I'm very wicked," she went on. "I know I'd be in trouble with the police if anyone found out. And as for Felix . . ." She blew out a breath.

"I don't think you're wicked," I said. "I know I haven't been here long, but I can see how tough things are for you, running the farm and looking after Billy." I was tempted to say what a nightmare it must be, being married to a man like Felix; to tell her about the repulsive way he'd behaved when no one was looking. But I sensed that that would only make things worse. Instead, I asked if she regretted marrying him.

"He's changed since we came to live here," she said. "When we were in Singapore, I never saw that side of him—the mean, bad-tempered side. Life out there was so much easier. Then, suddenly, he found himself having to be a farmer, and before we knew it, the war broke out."

"It must have been a strain for both of you, losing the farmhands, having to manage everything on your own."

"It was. But it's harder on him. I didn't realise what had happened to him in the last war until it all came out in a blazing row we had just after we moved here. His ship was torpedoed by a German U-boat, and a piece of metal went flying into his head. He was lucky to survive. But he said he's never been the same since. He gets these black moods and can't shake them off. I've tried to be understanding, but it isn't easy."

I took her arm and squeezed it as we walked up the track. What she'd told me explained a lot. I suppose it should have made me feel more sympathetic toward Felix, but like she'd said, it wasn't easy.

"You won't say anything, will you," she whispered as we crossed the farmyard.

"Mum doesn't know, then?" I whispered back.

"I can't tell her. She's being so brave, with your dad in prison. She'd never forgive me for cheating on Felix."

It was strange, hearing my aunt voice her fears about Mum. It reminded me so much of my own dread of being found out. All the lies and the subterfuge. Sometimes I'd longed to tell Mum the truth. Especially after I lost him. I longed to confide in her then. But what would she have thought of me, deceiving her for all that time? I needed her to love me then—more than at any time in my life—and I couldn't risk losing that love.

Mum was sitting in the kitchen with a cup of tea when we let ourselves in. She was all smiles as she told us how good Billy had been. Then she asked about the movie. Aunt Ruby said she had a bit of a headache and went off to bed, cleverly avoiding being caught out.

Once again, I had to tell Mum the necessary lies—but this time it was to cover my aunt's tracks, not my own.

It was nearly eleven o'clock when I went to bed—much later than usual—but I wanted to read some more of the journal before I went to sleep. This time it wasn't so much to distract me from memories of Taslim—it was to take me away from the swirl of thoughts and images generated by the evening in Bodmin.

> *The Third Day of February 1606*
> *Last evening Jago and I kept Candlemas together. In days gone by, the blessing of candles was done in church on the first Sunday of February. To me, it is a beautiful way to mark the returning of the light after the long darkness of winter. But like so many of the old ways, it is counted as Papist lore, so the candles were blessed by none but ourselves.*
>
> *Afterward he bade me say when I had last made confession. I told him that it was years since I had been able*

to confess in the proper way, but that lately I had been striving to keep a tally of my sins by writing them down.

"Is there aught you would confess to me now?" He glanced down at his rough smock and breeches. "I may not have the look of a priest, but I can still hearken to what troubles the soul."

"I think that you already know my sins," I replied. "I hope that I can be forgiven for committing them for the sake of one of God's representatives on earth."

"Be assured of that," he said. "But tell me, is there nothing else that lies heavy on your conscience?"

I felt myself redden then. I hoped that, in the dim light of the candles, he might not perceive it. How could I confess what truly troubled my conscience? Not the lies I have told to protect him, nor the dishonour I have done my grandmother by concealing him on her farm without her knowledge. Both these sins seem to pale beside the one I cannot reveal: that I burn with unholy fire for him, every waking moment.

"The dread of you being captured afflicts me most of all," I said. My eyes were fixed on the wooden planks of the floor, not on him. "There is no room within my head for any other disquiet." It wasn't a lie. But nor was it the whole truth.

"Well, in consequence, I must ask you to pray for me," he declared. "For I fear that I enjoy my time with you too much. That my anticipation of your visits fills me with unseemly joy."

I looked up. Had I heard aright? Had he just confessed to feelings that matched my own? His eyes were cast in shadow by the candlelight. I longed to take his face in my hands, to look into those eyes and read the secrets of his heart.

My lips trembled as they parted. "You wish me to pray that you would like me less?"

"Aye." It was only one word—but spoken with such anguish.

My tongue would not allow the words he craved to leave my mouth. I could not promise to pray for his heart to grow cold. After a long silence, he spoke again.

"I must do my part in this," he said. "I will fast until word comes of a ship bound for Spain. You will not have to bring me food twice daily, as you have done so faithfully since I arrived."

"You will eat nothing?" This only added to my misery. There was no telling when that ship would come. How could he escape the king's men if he was too weak to run?

"I will pray that God will give me strength," he replied. He turned away from me then, sinking to his knees on the hard planks beside the straw pallet where he took his rest.

I stumbled forth from the hut and back across the field, my hand shaking so badly I could scarce hold the lantern.

And this morning I awoke with such emptiness in my heart.

Emptiness. The letters on the page began to swim before my eyes. The woman who had lived in this house more than three centuries ago had used the very word that had come to me in the days after Taslim's death.

Was it better for her, I wondered, to have this burgeoning passion nipped in the bud? Would it make it any less heartrending if he was captured and executed? I already knew the answer to those questions. Because if someone had asked me if I wished I'd never kissed Taslim, had never breathed in the scent of his skin as we lay together, I would say no. To never have known such love was unthinkable.

But if you'd never loved him, he'd still be alive. The demon voice whispered in my head. I turned the page, desperate to drive it away, but the writing was a blur. I closed my eyes to stop tears from falling onto the paper.

I must have fallen asleep with the book still open, because when I woke up, it was there on the eiderdown, the feather lying across the unread page.

As I tucked it away beneath the bed, I played back the images that had crowded my unconscious mind. In my sleep, Taslim had transformed into the man I'd seen kissing my aunt. I was pulling at the sleeve of his jacket, trying to get him away from her, screaming that she'd stolen my boyfriend. He turned to push me away, and I caught a glimpse of a cross dangling from his ear, like the one Jago Carlyon wore in the painting.

I ran across the street to the cinema, where Rex Harrison was shaking hands with the moviegoers. I called out to him for help, but before he could reach me, Aunt Ruby came across the street with a hawk perched on her wrist, wiping lipstick from her face with her free hand.

"What's the matter?" Her dream voice echoed inside my head. "You know you can't help who you fall in love with."

Recalling it triggered the same sense of danger I had felt on the bus back from Bodmin. *Just a bit of fun.* That was how she'd tried to pass off what I'd seen in the shop doorway. Could kissing another man like that when you were married ever be excusable? Even if your husband was Felix?

I feared what might happen if someone else had seen her. Someone who lived in St Columb Minor and had just happened to be in Bodmin last night. Felix went to the pub in the village nearly every evening. How long would it take before the gossip reached him?

As I got ready to go and do the milking, I heard Billy crying, followed by the distant creak of footsteps on the landing. I paused for a moment, just listening to him. I couldn't bear to think what might happen if his father discovered what his mother was doing.

Opening the door of my room, I felt as though I were about to step out into a minefield.

Chapter 12

I didn't see Aunt Ruby when we came in from the cowshed. Felix asked Mum to cook the bacon and eggs. He said my aunt was upstairs with Billy, who had been sick during the night. Mum asked if she should take up some breakfast for her sister, but Felix said no. The tone of his voice sent a frisson of fear through me. Had he suspected something when he came home from the pub? Had they had a row? I had no way of knowing.

He told me that I would return to fence-mending duty because the truck that brought the prisoners to the farm had been repaired. He set off with the horses while Mum and I boiled kettles for the tea I was to take to the field.

The hawk appeared as I pushed the wheelbarrow along the track. It alighted on the thatched roof of the old barn. The memory of my aunt's confession flashed through my head as I looked up at the bird. The barn was where her boyfriend had hidden while he waited for Felix to go to The Farmers Arms. I wondered how long they had been meeting like that before we'd arrived to spoil everything. And how did she communicate with him, now that he couldn't come to the farmhouse? Perhaps she would ask me to go to Bodmin with her every Tuesday, if that was Carlo's night off.

I didn't like the idea of lying for her. Lying on my own behalf had become a way of life when I was seeing Taslim, but this was different.

My aunt had a husband and a child. However much I loathed Felix, I felt bad about helping her to cheat on him.

How could she say it was just a bit of fun? The way I saw it, once you betrayed someone, that was it. The bond you'd had with them was broken. Did she imagine some sort of future with Carlo if this war ever ended? And where would Billy fit into that picture? Even if Felix let *her* go, I thought, he'd never allow her to take their son.

"What's she going to do?" I was looking at the hawk as the words came out, but I imagined it was Taslim I was talking to. I heard no reply inside my head. The sound of my voice must have alarmed the bird. Its great wings unfolded as it rose from the roof and glided away.

When I got to the field, I saw that a different guard was on duty. He was younger than the previous one and seemed more relaxed. He left the men to line up for their tea while he went over to chat with Felix.

The prisoner I'd spoken to before greeted me by name when he held out his tin mug. I felt bad because I couldn't recall his. There had been so many names to record in the account book—all unfamiliar—that my memory couldn't contain them. He had kind eyes—a very dark brown, fringed with black lashes. Remembering what I'd seen happen to him at the camp, I asked him if he was okay. He gave me a puzzled smile. There wasn't time to explain that I'd seen him get shoved—the other men were waiting to be served.

It was frustrating, not being able to have a proper conversation. But a few minutes later, when the men were divided into separate groups, I saw that he'd be working in the same field as me.

The new guard didn't seem concerned about me working alongside the POWs. I'd already marked the posts that needed replacing, so I went around with a pair of pliers, pulling out the staples that held the wire fencing so that the men could pull the posts out.

Before long I found myself standing beside the prisoner who knew my name. As I worked away with the pliers, I told him what I'd seen after he'd left the mobile shop.

His eyes clouded. "It is nothing," he said. "It happens."

"You mean it's happened to you before?"

He shrugged. "Since I start working here. One of the guys at the camp is from the same place I live in Italy. He doesn't like that I help the British."

I nodded, remembering what Dorothy had said about one faction in the camp calling these other men traitors. From the tone of his voice, I got the sense that he didn't like talking about it.

"I'm sorry, I was in a bit of a rush at the camp," I said. "I've been trying to remember your name."

"Francesco Marelli." He held out his hand to me.

"Pleased to meet you." I smiled at him as I shook it. The warmth returned to his eyes.

I helped him yank the pole out of the ground, and he told me that he and the others had asked if they could take the unwanted wood back to the camp with them.

"What are you going to do with it?" I asked.

"We make a little church. It is nearly ready. But we need to make some things to sit on."

"How did you build it?" I couldn't imagine the camp authorities providing bricks and cement for the benefit of enemy soldiers.

He shrugged. "We use an old hut where nobody sleeps. We make paint to decorate the walls from plants that grow around the camp. We carve statues and a cross from a tree the wind blows down. And we use empty corned beef tins to hold the candles."

I stared at him in awe. He and the others must have a very strong faith to want to create a place of worship out of so little. I couldn't help feeling envious of such conviction.

From another part of the field, the sound of singing rose into the air. It was a song the men often sang while working. I smiled as I glanced across the pasture. "What is that song called? I wish I understood the words."

"'The Soldier in Love,'" Francesco replied. "It's about a man fighting in the last war. He misses his girlfriend. She is his first love, and he says she will also be his last."

I wondered how such a melancholy song could feel so uplifting. Whenever I heard it, my heart seemed to swell. A first and last love. That was my story, too.

I was about to ask him who he missed, back home in Italy, but our conversation was interrupted by the arrival of Mum, Ruby, and Billy with the sandwiches. I was relieved to see Billy running around the field. He was full of energy and apparently over the sickness he'd had during the night. Mum came toward me, waving something in her hand.

"A letter from Dad," she called out from a few yards away. I ran over to her.

"Is he okay?"

"I think so." She was out of breath. I led her to the pile of fence posts, and we sank down on them. "They've moved him to a different place. He's working in a factory now. He says it's tiring but better than doing nothing all day." She handed me the letter.

The sight of Dad's familiar handwriting made me well up. He wanted to know how we were getting on in Cornwall, and whether we had enough to eat. He said that the only meat on offer at the prison camp was horseflesh, and that vegetables were a rarity. But he'd recently received a Red Cross parcel with a bar of chocolate and a pack of cigarettes in it, which had cheered him up. He didn't mention us leaving the shop in London. If the news had upset him, he didn't say.

I passed the letter back to Mum, blinking back tears. "He sounds quite cheerful, doesn't he?" I tried to keep my voice even. She looked as if she'd been crying, too. I didn't want to set her off again.

She nodded. "I only wish he was being treated as well as this lot." She glanced at the men, who were sitting on the ground, eating their lunch. "Doesn't sound like he's getting enough to eat, does it?"

I stared at the sandwich she'd brought for me. Two thick slices of bread with a hunk of cheese and pickle. I felt guilty just looking at it.

"I wish we were allowed to send him something." Mum blew out a breath. "Thank God for the Red . . ." She didn't get to finish the sentence. Billy came running over to us, launching himself at Mum, trying to scramble onto her lap. She laughed as she scooped him into her arms. Then he made a grab for my sandwich, which made me laugh, too.

"Should I give him some?" I asked. "It won't make him sick, will it?"

"A bit of cheese wouldn't hurt, I don't think," she said. "He's already had some toast—he kept that down all right."

As I fed Billy, I thought what a blessing he was. Back in London, Mum would worry endlessly after receiving a letter from Dad. She would keep it in the pocket of her apron, taking it out and poring over every word again and again, as if she'd find some secret message to decipher if she could only puzzle it out. But Billy had the unique ability to distract her. I leaned across and kissed him on the nose, which made him giggle.

When they'd gone, I went back to the far side of the field with my pliers. The men were still sitting where they'd had lunch. They were chatting to the guard, who seemed to be in no hurry to get them back to work. A cloud of cigarette smoke hung in the air above their heads.

I thought I might as well start pulling out staples on one of the marked posts so that it would be free of the wire when the men came to it. I was thinking about Dad as I grasped the metal between the arms of the pliers. He hadn't said what sort of work he was doing in the German factory. Probably wasn't allowed to put that in a letter. I don't know whether I tugged too hard, or whether I just lost my concentration, because the next thing I knew, the post came right out, striking me on the head as it fell to the ground.

I must have passed out momentarily. When I opened my eyes, Francesco was inches from my face.

"Violet! Can you hear me? Are you in pain?"

I stared up into his dark brown eyes. I could see the sky around his hair. I felt something under my shoulders. It was a shock to realize it was his arm.

"Don't try to move." He turned and shouted something I didn't understand. Another man appeared beside him. "Giovanni is a doctor," he said gently. "He will take care of you."

"I'm okay." My voice came out all croaky, but I managed to sit up. Francesco sat beside me, supporting my back, while Giovanni asked a series of questions and held his fingers up in front of my face. By this time the guard had arrived as well. He asked me if I needed to go to the hospital.

"I don't think so." I got to my feet, a little unsteady, feeling the side of my head.

"Let me look." Giovanni lifted the scarf I'd tied around my hair and peered at my scalp. "No blood. But you have . . . how you say? A chicken."

It took a moment to grasp what he was trying to say. "You mean an egg?" I laughed, and the others laughed, too.

"I reckon you should go and have a rest, miss," the guard said. "A nice cup of tea and a lie down. That's what you need."

I looked at the doctor, who nodded.

"I walk with you to the farmhouse," Francesco said. He turned to the guard, holding up his hands, palms out. "I make no trouble—I promise to you."

"Hmm." The guard looked him up and down. Then he glanced across at the neighboring field. But Felix and the horses were dots in the distance, with the seed-planting team following in their wake. "Well, I suppose I could let you," he said. "We don't want this young lady keeling over on the way home. But no funny business. And if you're not back here in twenty minutes, you'll be in solitary for a week, you hear?"

I didn't protest when Francesco took my arm and guided me across the rough grass where the sheep were grazing. Despite saying I was okay, I still felt a little dizzy.

I leaned against the fence while he opened the gate to the road. He put his arm around my shoulders as we crossed over, looking over the top of my head to make sure there were no vehicles coming. It was a strange sensation, walking along like that. I'd forgotten what it felt like.

He didn't try to speak to me as we made our way along the track. I was grateful for that. I wasn't sure I was up to making small talk. The guard had been right. What I needed was a cup of hot, sweet tea and a lie down.

When we reached the old barn, he asked if I needed to stop for a rest.

"Better not," I said. "I don't want you to be late getting back."

"It's okay," he replied. "I can run. I am champion runner back in Italy."

"Were you?" I smiled. "I've never been much good at sports."

"But you are strong." He made a fist with his free hand and punched the air. "You lift those big baskets of sugar beets, no problem."

"I don't know about that." I shrugged. I didn't feel strong. He guided me to a rusty old hay trailer that lay half buried in the grass in front of the barn, and I sank down on the edge of it.

He sat down, not beside me, but at the other end of the trailer. "Where do you live, before you come here?" he asked.

"London," I replied.

"Ah, London. That is a bad place to live now?"

I hesitated. For all I knew he could be fishing for information to pass on to the enemy. "I don't like to talk about it," I said. That was quite true.

"I understand," he nodded. "In the camp, we don't talk about what happen to us in Africa. Bad memories."

"Africa?"

"Where they capture us. By the sea. A place called Tobruk."

I'd read about the siege of Tobruk in the newspaper. Thousands had died there.

"I am lucky," he went on. "Many of my friends are not."

"I . . . I'm sorry." I could barely get the words out. I had a mental image of bodies lying in the sand among camels and palm trees. I wondered how many of his friends had died in that battle. It must have been bad—very bad—for the men at the camp to make it a taboo subject.

"I lost someone in London." The words came out of my mouth as if someone else was controlling my voice. "My boyfriend. His name was Taslim."

Why was I telling this stranger what I'd been unable to tell anyone else? Was it the bump on my head? Had it done something to my brain? All I knew was that letting it out released something inside of me. Tears streamed down my face. I couldn't stop them.

"Violet!" He was on his feet, coming toward me. He pulled a handkerchief from his jacket pocket and held it out to me.

"I . . . I'm . . ." I struggled to my feet, wiping my face. "You must go. I'll be okay now."

He insisted on walking with me until we were in sight of the farmhouse. When I thanked him, I felt myself welling up again. After he'd gone, I had to go and sit in the privy next to the pigsty. I couldn't face Mum and Aunt Ruby until I'd calmed myself down. I tried taking deep breaths—but the rancid air just made me feel sick. After a while, I decided to avoid the kitchen and go straight up to my room via the dairy. I could have a rest and come downstairs later.

I sneaked across the farmyard, keeping close to the wall, hoping I wouldn't be spotted through the kitchen window. The cat was the only witness to my subterfuge. When I went into the dairy, Kuching jumped off one of the shelves and rubbed himself against my legs. Then he followed me up the stairs. I could have shut the door on him, but instead I let him come into the bedroom. When I got under the covers, he snuggled up next to me on the eiderdown.

There was something very comforting about the weight of Kuching's body against my back. I must have drifted off to sleep very quickly. When I woke up, I lay quite still for a moment, staring at the pattern on the curtains. For the first time in more than a year, I had no dreams, no nightmares. I glanced at my watch, which I hadn't taken off when I'd got into bed. Two precious hours of peaceful sleep. Was it the cat? I wondered. Or was it talking to Francesco?

I went downstairs a few minutes later, feeling refreshed and ready to deal with the volley of questions I knew I'd get from Mum. When I told her what had happened, she seemed more worried about me being escorted home by a POW than being knocked to the ground by a fence post.

"I hope he kept his filthy hands off you!" She stood by the range, hands on her hips. "I can't believe the guard allowed that, can you, Ruby?"

My aunt was feeding Billy. She didn't look up, just shook her head.

"He didn't have much choice, Mum," I said. "He couldn't leave the other prisoners, and he was worried about me walking all that way on my own."

"But your Uncle Felix was in the next field," Mum insisted. "Why couldn't the guard have asked him to bring you back?"

I was about to explain why that hadn't been possible when Billy derailed further conversation by choking on the piece of bread he'd stuffed into his mouth. There was pandemonium in the kitchen until the crisis was over. Then Mum offered to take him up to bed and read him a story. Aunt Ruby stayed downstairs, and we started peeling vegetables for the evening meal.

"I couldn't look at you when your mum was going on about that Italian." She huffed out a breath as she sliced into a potato. "God only knows what she'd say if she knew about Carlo."

"Well, she won't hear it from me," I said. "But aren't you worried that someone might see you? When you're out with him, I mean?"

"I didn't think anyone in Bodmin would recognise me." She shook her head. "But you did."

"Only because of your hat," I said. "Maybe you should wear something a bit less eye-catching next time."

The sound of the door opening made us both look up. Felix came into the room, frowning when he caught sight of me. He opened his mouth, and I thought he was going to make some snide remark about me shirking the afternoon's work. But he just asked when supper would be ready, then disappeared again.

Aunt Ruby turned to me, her face pale. "Do you think he heard us?"

I glanced toward the door. Could Felix have been listening before he came in? I thought about the time I'd found him standing outside my bedroom. I'd had no idea how long he'd been there, nor whether he'd been peering through the keyhole. I'd suspected that he was in the habit of spying on people. For my aunt's sake, I hoped I was wrong about that.

~

I wasn't particularly tired when I went to bed. The afternoon nap had left me wide awake when everyone else in the house was yawning. Kuching had returned to his lair in the dairy. He opened his eyes as I went past, and I tried coaxing him to come upstairs with me. It would have been nice to have a companion as I sat reading the journal, but the cat was having none of it. With a look of disdain, he went back to sleep.

I sat for a while, listening to the sounds of the house, before I started reading. I strained my ears for voices, half afraid that I'd hear Felix challenge Aunt Ruby about what he might have caught of our conversation. But all I could hear were the creaks of the timbers as the house settled for the night.

Taking the feather from its place between the pages, I shone my flashlight on the sloping script.

> *The Fifth Day of February 1606*
> *Three days have passed since I have spoken to Jago. I thought that hunger would overcome his scruples about being in my company, but it has not. He will not break his fast. I have seen him from a distance, drawing water from the well and guiding lambs across the farmyard to the field. The pain of catching sight of him is beyond the power of words.*

This morning, I went to church alone, for my grandmother remains in Falmouth. In the pulpit, Robert Archer gloried in recounting the horrid deaths of the men who were arrested for their part in the plot to blow up the king.

He gave a fulsome account of what befell Guy Fawkes and other conspirators on the day of their execution, from being dragged on wicker sledges from the Tower of London to Palace Yard in Westminster, where the hangman waited.

I swear that he was smiling when he told us what followed the placing of the noose around the necks of the unfortunate men. Afore they were dead, they were taken down, their bellies sliced open, and their entrails pulled out and burned. Their privy parts were cut off and disposed of in a similar manner.

A woman in the pew in front of me fainted away at this, but it did not still his tongue. He proceeded to recount how Guy Fawkes had hastened his death by jumping from the ladder when the rope was first put upon him, breaking his neck and so evading the tortures endured by the others. Such a man, he avowed, was bound to burn in hell for all eternity.

Then came the pronouncement that the king's men were searching houses up and down the land for the three priests who are still at large. The town of Bodmin, he said, was among the chief places for these raids, as it was the birthplace of the Cornishman Jago Carlyon.

"If anyone here present has any intelligence of this traitor," he declared, "it is their bounden duty to report it. No retribution will be served upon that person—but woe betide the one who keeps such knowledge secret."

I could not behold him as he spoke these words. I kept my eyes firmly fixed on the prayer book in my hand. If the king's men are already searching houses in Bodmin, it can only be a matter of time before they cast the net wider and come looking in our village.

When the worship came to a close, there was no way to evade the rector. He was standing at the door, shaking the hand of each person as they left. When I passed by him, he gripped my fingers.

He enquired after my grandmother, saying he hoped her absence from church was not due to ill health. When I told him of her visit to Falmouth, his eyes narrowed, like a fox's when it lurks around a henhouse. I could feel the dampness of his palm against my skin. The smell of unwashed feet seems to linger about him.

When at last he released my hand, it was with a promise to call at the farmhouse when my grandmother returns. God grant that she will stay away until Jago has the means to escape to Spain. But my heart breaks to think on that day.

Since returning home from church, I have battled to stop myself from going to the field and knocking on the door of the shepherd's hut. In a bid to distract myself from sinful thoughts, I have laboured to paint Jago's image. I am no artist, but it is a fair likeness. If he will not permit me to see him, I can make believe that he is with me, in this room. I can tell him what is in my heart and imagine his voice, soft and low, his lips brushing my ear.

I slid the portrait from its place at the back of the journal. She was too modest. The quality of the work was as good as anything I'd seen in an art gallery. The intricate lace on the collar of his shirt must have taken many hours to execute. The delicate cross hanging from his ear would have required the lightest of brushstrokes and a very steady hand. But most of all it was the eyes that made the image so captivating. There was a depth to them that conveyed something of the character of the man. I searched for the right way to describe the expression she had captured. Tenderness tinged with defiance. Those were the words that came to mind.

One of my deepest regrets was that I had no photograph of Taslim. Neither of us had owned a camera. We could have gone to one of the professional studios in London to pose for a portrait, but that would have been an uncomfortable experience. And I would have had to hide the resulting prints from Mum.

Looking at the painting, I wished I had the ability to recreate Taslim's face on paper. It would be such a comfort to be able to look into his eyes. The thought of it made me well up. The image, seen through tears, distorted into something grotesque. The fiery background swirled and spread across the face. Why had she painted those flames? Had she added them later? Had Jago been caught when he tried to board the ship for Spain? Had he been executed? Robert Archer had described the burning of the entrails of the men accused of plotting to kill the king. Had Jago endured the same gruesome fate?

With a shudder, I tucked the portrait back into the book and turned the page.

The Seventh Day of February 1606
Yesterday was the fourth day of Jago's fasting. The thought of him lying in the hut, weak from hunger and afraid for his life, was more than I could bear. I spent two hours on my knees in the morning, begging for God's help. It was sent in a way I least expected, when a ragged crone came knocking on the door of the farmhouse late in the afternoon.

At first, I thought she was a Gypsy fortune teller come begging for a piece of silver, but when I tried to send her away, she put her hand inside her cloak and drew out something that stilled my tongue. It was an Agnus Dei—*the same waxen image held in glass that Jago gave me for safekeeping. This was no old woman, but a man in disguise: a man with a message about the ship that Jago awaits.*

He passed me a fragment of paper, then shuffled off down the track without a word. The paper was blank till set to a candle flame. The ship will anchor at Porth harbour on the morrow and will sail at high tide.

I forbore to rush across the field to the hut, afeard that if I did so, one of the farmhands might suspect a connection between this visitor and the man they believe to be a shepherd. It was pure torture, remaining in the house when I longed to be with him and had the noblest reason to go knocking on his door.

It was near dark when I departed the farmhouse. There was no moon, but I know my way so well I swear I could go blindfolded. I crept across the grass as softly as a cat, but Jago hearkened to my coming while I was yet a distance from the hut. He must have been sitting in the doorway, as a good shepherd should, listening for any sound that might herald danger—to himself as much as the lambs.

He cried out, "Who goes there?" The sound of his voice made my heart flutter like a bird trapped in a cage.

I called back my name, saying I brought word from a friend. That sounded innocent, should anyone out in the woods be close enough to overhear. It also conveyed to Jago that I had not come to put temptation in his way.

I heard a thud as he jumped from the hut to the ground. In a moment he was beside me. He bade me tell him if it was true. When I answered yes, he took my hand

and led me back to the hut. The feel of his skin on mine was a balm to my soul after all these days away from him.

He helped me up the steps, which were invisible in the darkness. Inside, a single candle was burning. We sat down on the straw pallet where he sleeps, just as we used to, and he listened in silence as I told him of the ragged visitor with the Agnus Dei *hidden beneath his cloak.*

We talked for a while about practical affairs: the route he would take to reach the ship, and the time of high tide. When he thanked me for all I had done for him, I could not stop my tears. He wiped them away with the hem of his smock, and, as his body drew closer, my hand brushed the skin of his belly. He made a small sound, like the gasp of air from bellows stoking a fire. My fingers lingered on the soft flesh above his breeches, and then his hands were upon my body, stroking my neck, releasing the ribbons of my cloak. When our lips met, I thought I would die of happiness.

We lay together all the night long, entwined on our bed of straw. Can it be a sin, to love like this? If the very gates of heaven were thrown open, there could be no greater joy. He told me that he loved me; that somehow, when he is safe in Spain, we will find a way to be together.

I asked him how that could possibly come to pass, with him a priest.

"I have tried to fight it, but my soul cries out that I need you in order to be who I am," was his reply. "If that means I can no longer be a priest, then so be it."

This was sweet music to my ears. I asked him by what means we might make a living in a foreign country. He said that he had a friend in Spain. He had met this man while on a pilgrimage from France to a place called Santiago de Compostela. The friend was a printer of books and had liked the Spanish town so well he had decided to set up in business there. His chief endeavour was the establishment of a printing press in the English language. Jago believes he could find employment there.

Dawn was breaking when I left him. I would have stayed until it was time for him to go to the ship, but I could not risk being missed at the farmhouse. I told him I would return in a few hours' time with food for his journey.

As I write these words, my hand trembles for fear of what lies ahead. This day, I must bid him farewell and send him on his way. He has left me a beautiful dream of what our lives may be one day. Shall I ever behold him again? God grant it so.

I turned the page, desperate to know what would happen. But there was nothing there. Just blank paper. I leafed through the rest of the book, thinking that she might have missed a page by accident. But there were no more entries. Her story stopped on the seventh day of February 1606.

I lay awake for a long time, wondering what had become of her. Did Jago escape on the ship to Spain? Was she able to follow him? Had he meant it when he told her he loved her? Would he leave the priesthood so that he could marry her?

When at last I drifted into sleep, I dreamed of the shepherd's hut. I was walking barefoot across the pasture, the grass like needles of ice against the soles of my feet. But I knew I must endure the pain, because Taslim was waiting for me there. He was dressed as Jago Carlyon had been, in a smock and breeches. As he drew me to him, I could smell the mingled scent of spices on his skin. We undressed each other slowly, until both of us stood naked in the candlelight. The flame guttered, casting shadows across his face, and I cried out, terrified of the hut catching fire. He told me not to be afraid, that fire couldn't hurt us because we had stepped through time into a place of safety.

Afterward, as we lay together on the straw, he whispered words from the journal.

Can it be a sin, to love like this?

Chapter 13

As I wheeled the cans of tea across the farmyard the next morning, I was still thinking about the abrupt end to the journal. Why had she suddenly stopped writing? Had someone seen her leaving the shepherd's hut early in the morning? Had the king's men come to the farm to arrest her for harboring the runaway priest?

Pushing the wheelbarrow over a loose cobblestone, I felt the silver whistle shift on its chain beneath my sweater. At the same moment, I heard the shrill cry of a hawk. Looking up, I saw it perched on the roof of the milking shed. It seemed to be staring right at me, and it gave me the strangest feeling, as if there were something it wanted to tell me.

It knows how the story ends. Taslim's voice whispered inside my head. As if *he* knew. As if his spirit really had reincarnated in the form of a hawk.

Stop it! I hissed the warning to myself, under my breath. *It's just a bird.*

I glanced over my shoulder, afraid that Felix might spot me through the kitchen window. If he saw what I was looking at, he might come out with his gun. I tried to move faster. When I reached the gate, I went a few yards down the track, then pulled out the whistle and blew it.

The sound had the desired effect. The hawk rose from its perch and glided over my head, away from the farm. When I reached the barn, it was waiting there for me. It had flown onto the rusty hay trailer where I had sat with Francesco. I cringed inside, remembering the tearful confession I had made. Why had I opened my heart to him when I had kept the secret of Taslim so close for so long? It was going to be embarrassing, seeing him now, after revealing so much of myself.

But when I got to the field and the men came to queue up for their tea, I saw that Francesco was missing. Had he been punished for taking too long to escort me home after my accident? I asked the guard what had happened to him.

"There was a fight at the camp last night," the guard replied. "The feller that helped you was in the thick of it. He's in the cooler for a couple of days."

"Is he okay? Was he hurt?" I couldn't bear the thought of those kind eyes swollen with punches, or, even worse, his body bleeding and bones broken. Remembering the force with which that other prisoner had nearly pushed him to the ground by the mobile shop, I feared the worst.

The guard didn't answer my question. He simply shrugged and moved off to greet Felix, who was coming through the gate with the horses.

It wasn't until after lunch that I managed to speak to Giovanni, the doctor who had examined me after my accident. He told me that news of Francesco walking me home had quickly spread among the prisoners. One of the men who refused to work outside the camp had waited for Francesco outside the mess hall and beaten him up. The guards who had intervened blamed both men for getting into a fight and wouldn't listen to any explanation.

"Was he badly hurt?" I held my breath.

"Just cuts and bruises," Giovanni replied. "He'll be okay." He gave me a tight smile, and I wondered if he was holding something back.

Francesco was still on my mind as I walked back to the farmhouse at the end of the day. I raged inside to think of him being attacked for an act of kindness. It was my fault. If that stupid pole hadn't knocked me sideways, he wouldn't be locked up now with painful injuries.

It wasn't your fault. You didn't do it on purpose. I heard Taslim's voice, repeating words I'd imagined him saying countless times. He was right, of course. I hadn't injured myself on purpose to get Francesco into trouble, just as I hadn't willed the Germans to drop bombs on the wharf where Taslim and I were hiding. But *I* was the reason that both had come to grief. As if I were a magnet for disaster.

As I neared the farmyard, the sound of raised voices broke my chain of thought. It was Felix and Aunt Ruby. They were in the milking shed. I could only hear snatches, but it sounded like an almighty row.

I scurried past, heading for the house, feeling like a coward but afraid to face Felix when he was in full flow. Had he found out about Carlo? I hovered about in the kitchen, picturing him going for her, hitting her, or . . . I glanced at the wall. The gun was there. *Thank God,* I thought. As I stood staring at it, my aunt came through the door. She slumped down at the table and put her head in her hands.

"What's happened?" I sat down beside her. "I heard shouting when I came back from the field. He hasn't hurt you, has he?"

She shook her head. "Someone told him about me throwing a pack of ciggies to the prisoners on the truck," she said. "He was furious. Pushed me against the wall and threatened to break my neck if I went near them again." She took in a long breath and huffed it out. "I think he'd keep me locked up in here all the time if he could."

"He doesn't know about . . ."

"God, no." She put her finger to her lips, glancing over her shoulder toward the door.

"What are you going to do?"

"Well, I won't be going to Bodmin any time soon. It's too risky. We might have to knock things on the head for a bit. Wait until Felix has simmered down."

It was a relief that I wouldn't have to act as her accomplice—at least not for a while. She'd painted a terrifying picture of what Felix was capable of. I dreaded to think what he'd do to me if he had any inkling that I'd been covering for her.

The sound of the door opening made us both jump. But it wasn't Felix. It was Mum, who'd taken Billy out in the pram.

"He's fast asleep," she said. "I left the pram by the dairy. The cat won't jump on him, will it?"

"I doubt it. He's only interested in mice." Aunt Ruby's mask was back on. She smiled at Mum and asked her if she'd like a cup of tea. As she put the kettle on the range, she turned to me.

"I forgot to tell you—I bumped into the rector's wife in the village this morning. She asked if you might be able to spare an hour tomorrow afternoon to help her restock the mobile shop. She said any time between four and six would do."

"Oh—okay," I nodded. "I'll go straight there after I finish in the field."

I heard Mum sigh as she pulled out a chair. "I wish you hadn't volunteered for that, Violet. I'm worried about you overdoing it. You've hardly had time to get over that knock on the head."

"I'm fine, Mum, honestly." That wasn't entirely true. My head was still sore where the pole had hit it. I had to avoid the lump when I brushed my hair.

From the look on her face, she didn't believe me. But before she could say anything else, a wail came from outside. Billy had woken up.

"I'll go and get him." When I scooped Billy out of the pram, I caught sight of Felix on the other side of the farmyard. He was chopping wood. The ferocity with which he brought the axe down on the block made me shudder.

~

When I went to bed that night, I lay awake for ages, thinking about Francesco. I hated the idea of him being locked up, very likely in pain after the beating he'd received, all because he'd been kind enough to look after me when I was hurt.

As the feelings of guilt swirled around in my head, I wished I had more of the journal to read. I had come to rely on it when dark thoughts threatened to engulf me, but now that solace had ended. Not knowing what had happened felt like being in a cinema when the reel breaks during a movie. But with a movie, there was always the chance to go and see it again.

I wondered if there was any way of finding out what had become of the woman and the priest without asking Felix—who may or may not know anything about them. It seemed unlikely that he did know. Remembering the ghoulish pleasure he'd taken in telling me about the witch marks, I couldn't imagine him passing up the chance to shock me with a story like that—especially if it had ended with an execution.

I took the old book in my hands, running my fingers over the cracked leather binding, as if I could divine the two lovers' fate by some form of telepathy. The ace of hearts with the portrait attached to it slipped out from between the pages. I held it in the beam of the flashlight, staring into Jago Carlyon's eyes until his features began to blur.

"What happened to you?" I whispered the words, but they sounded loud in the silence. "Did you get to Spain? Did you keep your promise to her?"

But if he had managed to escape, the chances of them having a future together seemed remote. Her part in his disappearance might have come to light, in which case, she would almost certainly have been arrested. For a crime like that, she would have gone to prison. She might even have faced execution. Even if she'd evaded the law, there was the possibility that, once in Spain, Jago might have gone back to being a priest and conveniently forgotten all about her.

I thought of the graveyard behind St Columba's church. I'd seen it when I went to the shed where the mobile shop was parked. I wondered if the writer of the journal could be buried there. No doubt Dorothy would know the date of the earliest gravestones. I could ask her tomorrow, when I went to help her with the stock.

But with a sinking feeling, I realized that it would be no use searching for a gravestone unless I knew the name of the writer of the journal.

I fell asleep thinking about it, weighing the idea of telling Felix about the journal in the hope of getting that name. But I hated the thought of him reading her words. I could just imagine the lascivious smile on his face as he found out what had happened in the shepherd's hut.

In my dreams that night, the hawk appeared again. It perched on the roof of the milking shed, as it had in reality that morning, but the dream version of the bird could speak. It told me to follow it, so I left the farm track to cross the field, where it was gliding toward the woods. I passed the shepherd's hut and stopped to look inside, but it was empty, except for a tiny cross inlaid with pearls that lay on the floor. I picked it up and tried to insert it in my ear, but my piercing had healed over, and it made my earlobe bleed.

I saw that the hawk had come to rest in a tree covered in bright red berries. When I reached it, it asked me if I knew the name of the tree. I knew that I should know it, but I couldn't remember what it was called. The only word that came out of my mouth was "jelly."

Slipping out of unconsciousness, another image formed. It was Aunt Ruby, setting food on the table the first night we spent at the farmhouse. She brought cream cheese from the larder and set down a jar with something bright red inside it. Jelly. Now I remembered. She'd said she'd made it from berries growing on a tree she could see from the farmyard. Rowan berries. That was the name. But what was the significance of that tree? Why had the hawk perched in it in my dream? And why had those scarlet berries looked exactly like the drops of blood falling from my ear?

~

I looked for the hawk on my way to the field the next morning, but there was no sign of it. Walking along the track, I blew on the silver whistle, but the only response came from a startled rabbit, which ran across the path in front of me.

Over the hedge on my right, I could see the tops of the trees at the edge of the woodland. I wondered which one was the rowan. Most of the trees had lost their leaves, and any berries were long gone. I had no chance of identifying the tree that had appeared in my dream.

When I got to the field and the Italians came for their tea, I asked Giovanni if there was any news of Francesco. He shook his head and said he hadn't seen him.

"Tomorrow he is out of the . . . how you say? Icebox?"

"The cooler, you mean?" The mistake made me smile. It was a relief to know that Francesco's punishment was nearly over. He would be free to come to the mobile shop. I could see for myself how he was doing.

Mum arrived with the sandwiches at lunchtime. She said Aunt Ruby had had to go into the village to pick up the orange juice ration for Billy. I wondered if Felix had forbidden my aunt to bring food to the Italians after their row, and the errand was an excuse she'd made to Mum.

As I sat eating my sandwich, it struck me that neither Aunt Ruby nor I felt able to confide in Mum. I wondered if it had always been like that for my aunt—whether, growing up, there had been an emotional distance between the sisters because of the age gap between them. Or was it just because Mum was so judgmental?

As a child, I had idolized her. The bond between us had loosened when I got older, but things really changed when I realized how mean and snobbish she could be about people she considered to be different from us. I remember when the Taj Stores first opened, and she came in with a look of disgust on her face, saying she'd just walked past the Indian shop, and the smell coming out of the door had made her feel sick.

After that, she had never missed an opportunity to make snide remarks about Taslim's family—about what they wore, the food they sold, and the color of their skin. Sometimes I wondered how Mum and I could be so unlike one another. I loved her—of course I did—but I often felt that I didn't *like* her.

When Dad went off to war and then got captured, the guilt I felt about not confiding in her was even harder to bear. She was so vulnerable and trying to be so brave. But it didn't stop her from saying spiteful things about other people. Taslim had been waiting for his call-up papers when he was killed. It had taken longer for his name to appear on the official list because he wasn't born in Britain. But in that first year of the war, Mum was always looking across the street at him, complaining loudly that the Indian lad was living the life of Riley while Dad was risking life and limb fighting the Germans.

I watched her as she handed over the sandwiches to the POWs. Never once did she smile when they thanked her for their lunch. She kept her mouth set in a tight line. She delivered their lunch because she had to, not because she wanted to. In her opinion, these men didn't deserve good food. If it had been up to Mum, they would be made to work all day in the field without a morsel of nourishment. I dreaded to think how she'd react if she knew that her sister was having a secret affair with an Italian.

~

At half past four, when the POWs were waiting for the truck to come and take them back to the camp, I headed off down the road to the rectory.

When Dorothy answered the door, I was relieved to see that she wore clothes almost as scruffy as mine.

"Sorry I look such a fright," I said. "I've come straight from the field."

"Nonsense, dear." She smiled. "You'd look as pretty as a picture if you wore a potato sack!"

She asked me to come in while she went to get the stock list. The aroma of fried onions came from the kitchen, which made my stomach rumble. Through an open door in the hallway, I could see the rector working away in a room full of books. He had his back to me and didn't turn around when I called hello.

"Please excuse Humphrey," Dorothy said when she returned to me. "He's not being rude—he can't hear a blessed thing unless you're standing right in front of him." She handed me a basket to carry. "I thought you might be hungry after slogging away outdoors all afternoon. There's cake and biscuits and a flask of tea in there to keep us going."

When she opened the door of the shed behind the church, I saw a pile of boxes that reached almost to the roof. Dorothy said she'd hurt her back digging in the garden and didn't like to risk moving them on her own. She pointed to a stepladder in the corner of the shed and asked if I could bring it over.

The boxes weren't heavy, but they were an awkward size. I nearly overbalanced on the ladder getting the first one down. When I'd laid the last one on the ground, I felt a bit dizzy. I reached out for the wall of the shed to steady myself.

"Are you all right, dear?" Dorothy put her arm around my shoulder. "Do you need to sit down?"

"It's okay," I mumbled. "I'll be fine in a minute. Just a bit tired, that's all."

"I'm so sorry—I shouldn't have asked you to come. I should have realised you'd be worn out, working on the farm."

"It's not that," I said. "It's just that I don't seem to sleep very well." I hesitated, wondering if I should tell her about the nightmares. I'd intended to ask her about the gravestones in the churchyard, and she would likely ask why I was interested. I hadn't known her very long, but she seemed like someone I could trust.

"I thought you looked a bit peaky," Dorothy said. "Shall we have a break before we start unpacking these boxes?"

There was nowhere to sit but inside the truck. She poured me a cup of tea as I settled into the driver's seat, then passed me a slab of fruitcake to go with it.

"Is there anything worrying you, to keep you awake at night?" she asked.

"This is going to sound silly, I know," I replied, "but I found something in my room, and it's been giving me nightmares." I told her about my discovery of the box with the book and the hawking whistle inside. I explained how the writing had changed from a record of sins to a detailed journal of the dramatic events that had unfolded at the farm. Then I described some of the dreams I'd had after reading the journal. I didn't mention that Taslim had featured in them. It was bad enough that I'd told Francesco about him. I couldn't be sure that Dorothy's views on romance between a white girl and an Indian boy would be any different from Mum's.

As I spoke, she stared at the steering wheel, a look of intense concentration on her face. "Was there a date in the book you found?" she asked.

I nodded. "Sixteen hundred and six. All the entries were from the first two months of that year. It ended the day before the priest she was hiding was due to escape on a ship to Spain."

She took in a long breath before replying. "I'm reluctant to tell you this, because I worry it might scare you," she said. "But by the sound of it, knowing some of the history of the house might help you deal with what you've discovered."

My heart shifted against my ribs. "What happened there?"

"In the year sixteen hundred and six, a former rector of St Columba's was said to have been murdered by a witch who lived at Lowartha Farmhouse."

My mouth went dry. A *witch*? Nothing I had read in the journal had suggested that. Was this the same woman?

"What was her name?"

"Maria Wolveden. She was the daughter of a Catholic lord whose house and land had been confiscated. In those days, it was against the law to be a Catholic."

So, it *was* her. And she had *murdered* Robert Archer? Why would she do that? Had he seen her leaving the shepherd's hut after she'd spent the night with Jago? Confronted her in a jealous rage?

"What happened to her?"

"I don't know." Dorothy leaned across to top up my cup of tea. "Witchcraft and murder both carried the death penalty. By that time, they'd stopped burning witches. She would probably have been hanged. I did some research a few years back, but I couldn't find any mention of a trial in the county archives. Nor is there any record of her burial."

They'd stopped burning witches. Her words set off an automatic surge of panic. Just thinking about it was enough to trigger the phobia. "Could she have escaped somehow?" I could hear the tremor in my voice.

"It seems unlikely," Dorothy said. "She could have died in prison awaiting trial and been buried in an unmarked grave. That would explain why there are no court documents relating to the charges against her."

"Why was she accused of witchcraft?"

"The rector, Robert Archer, denounced her. He'd written a letter to his bishop about it. He said that she'd bewitched his horse by giving it a remedy that had turned it wild and caused the animal to unseat him. The letter was discovered in the rectory after he was found dead in the woods near Lowartha Farmhouse. Humphrey has a copy of it in a book in his study."

"So, she got the blame just because of that?"

"That's how it looks," Dorothy replied.

"But she wrote about that horse in the journal," I said. "It had an injured leg, and she offered to help. She said she'd been taught the cure by a man who used to work in her father's stables."

Dorothy nodded. "I don't doubt it. But in those days, a woman could be accused of witchcraft for just looking at some person or animal who subsequently fell ill or had something bad happen to them."

"Really?" I stared at the steering wheel. Words from the journal echoed inside my head. *Superstitious fools. Mired in witchcraft.* The fact that Maria came from a Catholic family would have marked her out for scrutiny in the eyes of a man like Archer.

I pictured armed men seizing her and dragging her off to some god-awful jail. Had she died there, of hunger or disease, as Dorothy believed? Or was there a chance that she had managed to escape and found some way to reunite with Jago?

"Do you know what happened to the priest?" I held my breath.

"He was arrested in February of the same year, about to board a ship in Porth harbour. They took him to the Tower of London because he was suspected of having been involved in the Gunpowder Plot." Dorothy shook her head. "It was never proved that he was in league with those men, but anti-Catholic feeling was so strong that he was sentenced to be burned at the stake for heresy."

My mouth opened but no words would come out. The image attached to the ace of hearts flashed across my mind's eye: the flames behind the figure of the priest, ready to consume him. Maria must have *known* how he was going to die.

"There's no record of his execution, though," Dorothy went on. "I thought that was odd, given the publicity Guy Fawkes and the others attracted. Their deaths were portrayed in grisly detail on pamphlets that were circulated up and down the land. You would think that Jago Carlyon's burning would have been publicised in a similar way. It was all about propaganda—trying to scare people away from the Catholic faith." She clicked her tongue against her teeth. "What terrible things men have done in the name of religion."

My heart was beating so fast I could feel the pulse in my temple vibrating. The darkness was closing in: that same terrifying sensation I'd had when the bombs fell on the docks and my world caught fire. I remembered searching the wards of the hospital for Taslim, and that terrible morning when Mum brought me home in a taxi, and we saw the blinds down in the windows of the Taj Stores. I could imagine Maria feeling just as I had: that desperate, all-consuming sense of loss, and the sheer horror of knowing how it had come about.

"Could *he* have escaped?" Even as the words came out, I felt I was clutching at straws. He'd been held in the Tower of London—the strongest fortress in the land.

"I suppose it's possible," Dorothy replied. "History tells us that a few people found a way out of the Tower during the centuries when it was used as a prison. But I couldn't find any evidence for Jago Carlyon escaping."

I stared at the dregs of tea at the bottom of my cup. "Do you believe in ghosts, Dorothy?"

"Goodness me—what a question to ask a rector's wife!"

"I don't really mean ghosts—not most people's idea of them, anyway," I said. "I was thinking more about the idea of getting messages from people who've died. Do you believe that's possible?"

She was silent for a moment. "I believe in the power of the human mind," she said. "When I think about you reading that journal, late at night, I can imagine your sleeping brain trying to process what it's taken in. That could lead to dreams that might seem like some kind of message."

"But it's not just the dreams." I told her about the hawk that had appeared nearly every day since I'd arrived at the farmhouse. About the feather I'd found in my room. "It feels as if the bird is trying to tell me something," I said.

She went silent for a moment. "I don't mean to pry." She turned to me, searching my face. "But have you ever felt this kind of thing in the past? Before you came to Cornwall, I mean?"

I must have failed to switch on the masklike expression I always wore when Mum asked awkward questions. My mind was in turmoil with everything Dorothy had told me. Images tumbled around my head. Things I'd tried to shut out of my mind. That was what fire did to me. The very thought of it had the power to unbalance me.

"What happened to you, dear?" Her voice was gentle. "Can you tell me about it? I promise that anything you say will go no further."

Somehow it all came pouring out. I told her much more than I'd told Francesco. About talking to Taslim this whole past year since he died, about hearing his voice inside my head. I even told her how I'd rubbed the silver hawking whistle between my fingers to summon him when I needed him most, because I sensed that his spirit had entered the body of the hawk.

She said nothing until I'd finished talking. Oddly, I wasn't crying. I'd managed to say all that without shedding a single tear.

"Does your family know about any of this?"

I shook my head. "My father's in a prison camp in Germany. He went to fight in France a few months after I started seeing Taslim. He doesn't know anything about what happened—not even about me being in the hospital after the bombing of the docks. And I can't talk to Mum about it. She would never have approved of me dating an Indian boy. She didn't even like the fact that his family had opened a shop across the road from ours."

"But I'm sure she loves you very much. No mother would want her child to suffer the way you have." Dorothy put her hand on my shoulder. "Can't you let her in?"

I couldn't answer. I'd hidden it from Mum for so long. How could I unravel all those lies? I stared at my hands, uncomfortable in the silence. When, eventually, I looked up, I saw that Dorothy's eyes were closed. I wondered if she was praying for me.

~

I didn't leave the shed at the back of the church until I'd unpacked all the stock for the mobile shop. Dorothy had tried to persuade me to go back to the farmhouse and get some rest. She'd said that she could cope on her own now that all the boxes were at floor level. But I felt I had to make up for the weakness of opening my heart to her. I had to show her that I was tough on the outside, even if I came across as broken and pathetic.

It was twilight when I made my way back up the road. I could hear the sheep calling to one another in the field as I climbed higher. The smell of them mingled with the scent of damp grass as I turned off the road onto the farm track.

The sight of a light coming toward me in the gathering gloom took me by surprise. It was Felix on his bicycle. On his way to the pub already, I supposed. I had nowhere to hide. He'd already seen me. Every sinew of my body tensed at the thought of what he might do, with no one else in sight.

He braked hard, skidding to a halt right in front of me. "Oh, it's you." His tone was menacing. "Decided to come back for your supper, then? We thought you'd be getting something fancy at the rectory."

"They're not like that." I took a step back as he climbed off the bike and propped it against the hedge. "Dorothy's very down to earth. There's nothing fancy about her. And anyway, I wasn't at the rectory—I've been down by the church, unloading boxes."

"Oh, it's *Dorothy*, is it? How very cosy! She's got a hell of a cheek, the old bag, dragging you away from the farm yet again."

His face was inches from mine. I could smell his rancid breath. "You want to watch yourself, girl," he snapped. "It doesn't pay to get too cosy with folk around here. You never know what they might be saying about you. A little bird told me that you were necking with an Eye-tie in Bodmin the other night."

"I was *not*!" I felt the blood surge through my neck to my cheeks. "Whoever told you that is a liar! I was in the cinema, on my own, all evening." As soon as the words came out, I realized it was a trap. "With Aunt Ruby right beside me." The extra line came out in a rush. It sounded lame—even to me.

He grabbed the collar of my jacket and pushed me up against the hedge. "Who's the liar now, you little bitch!"

His body was jammed against mine. Thorns from the hedge dug into my scalp. I was so scared I could hardly breathe. "I . . . I don't know what you're talking about."

"Was she with you all evening? Is that the truth?" I caught something in his voice. It was the slightest change of tone that betrayed his desperation to be proved wrong. I seized on that chink in his armor. Pushing against him with all my might, I managed to throw him off-balance.

"Yes, it's the truth," I hissed. "Now leave me alone!" I marched off down the track, shaking with fear, terrified that he'd come after me. When I reached the old barn, I dared to look over my shoulder. To my utter relief, he was a blur in the distance, cycling in the opposite direction.

Who's the liar now? His words rang in my head as I neared the farmhouse. What was I going to say to Aunt Ruby? I would have to tell her. Warn her how close he was to guessing the truth.

Chapter 14

The curtains were drawn across the kitchen window. I could hear Mum's voice. When I opened the door, I saw that they were playing a game of cards.

"Your supper's in the range." Aunt Ruby glanced up when she heard me come in.

"You're late, love," Mum chimed in. "Was there a lot to do?"

"Quite a few boxes to sort out," I said as I reached for the oven glove. Beef stew and dumplings had been set aside for me. I didn't think I could face eating after all that had happened, but it smelled delicious.

I picked at my food as they continued with their game. Mum said I could join in the next round, but I said I'd planned to write a letter to Dad. It wasn't a lie. I'd been meaning to write to him ever since his letter had arrived. But it was also an excuse to be on my own, to allow myself the time to calm down after the encounter with Felix and to mull over everything Dorothy had told me.

"Well, make sure you don't mention the Italians," Mum said. "Can you imagine what he'd say if he knew you were working with them?"

"I'm not that daft," I replied.

I tried to catch Aunt Ruby's eye as I said good night, hoping she might follow me out of the kitchen so I could tell her what had happened. But she was concentrating on the fan of cards in her hand.

It didn't take me long to pen a few lines to Dad. There was so little we were allowed to say, such was the fear of giving away information that could be of use to the enemy. I told him about taking the heavy horses to prepare the field for sowing wheat, and how surprised I'd been to find they were so gentle. I described learning to milk the cows, but I couldn't bring myself to write anything about Felix. I just said that Aunt Ruby had made us very welcome at the farm, that the food in Cornwall was good and plentiful, and that I hoped my mentioning it wouldn't make him envious.

I didn't put the letter in an envelope because it would have to go in the same one as Mum's. Prisoners were permitted only occasional correspondence from loved ones, so we had to be careful how much we sent.

I lay back on the pillow, thinking of him, wondering what he would be doing in that faraway place whose name I could hardly pronounce. My thoughts drifted to Maria Wolveden, the writer of the journal. I wondered how she would have found out about Jago's capture and his imprisonment in the Tower of London. Had Robert Archer announced it from the pulpit, lingering over the details with the same twisted pleasure he had taken in describing the execution of Guy Fawkes and the others?

I thought of Maria, sitting in church, having to listen to that. How long was it afterward, I wondered, before Robert Archer was found dead in the woods near the farmhouse? Did Maria kill him? Or was she framed for his death by the letter he'd written about her?

It was heartbreaking, thinking of her being locked up, facing execution. There had been such joy in that last journal entry. Even though she knew the odds were stacked against her, she reveled in the love she'd found with Jago. I couldn't bear to think of that love being snuffed out, as mine had been when the bombs fell.

Did Maria and Jago haunt my dreams because they had both suffered horrible deaths? Was I sensing their spirits because of what happened to Taslim? I tried to imagine explaining that to Dorothy. I probably shouldn't have told her about the hawk. The idea of a human spirit communicating through an animal wouldn't sit well with anything Humphrey preached on Sundays. If she had me down as delusional, I couldn't blame her. It *sounded* outlandish. But it had felt so real. And so had the nightmares about Maria and Jago.

They're just trying to tell you how it felt to be alive. Taslim's words came back, loud and clear, even though he'd never said them in life.

"But what became of them?" I whispered the question, looking up at the sloping ceiling. "Why can't they tell me *that*?"

In the silence, all I could hear was the distant hoot of an owl.

I slid off the bed and reached under it for the Jacobean box. I'd put the book back inside and turned the key in the lock after reading that final entry. But something nagged away in a corner of my brain. Dorothy had said there was no record of the execution and burial of either Maria or Jago. Was there something in the journal that might provide a clue to where they could have gone if, by some miracle, they'd both managed to escape? I was sure I'd read of a specific place in Spain—but I couldn't remember the name of it.

It didn't take me long to find what I was looking for. On the last page, Maria had written about the friend Jago had met on a pilgrimage from France to Spain. He had moved his printing business to a place called Santiago de Compostela, and there was a possibility of Jago getting work there.

I had never heard of it. But I thought that Dorothy might know where it was. I could ask her when we went to the prison camp. The chances of it shedding any light on the mystery of what had happened to the condemned lovers seemed slim. But she would know whether it was worth pursuing, and how to go about it.

I lay awake for a while after that. My thoughts had turned to Francesco. I pictured him cooped up in a cell, counting the hours until his release. He might have cuts on his face. A broken nose. Or, at the very least, a black eye. And that would be my fault. If I'd been more careful when I was checking that wretched fence post, it wouldn't have fallen on my head. I wouldn't have been hurt, he wouldn't have walked me home, and he would have avoided a beating.

You need to stop blaming yourself. I heard Taslim's voice as I closed my eyes. *People filled with hatred do bad things. That's not your fault.*

"Thank you," I whispered back. But it didn't take away the guilt I felt. If only I'd been more careful with that fence post. If only I hadn't persuaded Taslim to go to the warehouse on that fateful Saturday afternoon. *If only.* Those must be the two saddest words in the English language.

I fell asleep with both Taslim and Francesco on my mind, but neither of them appeared in the nightmare I had that night. It was the kind of dream in which you think you're still awake, which made it even more disturbing. I was sitting up in bed, crying. But I didn't know what I was crying about. I got up, intending to distract myself by going outside, but when I pulled back the curtain to get my clothes, the only things hanging there were the long dresses Maria would have worn.

I put one on, and as I fastened the buttons on the bodice, the bedroom window swung open. Maria's hawk came flying in and landed on my wrist. Just like in my previous dream, it spoke to me with a human voice. It told me that Jago was in the Tower of London and that the men who had arrested him would soon be coming for me.

I knew I had to leave the house and hide somewhere. The hawk led me across the field to the same tree it had perched in before. This time I remembered the name: It was a rowan tree. As I drew closer, a man stepped out from behind it. I recognized his green eyes and thinning hair. Robert Archer. He leered at me and grabbed my arms, pushing me against the trunk of the tree. Unless I promised to marry him, he said, he would denounce me as a witch.

As his mouth closed over mine, I heard a piercing cry and felt a rush of air. The hawk swooped down, clawing at Archer's face. The ambush knocked him off-balance. He fell sideways, and his head struck a gnarled root at the base of the rowan tree.

He lay there, very still, the blood oozing from his head. *I* hadn't killed him, but I knew that if I was found there, people would believe that I had.

I told Phantom to fly away, for fear that the telltale scratches on the rector's face would give away what had happened. Then I ran back to the farmhouse and hid the hawking whistle with the journal in the box.

I woke in the dark, caught in a no-man's-land between dream and reality. For those few seconds, I was her, not me. I was Maria Wolveden. The woman with the hawk. And soon the whole village would know that Robert Archer was dead.

I jumped out of bed in a panic, groping around for my flashlight. When I switched it on, I saw my own face in the mirror. But something was missing. My hand went to my throat. The silver whistle wasn't there. I knew that I hadn't taken it off when I went to bed.

I pulled back the sheet, the blankets, and the eiderdown, but it wasn't there. Then I knelt on the rug beside the bed, thinking it had fallen onto the floor. But there was no glint of metal when I ran the flashlight over the boards.

I don't know why I reached for the Jacobean box, because I had left it empty when I'd retrieved the journal. When I opened it, I found the silver pendant lying inside. Had I put it there in my sleep? Acted out the final part of the nightmare?

I slipped it over my head and climbed back into bed. Images chased each other around my head. Was it true? Had Phantom attacked Robert Archer to protect his mistress? Was a bird of prey capable of that kind of loyalty?

My mind flitted to another question: Was it possible to dream the solution to a mystery? And could that information come from beyond the grave, from a departed spirit taking over the brain of someone living?

Be careful, dear. It was Dorothy's voice I heard then. Her tone was gentle, but there was no mistaking the warning it carried. How would she react if I told her that I knew Robert Archer's death had been an accident because I'd seen it in a dream? She must already be worried about my mental state. Was it a kind of madness, allowing myself to believe that Maria Wolveden had taken temporary control of my unconscious mind?

It's the only way she can communicate. This was a different voice. Taslim was talking to me now. *They called her a murderer. She wants you to know that it wasn't her fault.*

The message was so familiar. *It wasn't her fault.* Just hours ago, he'd used the same words about my part in the beating Francesco had received. And he'd said it repeatedly over the past year: every time I'd cried over my guilt about the way his own life had ended.

Was it any more bizarre, I wondered, to imagine hearing the voice of a departed loved one than that of someone who had lived more than three centuries ago?

So many questions. And there were no real answers. I needed sleep. But I was afraid of what it would bring with it.

In the moments before I drifted off, I wondered if this was what hell would be like. Were these nightmares my punishment for the awful, avoidable results of my actions? I thought that if there was such a place as hell, it could hardly be more wretched.

Chapter 15

Lack of sleep made me clumsy the next morning. I knocked over a bucket when I shifted the milking stool from one cow to another. Mum helped me mop up the mess so that Felix wouldn't see it when he came to move the herd back outside.

She asked me if I was feeling all right. I forced a smile and said I'd been miles away, thinking about Dad and wondering if I could have said more in my letter to cheer him up. I felt bad using him as an excuse. But if I'd told her I was bleary eyed from lack of sleep, she would probably have tried to talk me out of going to the prison camp with Dorothy later. And I couldn't risk that. I needed to see for myself that Francesco was okay.

Aunt Ruby was on my mind, too. I needed to get her on her own somehow, to warn her about Felix's suspicions. Before we'd finished the milking, I told Mum I needed to go to the privy. Instead, I dodged into the kitchen, where my aunt was giving Billy his breakfast.

Her cheerful face clouded when I told her how Felix had interrogated me. I left out the part about him pinning me up against the hedge, but I explained how he'd tricked me by saying he'd heard gossip about me kissing an Italian in Bodmin.

"What did you say?" She was holding on to the back of Billy's high chair. I could see the whites of her knuckles.

"That I'd been on my own all night at the movie. Then I realised I'd fallen into his trap. So, I quickly added that you'd been right beside me."

"Did he believe you?"

I hesitated. "I hope so. I think he wanted to believe me." I glanced at the window. "I'd better go. I'll see you later."

~

Breakfast that morning was a tense affair. My aunt hardly spoke as she doled out the bacon and eggs. Felix sat at the head of the table, stone faced. Mum's chatter to Billy was the only thing that broke the silence. I kept running the confrontation on the track through my head, wondering how I could have been so stupid as to make that slipup. I dreaded to think what was going on inside Felix's head.

When he'd finished eating, he pushed his plate away and got up. The scrape of his chair against the flagstones made us all look up. He stood, drumming the table with his fingers as if he were about to say something. I quaked inside, glancing at Aunt Ruby. She'd turned away, bending over the sink. She looked as if she were trying to make herself as small as possible.

"I've sent a message to White Cross," he said. "No more prisoners to come to Lowartha."

Nobody spoke. Mum and I exchanged glances. My aunt scrubbed away at something in the sink.

"Now the beet harvest's in and the winter wheat planted, we can manage without them," he went on. "Just the animals to look after now." He looked at me. "I expect you'll be glad to stay in the farmyard now the weather's turning colder." Then he turned toward the sink. "No reason for any of you to be going out to the fields anymore."

Aunt Ruby didn't turn around. Felix went to where his gun rested on the hooks on the wall and took it down. He stood for a moment, examining it, before heading out of the kitchen.

Mum was the first to speak. "Well," she said. "It'll make life easier, won't it, not having to make tea and sandwiches for them every morning?"

She turned to me. "And he's right about the weather. There was a real nip in the air when we got up for the milking, wasn't there, Violet?"

I nodded. I was thinking about what really lay behind his decision. He must suspect that Aunt Ruby was interested in one of the men who came to the farm each day, that a romance might have developed before we came to Cornwall, when she'd worked alongside them. If he *did* suspect that, it meant he didn't know about Carlo. But how on earth did he think my aunt could carry on an affair with a man from White Cross when the prisoners were locked up every night?

I couldn't be certain what he was thinking, but no doubt he would watch her every move from now on. I hoped she wouldn't ask me to help with any subterfuge. I wasn't sure I would be able to brazen my way out of another interrogation from Felix. And the thought of running into him while he had that gun in his hand was utterly terrifying.

That Saturday morning, I was given the job of clearing out the stock shed so that the cattle could be brought in from the fields to spend the winter inside. I would be responsible for making sure the animals were fed and watered and regularly mucked out over the coming months.

It looked as if no one had entered the shed since the cows had been put out to pasture in the spring. Dust motes hung in the air when I pushed the door open, and there was a lingering smell of dried manure. I got to work with a shovel and a broom. But it was a vast space. It was going to take hours to get it clean.

While I worked, I thought about the Italian POWs, wondering where they would be taken now that Felix no longer wanted them on the farm. I hadn't realized how much I would miss them. Even though we couldn't communicate much, it had felt companiable, working alongside them. There had been a sense of everyone pulling together to get the job done. And it felt so unnaturally quiet without their singing.

I wondered if Francesco had returned to the work party after his time in the cooler. I hoped that I'd have a chance to speak to him when I went to the camp with Dorothy later. I wanted to apologize to him for what had happened, even though, as Taslim kept reminding me, it wasn't really my fault.

By midday the shed was beginning to look a bit cleaner. I still had to hose down the floor and lay fresh straw, but Aunt Ruby appeared in the doorway, beckoning me out with a gloved finger. She was all ready for the weekly outing for lunch in the village.

This time I insisted on changing out of my working clothes. I looked even scruffier than usual, with bits of straw in my hair and manure caking my boots. She gave me five minutes—which wasn't long enough to do much with my hair other than comb it out. I wriggled into a pair of nylons and pulled on a skirt and sweater before grabbing my coat and hat from the hook on the door.

"You've got something on the side of your face," Mum said as I caught up with them by the farmyard gate. "Looks like a bit of mud." She pulled out her handkerchief, spat on it, and wiped my cheek, as if I were Billy's age again. I hoped it *was* only mud and not something worse.

"Are you sure you're going to be warm enough?" She looked me up and down. "You could do with a scarf and gloves in this weather."

"I'm absolutely roasting," I said. I could feel sweat on the back of my neck. It was going to take ages for me to cool down.

We set off along the track, with me pushing Billy, who was asleep in his pram. I thought the bumpy ride would wake him up, but he didn't stir.

"I hope there'll be something a bit more exciting than mushrooms on toast for us this week," Aunt Ruby said as we turned onto the road. "They used to do fish and chips—fresh haddock landed at Porth harbour—but I haven't seen that on the menu for ages."

She and Mum chatted for a while about foods that had become scarce or unobtainable since the war had started. It made my stomach rumble—I hadn't realized how hungry I was.

When we passed the rectory, I spotted Dorothy hanging washing out. I waved and she called out that she'd see me later.

"Gosh, that's just reminded me." My aunt glanced at Dorothy, who was struggling to peg out a white surplice that was billowing like a sail. "I'm supposed to be doing the flowers for church tomorrow. I'll have to get some in the village and take them round."

"I can do it if you like," Mum said. "Will the shop be open after lunch?"

"No, they close at one o'clock. I'll nip down there now if you two don't mind looking after Billy." She set off at a brisk pace. "Order for me, will you," she called over her shoulder. "Anything but mushrooms on toast!"

The café was packed when we got there. Billy was still asleep, so we left the pram outside with him in it. Mum said we'd hear him if he woke up, but with the volume of chatter, I wasn't sure about that. We had a table by the window, but the glass was so steamed up it was impossible to see out.

"Ooh! Tripe and onions!" Mum was reading the menu. "With sauté potatoes!"

I pulled a face. I'd never been able to fathom how people could get excited about a dish made from the stomach lining of a cow.

"Well, it's that or the mushrooms again," Mum said. "Not much of a choice, is it?"

Hungry as I was, I couldn't face the tripe. I asked the waitress if I could have a double portion of the fried potatoes on their own.

Aunt Ruby still hadn't appeared when our food arrived. Mum asked the waitress for a plate to put over her sister's dish of tripe and onions so that it wouldn't go cold. We'd almost finished our meals when she bustled in, squeezing past the chairs and tables to get to us.

"Sorry it took so long." She wriggled out of her coat, blowing out a breath as she sat down. "I couldn't get into the church. I had to go round to the rectory for the key."

"Well, never mind," Mum said. "You're here now—and this tripe's delicious!"

I studied my aunt's face as she tucked into the food. Her cheeks were pink from rushing around in the cold. But there was something else about her—something that made me uneasy. She had that brightness in her eyes—the same sparkle I'd seen on the bus back from Bodmin. She couldn't have, could she . . . ?

I munched silently on the last of my potatoes as she and Mum chattered away. Was it possible that my aunt had cooked up the story of the flowers to get away for a meeting with Carlo? Had he ridden to the village on the borrowed bicycle for an assignation?

I thought about the practicalities of such a bold plan. How would they have arranged it? There was no telephone at the farmhouse. She could have made a call from the booth in the village if she'd come shopping during the week, but I doubted whether the farm where Carlo was staying had a phone, either. Could she have written to him? That would be a very slow way of arranging things.

Perhaps he knew that she always came into the village at this time on a Saturday. Maybe there was a place they'd met before where there was no danger of being seen. I racked my brains to think of anywhere they could hide. It came to me almost immediately—probably because I'd had to do so much of that kind of thing with Taslim. The graveyard behind the church. There was a little shelter where people could sit if it was raining—I'd spotted it when I'd driven the truck out of the shed.

I hoped I was wrong. That I was letting my imagination run away with me. It would be such a dangerous game. She would be gambling on no one visiting the graveyard on a Saturday at lunchtime. I knew that feeling so well, that sense of the danger of being caught. But she had so much more to lose.

If Taslim and I had been discovered, I would have been banned from seeing him. And I would have had to live with Mum's anger and disappointment in me. But Aunt Ruby would be risking far more than that. Public disapproval and criminal prosecution were the least of her worries. Felix would probably beat her up and throw her out. She could lose Billy.

As if on cue, I heard a wail from outside. Before any of us could get to the door, a woman came in from the street and called out that someone's child was crying. That was the kind of place St Columb Minor was. People watched out for one another. But that could be a double-edged sword.

~

I carried Billy back to the farmhouse on my shoulders. Halfway up the road, he started fussing, so I hummed a tune in a bid to soothe him. The song that came into my head was "The Soldier in Love." Hardly surprising, in view of what I'd been thinking about less than half an hour earlier.

When I stopped humming, he started pulling my hair and wriggling to get down. We were going along the farm track now. Mum and Ruby walked ahead of us with the empty pram.

"Okay, Billy," I said, lifting him off my shoulders. "Let's have a little rest, shall we?"

I sat down on the edge of the old hay trailer—the same place I'd stopped when Francesco had brought me back from the field. The derelict barn was a few yards to my right—its doors held in place by a length of wood wedged into rusty metal brackets. I thought of Carlo, hiding there, waiting until Felix passed by on his way to the pub. How long had that gone on, I wondered, before Mum and I had arrived and ruined the arrangement?

I looked at Billy, who was pulling at the long grass growing around the sunken wheels of the trailer. It worried me to think how precarious things were at the farm, that his little world could be turned upside down with a few careless words.

As I watched him, a sharp cry overhead made us both look up.

"Chi-chi!" Billy pointed to the bird flying toward the old barn. It was his word for the farmyard chickens.

"No, it's not a chicken," I said. "It's a hawk. *Hawk.* Can you say that?"

"Haw!" He chuckled as he said it. "Haw-haw!"

The bird was perched on the edge of the roof, looking down at us. I was pleased to see it. It hadn't appeared for a couple of days, and whenever Felix went out with his gun, I feared for its safety. Watching it now triggered images from the nightmare about Robert Archer lying dead under the rowan tree.

I'd seen it all through Maria's eyes, as if I were living inside her body. I recalled the intense feeling of fear, seeing the bloody scratches Phantom had made on the rector's face, knowing they would betray what had happened. And I remembered the pain of telling my bird to fly away. That had felt so real.

It occurred to me that if what I'd dreamed was true, it would explain why the hawking whistle had been hidden away with the journal in the Jacobean box. Otherwise, Maria would have had no reason to take it off. It would still have been hanging around her neck when they came to arrest her.

I slipped my fingers inside my coat, feeling beneath my sweater for the pendant. "Tell me she didn't die," I whispered, staring up at the hawk. It was a stupid thing to say, because of course she had died at some time—a person who had lived three centuries ago. But I couldn't bear the idea of the woman whose body I had briefly inhabited dying young, slipping away from disease or starvation in some prison cell. Or having her life snuffed out by a hangman's rope, in front of a baying crowd.

For a moment the bird stared back at me. Then it rose into the air and glided off, out of sight.

Aunt Ruby made herself scarce that afternoon. She took Billy upstairs and stayed with him until it was time for me to go and meet Dorothy.

Whether she was afraid of me quizzing her, I don't know. But I soon found out that she'd lied about doing the church flowers.

Dorothy said that she needed to stop at the church before setting off to White Cross. She had to dispose of the floral arrangements on the altar because Mrs. Jennings, the butcher's wife, would bring fresh ones that evening.

I followed her into the church, still hoping I was wrong about my aunt, that she'd got mixed up and thought it was her turn to do the flowers when it wasn't. But as we walked up the steps to the altar, my heart sank. The petals on the yellow chrysanthemums were turning brown.

Dread rose from my belly at the thought of what she'd done. What if Mum mentioned the flowers at the service tomorrow? What if Felix came with us and heard his wife getting caught out by her own lies?

"Are you all right, dear?" Dorothy saw the look on my face. I had to tell her I was feeling a bit queasy after eating too many fried potatoes for lunch at the café.

"Are you sure you're up to driving?"

I assured her that I was. To change the subject, I told her about rereading Maria Wolveden's journal and finding the reference to a place in Spain where Jago had planned to settle if he managed to escape.

"Santiago de Compostela?" She peered at me over the rim of her glasses. "Yes, it's quite famous. The cathedral is reputed to contain a relic of one of the apostles. It's been a place of pilgrimage since medieval times."

"I suppose there's no way of finding out if he ever got there?"

She stood for a moment, her head on one side, looking at the ancient stone font that stood to one side of the church door. "You say that Jago Carlyon's friend set up a printing press in Santiago de Compostela?"

I nodded.

"I have a friend who works at the Bodleian Library in Oxford," she said. "They have hundreds of old manuscripts, from all over the world. There's a chance that a copy of a book produced by that press could have ended up there." She turned to me. "I could write to her. I'm not sure it'll get us any further, but it's worth a try."

"I don't want to put you to any trouble," I said. "I know it's ridiculous, wanting to know how it all ended. It's something about having held that journal in my hands. As if . . ." I trailed off, not wanting to tell her about the vision I'd had of Maria and Jago hovering in the air above my bed. If she was already concerned about my state of mind, I didn't want her to worry any more.

"I do understand," she said. "I felt something like that when I read the letter Robert Archer had written to his bishop. It was so venomous. I could picture him working away at it, the look on his face as he dipped the quill in the ink and composed those sentences, knowing the effect they would have on that poor woman's life."

"She didn't like him." I shook my head. "She wrote that she didn't believe he had the love of God in his heart, that he'd only become rector of St Columba's by right of birth."

"That's how it was in those days," Dorothy replied. "It wasn't a vocation, as it is now. Many men who weren't fit to look after people's souls went into the church that way. They got a house and a good living out of it." She glanced at her watch. "We'd better get a move on—we're due at the camp at six o'clock."

It was a good thing I'd done a trial run to White Cross in daylight. As darkness fell, the road became more hazardous. Because of the blackout, vehicles had to shield their headlights, which meant they gave out only a feeble beam of light. You didn't see something coming the other way until you were practically on top of it.

More than once, I had to slam my foot on the brakes. The boxes in the rear of the truck slid forward when that happened, banging into the back of our seats. I hoped there was nothing inside them that could get broken.

As I drove along, Dorothy told me that word had reached her of a fight between two POWs that had led to both prisoners being locked up. I wondered if she knew that what had happened was directly linked to me. She said that her husband was friendly with the camp chaplain, who'd told them all about it when he'd called at the rectory that morning.

"I think it was very unfair that the man who was picked on was punished," she said. "The chaplain thought so, too. He said the fight was about him helping a British woman who'd had a fence post fall on her in the field where they worked."

"Yes," I said. "That was me."

"Oh, my dear . . ." Dorothy's hand flew to her mouth. "Why didn't you say anything yesterday? The thought of you moving all those wretched boxes . . . No wonder you felt giddy."

"It wasn't anything, really," I said. "I was back at work yesterday morning. I feel far worse about what happened to him."

"Well, the chaplain's keeping an eye on the situation," Dorothy replied. "The trouble is, he can't be there all the time. These fights tend to break out when they're all locked up for the night."

I thought how frightening that must be, to be shut in a dormitory with someone who might attack you while you were sleeping. "Can't they separate the men who work on the farms from the ones who don't?" I asked.

"I don't think that's something Lieutenant Colonel Graves would even consider," she said. "When it comes down to it, they're the enemy. They're not considered worthy of any special treatment."

As we neared White Cross, I slowed the truck to a crawl. In the dark, the gates were difficult to spot. I overshot them by a few yards and had to reverse back. Luckily, nothing was coming up behind me.

We parked in the same place as before, in front of the mess hall, with the back of the truck facing the building. A group of men was already waiting for us. They crowded around the truck before we'd even had a chance to open the rear doors.

"Stand back, please!" Dorothy could be very forceful when she needed to be. I wondered why no guards were on hand to oversee the prisoners. Perhaps the attitude was that within the camp, there was a limit to what mischief these men could cause. But I knew that wasn't true. Had the guards simply turned their backs when Francesco was beaten up?

I scanned the faces gathered around us. Francesco's wasn't among them. Dorothy gave me the nod to pull out the sliding shelf from inside the truck. I arranged a selection of goods on it while Dorothy brought out the account book and the tin for collecting the tokens.

When the first customers had come and gone, I looked to see if Francesco had joined the line. But the only person I recognized was Giovanni, the doctor. When it was his turn to be served, I asked him where Francesco was.

"He stays out of the way, I think," he replied. "Not want to make more trouble."

It was understandable, but I couldn't help feeling disappointed. Now that he wasn't going to be coming back to the farm, I wouldn't have the chance to apologize for what he'd suffered on my account.

"Will you give him a message from me?" I asked. "Could you tell him that I'm so sorry for what happened, and that I've been thinking of him and hoping he's okay?"

I reached across the shelf for the pack of cigarettes Giovanni wanted to buy. He had the tokens in his hand, ready to pay, but as he went to give them to Dorothy, he accidentally knocked over the tin she collected them in. The plastic discs spilled onto the ground, creating a furor as the men in the line scrambled to retrieve them.

Dorothy banged her fist against the door of the truck and yelled out a warning: "If I find that a single token is missing when I total up, we won't be coming here again!"

You didn't need to understand English to get the message. The expression on her face was enough. One by one, the men came forward and handed over the tokens they'd picked up. Giovanni apologized for being so clumsy. He looked very anxious. I told him not to worry, that everything would be fine now.

Our time at the camp was limited to an hour, and when that was up, we slid the shelf back into the truck and headed for the gates.

"Goodness, I'm worn out!" Dorothy blew out a breath as we turned onto the road. "I thought we were going to have a riot on our hands when those tokens went everywhere."

"You handled it very well," I said. "I don't know what I'd have done, if it'd been up to me."

"I suppose it's all those years of being a teacher." She grunted a laugh. "Comes in useful sometimes."

On the way back, she asked me how I was feeling. "I don't mean the bump on the head," she said. "Have you been sleeping any better after those nightmares you were telling me about?"

"Not really," I replied. I told her about the latest one. But I didn't let on that I'd felt as though I'd been inside Maria's body as the dream unfolded—I was afraid she might think I was unhinged.

"It was so vivid," I said. "The hawk attacked Robert Archer because he had Maria up against the tree. He was threatening to denounce her as a witch unless she promised to marry him. When I woke up, I couldn't help wondering if that was what had happened in reality," I said. "Do you think that's possible? To be given the answer to something in a dream?"

"Well, yes," she said. "The Bible is laced with stories of people receiving messages or warnings through dreams." She paused for a moment. "What you dreamed was that someone accused of murder was innocent. It reminds me of what happened to Pontius Pilate's wife—the dream she had when Jesus was on trial."

"I don't remember," I said. "What was it about?"

"She told her husband she'd had a really bad dream about Jesus, that he was an innocent man, and Pilate should have nothing to do with the trial the Jewish leaders had called for."

"Really? I didn't know that."

"It tends to get lost in the story of the crucifixion. Pilate's gone down as one of history's villains, but he did listen to his wife. He didn't believe Jesus had done anything to deserve the death penalty."

And neither had Maria. I'd never imagined that dreams like mine would feature in the Bible. I found something very comforting about that.

"I was rather concerned about those other nightmares you told me about," Dorothy said. "And when you talked about ghosts . . . I was afraid there might be some sort of lingering evil in the farmhouse, and that because of the trauma of what happened to you in London, you might be susceptible to its influence. But I don't believe that now. Not after what you've just told me."

"You don't?" I glanced at her.

"A great wrong was done to that woman," she went on. "She never had the chance to clear her name. Somehow, you're picking up on that."

This was close to what I'd sensed Taslim telling me: that taking over my unconscious mind was Maria's only way of communicating the truth.

Dorothy put her hand on my arm. "Don't, for heaven's sake, tell Humphrey I said that, will you, dear? He's very anti this sort of thing. His view is that the Old Testament forbids people from trying to communicate with the dead, so that's all there is to say on the matter. But as far as I'm aware, there's nothing in the Bible that says *they* can't communicate with *us*."

That thought stayed with me for the rest of the journey back to St Columb Minor. Ever since discovering the Jacobean box, I'd had a sense of unleashing something malevolent and uncontrollable, that the spirits of those long-dead people were to be feared. Taslim had tried to tell me otherwise, but in my heart, I was still afraid. Now that I'd heard the same thing from Dorothy, it was as if something inside me had been released.

As we neared the church, she asked me if I wouldn't mind locking up the truck and the shed and putting the keys through the letterbox at the rectory on my way back to the farmhouse. "I've got the bishop coming for dinner," she explained. "I asked Humphrey to keep an eye on the roast chicken, but I don't entirely trust him, I'm afraid. When he gets his nose in a book, he tends to forget everything else."

I said I'd drive her up the hill to the rectory to save time. Climbing out, she thanked me for my help and said I was a treasure. I smiled as I watched her walk away from the dim beam of the headlamps. No one had ever called me that before.

The road was too narrow to do a three-point turn, so I reversed back down to the church. It was very quiet when I switched off the engine. I rummaged in my handbag for my flashlight, ready to switch it on as soon as I got out of the truck. As I reached for the door handle, I heard something that stopped me dead.

Violet.

My name, whispered in the darkness. It sounded so real. Whose voice was that, inside my head? Not Taslim's, I was certain of that. Was Jago Carlyon trying to communicate with me now? Was it *his* turn to tell his story?

A sudden movement behind me made me cry out. I thought a rat had found its way in and was burrowing among the boxes.

"Don't be scared." That voice again. "It's me. Francesco."

Chapter 16

He scrambled over the back of the passenger seat and slid down into the place Dorothy had just vacated.

"How on earth did you . . ." I trailed off, still in shock.

"I get inside the truck when Giovanni drop the tokens," he replied. "It is our plan, to make a big noise, so no one can see what I do."

In the dark, I couldn't see his face. My heart was pounding at the thought of what he'd done, of what would happen if Dorothy suddenly came back and caught us.

"The man who hit me, he says he is going to kill me," he went on. "So, I have to get out of the camp."

"*Kill* you?" I echoed.

"Already he hates me for working with the British. When he hears what I do for you, he says why don't you take her life when you are alone with her—as revenge for our people who are dying in the war."

"Oh my God." I blew out a breath.

"After the fight, we are both locked up. There is nothing he can do to me. But when they let us out, then I know he is waiting to get me. Giovanni, he tells me everyone is talking about what he will do, how he will creep up on me in the dark and slit my throat with the lid of a can of corned beef."

The grim picture made me shudder. No wonder he'd grabbed this chance to get away. "But what are you going to do now? Where will you go? It won't be long, will it, before they realise you've escaped? They'll be out looking for you."

"I need to hide," he said. "Can you help me, Violet? I don't want to get you into any trouble. But do you know a place where no one will see me?"

"I . . . I'm not sure." I hesitated. In that moment, it occurred to me that I'd been set up: that he'd gone out of his way to win me over as part of a carefully calculated escape plan. Remembering my name, chatting to me in the field, then offering to walk me home after the accident . . . had he done those things with an eye on using me when he broke out of the camp? And what about the threat to his life—how could I possibly know if he was telling the truth?

How would he have known that you'd be on your own now? That Dorothy wouldn't be with you when you locked the van and the shed? Taslim's voice cut through the confusion in my head. Of course, I thought. He couldn't have known that. He must have been so desperate that he made the plan to escape without knowing what he'd do once he got away.

Even so, there were a dozen good reasons for refusing to help him. I'd be putting myself and everyone associated with me in danger of criminal charges if word got out. But if I said no, what would become of him? In those prison camp clothes, he didn't stand a chance of getting away from here.

And if it was true that he'd only made this bid for freedom because his own life was in jeopardy, that was because of me.

~

As we crept along the side of the church, I heard a wave of laughter. Someone must have opened the door of the pub. I grabbed Francesco's arm to stop him from going any farther. When the noise subsided, we made our way onto the road. I was terrified of bumping into Felix. It was around the time he'd be cycling down to the village for his nightly session in The Farmers Arms.

Francesco followed me uphill. It was a clear night but there was no moon. Just the glow of the stars. I didn't want to attract attention by using my flashlight. It was lucky that I'd done this walk enough times to know every bend in the road.

When we reached the gate of the rectory, I told Francesco to crouch down by the wall while I went to put the keys to the truck and the shed through the door. When I walked toward the house, I could hear voices coming from inside. I was afraid that Dorothy might catch the sound of the letterbox opening and invite me in to meet the bishop. But there was no pause in the conversation as the keys dropped onto the mat.

I hurried back to where Francesco waited. "Come on," I whispered. "If you see lights from a car or a bicycle, you dive into the hedge, okay?"

We made it safely to the turnoff to the farm. "You remember when we walked along here?" I was still whispering, but my voice sounded very loud in the silence. "Not far to go now."

The old barn was a black silhouette against the inky sky. I almost tripped over the hay trailer as I led the way. Feeling for the edges of the wooden pole that kept the door shut, I pried it out of the metal brackets. The door creaked open, letting out a dry, musty smell.

Once we were both inside, I pushed the wooden latch down and turned on my flashlight. Now I could see Francesco's face. His left eye was puffy and tinged purple round the edges. And there was an inch-long cut on his cheekbone. My hand went out automatically. My instinct was to stroke that injured face. But I stopped short of touching him. He wasn't a child, like Billy—he was a man. A man I barely knew.

"I'm sorry," I mumbled. "I hope it doesn't hurt too much."

"It's nothing." He tried to smile, but the movement made him wince.

The flashlight almost slipped out of my hand as I shone it around the barn. I was drenched in perspiration and my heart was still racing.

There was nothing but a few rotting bales stacked against one wall alongside some rusty tools: a spade with a broken handle, an old scythe, and a hayfork that had lost its prongs. In the center of the space was a rickety ladder with some of its rungs missing. It was propped against a hatch in what appeared to be a loft area.

"You could hide up there," I said. "I'll hold the ladder. See if it'll take your weight."

The ladder creaked as he put his foot on it, but the rungs held as he made his way to the top. When he'd climbed into the loft, he held the top of the ladder so I could follow him up.

There was plenty of dry straw in the loft. Despite the dip in the roof, it didn't appear to have let the rain in.

"I can sleep here." Francesco patted a pile of straw in the far corner of the loft. "But what if someone comes?"

"It's not used anymore," I replied. "I'll bring you some food and water later tonight. I'll leave my flashlight for you. I'll get you a lamp when I come back."

"No," he said. "You need the light now. I will be okay."

"Are you sure? I'll have to shut you in." I was thinking of Felix. When he came past on his way back from the pub, he might notice if the pole was out of its brackets.

"Yes. I am not afraid of the dark. But if I hear something, how will I know it is you?"

I thought about it for a moment. I needed to give him some sort of signal; otherwise he'd think it was someone coming to look for him. The solution came to me in a flash: the hawking whistle. I retrieved it from under my sweater and blew a short blast.

"Like the bird," he whispered. *"Il falco."*

As I turned to go back down the ladder, he reached out and caught me by the hand. In one swift movement, he brought my fingers up to his mouth and kissed them. "Thank you, Violet," he murmured. "You save me."

I was shaking as I climbed down the ladder. I don't know if it was because the full gravity of what I'd done hit me at that moment, or whether it was because, for the first time in more than a year, a man had kissed me.

If I'd known what he was going to do, I would have pulled away. And yet there was nothing reprehensible in what he'd done. It wasn't the way an Englishman would have expressed his gratitude to a woman he barely knew, but perhaps, in Italy, this was the normal way of saying thank you.

~

Mum and Aunt Ruby were outside, in the farmyard, when I got back. They were tipping the bathwater into the drain. The tub was so heavy it took two people to shift it.

"Oh, Mum!" I ran over to them. "You should have waited for me to do that!"

"It's all right," she said. "I can manage. I think all the good food and the fresh air are making me stronger."

I followed them back into the kitchen, praying that my face wouldn't betray the agitation I felt inside.

"How did you get on at the camp?" Aunt Ruby went over to the range and took a plate out of the oven.

"Oh, it wasn't too bad." My voice sounded unnaturally high. I coughed and murmured something about being parched after the walk back from the church.

"There's tea in the pot," Mum said. "We were just about to have a cup." She fetched the crockery from the dresser and poured a drink for each of us. "We're going to take ours through to the living room," she said. "Come and join us when you've finished your supper—we can get cosy by the . . ." She checked herself. Sometimes she almost forgot about my phobia. She mouthed the word *sorry*.

"I think I might wash my hair," I said. I needed to find a way to sneak some food out to Francesco. "Is there any hot water left in the copper?"

"Should be," Aunt Ruby said. She kept her eyes on her teacup. She hadn't looked directly at me since the episode in the café.

When they'd left the room, I went straight into the larder. I cut a hunk of cheese and some thick slices of bread and wrapped them in waxed paper. I stuffed a couple of apples into my handbag as well. He would need water. How could I smuggle that past Mum and Aunt Ruby without them noticing? I cast around the kitchen for inspiration, and my eyes fell on the rubber hot water bottles we'd been taking to bed with us the past couple of nights. I could fill one of those with cold water.

I washed my hair in the sink and bundled it into a towel. When I went to say good night, the blazing logs in the hearth spat out sparks as I opened the door. I hovered on the threshold, not wanting to venture any closer. The familiar bubble of panic rose from my belly at the sight of the flames.

"What about your hair?" Mum's voice trailed after me as I headed through to the dairy.

"I towelled it dry by the range," I called back. "And I'm really tired." The last part wasn't a lie. I felt exhausted. But I had to stay awake until I was certain that Felix was back from the pub. I couldn't risk bumping into him on the way back to the barn.

In my room, I kept watch by the window. So long as I didn't switch on the flashlight, no one would see, from the outside, that I had the curtains half open. Even though the farmyard below was in darkness, I could see the outlines of the milking shed, the pigsty, and the gate that led out onto the track. When Felix returned, I would see the lamp on the front of his bicycle.

Waiting for that glimmer of light felt like an eternity. I turned everything over in my mind, trying to work out what would happen at the camp when they discovered Francesco was missing. Would they guess how he'd escaped? Would they come banging on the door of the rectory? And if they did, how long would it be before they came to interrogate me?

I worked out what I would say, just in case that happened. I would simply tell them that I'd locked the truck and the shed immediately after parking at the church, dropped the keys off, then made my way home. After all, I reasoned, if Francesco hadn't whispered my name, I would never have known he was hiding among the boxes in the back. He could have waited until I'd gone, let himself out of the truck, and then found a way out of the shed. There were plenty of tools in there. No doubt he could have sawed through the metal hasp that held the padlock if he'd worked away at it for long enough.

I wondered if the guards at the camp would question Francesco's friends. Giovanni would probably have cooked up a story to throw them off the scent. He'd staged the diversion that had allowed Francesco to get into the truck unnoticed, so he was bound to have prepared himself for what would follow. The clever thing to do would be to send them off in a completely different direction from St Columb Minor: to suggest, perhaps, that Francesco had talked of heading to London.

That thought made my mind jump ahead to how Francesco *was* going to get away. He would need clothes; that was the first thing. The kind that would allow him to pass through towns and villages without attracting attention. Could I steal clothes from Felix? That would take some careful planning. He'd left a jacket and an overcoat hanging up in the kitchen. But how long would it be before he missed them? Could I take a few things from the laundry basket on wash day?

I tried to imagine Francesco in those clothes. He was taller and slimmer than Felix. But with a few safety pins, I could make them fit. The prison-issue boots were no different from what most men in rural Cornwall wore, so at least that wouldn't be a problem.

Then I thought about money. He was going to need that, too. I had a few pounds in my Post Office Savings Account. I could go to the village and draw some out. But not until Monday at the earliest.

A distant flicker of light broke my chain of thought. It was Felix. His silhouette appeared at the gate as he dismounted and pushed the bicycle into the farmyard. Not long to wait now, I hoped.

After a while, I heard the creak of the floorboards. It came from the room across the landing. Was that Aunt Ruby getting ready for bed, or was it the two of them? I waited until everything went silent. Then I grabbed my bag and the rubber water bottle and crept down the stairs.

The cat jumped onto my shoulder as I tiptoed through the dairy. I clapped my hand against my mouth to stop myself from crying out. For a split second I thought it was Felix, grabbing me from behind. But the feel of fur against my cheek told me it was Kuching.

I let myself out of the dairy and crossed the farmyard as noiselessly as I could. I needed to get a paraffin lamp and some matches from the milking shed. I picked up a bucket, too. If Francesco was going to be locked inside the barn for a long period of time, he would need something to relieve himself into.

My flashlight was in my pocket, but I didn't use it to see my way along the track. I couldn't be certain that Felix was in bed. If he was still in the kitchen or the living room and happened to look through the curtains, there was a chance he would see the light.

When I reached the barn, I put the whistle to my lips and blew one short blast. It sounded incredibly loud in the still night air. I grasped the pole that held the door shut and slid it out of the brackets. It fell to the ground with a thud. A rustling in the hedge to my right made me freeze. What was it? As I stood there, the door was pulled open from the inside.

"Violet." There was a lilt in the way Francesco said my name that made it sound much prettier than the way English people pronounced it. "Are you okay?" he whispered. "You think someone follows you?"

"I heard a noise," I whispered back. "But I think it was just an animal—a rabbit or something."

When the door was safely latched behind us, I switched on my flashlight. He took the bucket with the paraffin lamp and the water bottle inside and climbed the ladder. I followed once he reached the loft. I didn't want to risk putting too much weight on rungs that looked as though they could give way at any moment.

"I wish I could have brought you a hot water bottle as well," I said as he unscrewed the top of the bottle and put the rubber mouth to his lips. "It's so cold tonight. Are you managing to keep warm?"

He smiled. "I make a hole in the straw. Like a little mouse."

His smile widened when I handed over the bread and cheese. He touched his cheek where the cut had scabbed over. It must be hard to remember not to smile. While he ate, I lit the paraffin lamp. I tried to keep my hand steady as I struck the match. The thought of it dropping onto the dry straw was terrifying.

"I'd better go now," I said. "I'll come back in the morning."

"I don't want you to have trouble because of me." His eyes searched mine. "If I leave now, I can get far away before the morning."

"But where would you go? How would you know what direction to take?"

He shrugged. "I will see the stars. I know where is north. The sea is west, yes? Not far from here?"

"It is," I said. "But what would you do when you got there? In those clothes, anyone who saw you would know you were a prisoner of war."

"I could hide on a boat."

I stared at him. In a strange trick of the lamplight, his features seemed to melt into another face I knew. It was as if he had transformed into the portrait from the Jacobean box. It suddenly struck me that history was about to repeat itself: that this man hiding away on the farm was planning an escape identical to Jago Carlyon's. That had ended in disaster. I couldn't let Francesco meet the same fate.

"Please, don't go tonight," I said. "Wait until I can get you some other clothes. And some money. You'll have a better chance then."

He shook his head. "Already you do so much for me. I cannot take your money."

"Well, I can't let you leave here with nothing but those tokens in your pocket," I said. "I don't have more than a couple of shillings back at the house, but I can draw more out on Monday."

I pressed my lips together, remembering my visits to deposit cash around the corner from our shop in London. The money I'd saved each month was meant to be *our* escape fund. Mine and Taslim's. For going to Scotland to get married. Would *he* approve of me offering that money to this man?

Yes, I thought. He would.

~

When I crept back into the farmhouse, via the door of the dairy, I paused to listen for the sound of anyone who might still be awake. The only thing I could hear was Kuching, scrabbling about in a corner, probably in pursuit of a mouse.

I took my shoes off and tiptoed up the stairs to my room. I didn't get undressed straight away. I knelt on the bed for a while, peering out through the curtains. Even in daylight, I couldn't see the barn from my window. It lay in a dip in the track, concealed by the hedges. But as I stared out into the darkness beyond the farmyard, at the stars twinkling in the moonless sky, I had the strangest feeling.

Scared wasn't the right word to describe it. I *was* scared, of course, of the potential consequences of hiding Francesco. But it was more than that. I felt a kind of exhilaration, a sense of having done something I wouldn't have believed I was capable of. It was as if I'd moved from an existence where everything was shades of gray into a world bursting with color.

Was that wrong, I wondered, when what I'd done was against the law? I couldn't answer that question. All I knew was that I felt good inside—for the first time since losing Taslim.

I don't know what time it was when I finally got into bed. I fell asleep running through the pros and cons of various escape strategies. I thought of taking Felix's bike. Francesco could go anywhere on that. I thought of Falmouth. It was a big port, not far away. And, according to what Dorothy had told me, it was crowded with refugees. In a place like that, he could blend in. His English was good enough for him to pretend he wasn't an Italian. He could say he was French or Belgian—any nationality that didn't make him an enemy alien. And perhaps, if he had money, he could bribe his way onto a ship.

Falmouth would be a much better bet than Porth harbor. I'd seen only a handful of small fishing boats there. With a war going on, I doubted that any would be sailing beyond British waters. The chances of Francesco pulling off what Jago had planned to do were virtually zero.

In the dream I had that night, I was back at the prison camp. Giovanni was chasing me as I drove toward the gates, and he was yelling Francesco's name. In my desperation to silence him, I threw the truck into reverse and knocked him down. Winding down the window, I saw guards running to arrest me. I knew that I was going to be accused of murder, and that I would hang for it.

I cried out to Dorothy to help me, but when I turned my head, someone else was sitting in the passenger seat of the truck. It was Maria. She had the goshawk perched on her wrist.

Don't be afraid. Phantom will set you free.

Her words echoed through my head as I drifted back to consciousness. I was still puzzling over them as I pulled on my clothes. What did it mean? How could a bird set someone free?

~

There was no time to go to the barn before the morning's work was done. Even on a Sunday, the cows had to be milked and given fresh hay to eat. It was so cold I could see the animals' breath as they lumbered across the farmyard. I hoped Francesco had managed to keep himself warm.

At breakfast, I slipped two rashers of bacon and a slice of bread off my plate when Aunt Ruby's back was turned. I had waxed paper ready in my pocket. I'd already hidden a jug of milk on a shelf in the dairy, ready to take to the barn later.

I considered saying that I didn't feel well, to get out of going to church. With everyone out of the house for a couple of hours, I'd have plenty of time to take Francesco his breakfast. But then Felix announced that *he* wasn't well. He said that the beer at the pub last night had tasted sour, and it had upset his stomach. He said there was no way he was going to be able to sit through the morning service.

I decided that my only option was to get down to the barn before we went to church. I wouldn't have long, but all I needed to do was hand over the food. At least I knew that Felix wouldn't be roaming the track, taking potshots at the rabbits. He'd gone off to the privy straight after breakfast, warning us all to stay clear of the place.

I told Mum and Aunt Ruby I needed to top up the hay for the cows before church. Mum was too busy feeding Billy to take much notice, and Aunt Ruby was lighting her first cigarette of the day. I went in with the cows for a couple of minutes, just in case either of them had followed me out into the farmyard. When I was certain no one was about, I doubled back to the dairy, retrieved the jug of milk, and set off down the track.

When I reached the barn, I blew the whistle. To my surprise, the hawk came gliding over my head and landed on the thatched roof. It watched me as I slid the pole out of the brackets to open the door.

Don't be afraid. Phantom will set you free. The words from last night's dream came back to me. What had Maria meant by that? It wasn't *me* hiding from the authorities.

"Violet!" The sound of Francesco's voice startled me. It hadn't come from inside. I whipped my head around and there he was, peeping at me from behind a corner of the barn. He looked up the track before darting across to where I stood.

"Quick! Let's get you inside." I ushered him in, then latched the door. "How did you get out?"

"Over there." He pointed to half a dozen hay bales stacked against the wall. When I went to look, I saw that the wood had rotted where the hay had rested against it. He'd pulled out a couple of pieces to make a gap. It was in the side of the barn that faced away from the track, so it wouldn't be visible to anyone passing by.

"Be careful, won't you?" Most mornings, Felix would be out here. Thank goodness for the dodgy beer, I thought.

"Of course," Francesco replied. "I only go out late in the night. Last night, I get more water."

"What?" I stared at him, open-mouthed. "Where from?"

"There is a tap in the yard—where the cows live."

"You came into the *farmyard*?"

"It is okay—everybody is asleep."

I shook my head. "I can't stop you, Francesco, but I have to warn you: Felix keeps a gun in the kitchen—if he heard you . . ." I trailed off, batting away the dreadful image in my mind's eye.

"Please, Violet, do not worry about me. Remember—I am a soldier."

But that won't help if he has a gun and you don't. I didn't say it out loud. I handed him the jug of milk and the bacon sandwich. "I can't stay," I said. "We're going to church. I'll come back this afternoon." I glanced at my watch. "Don't worry if you hear voices in about half an hour from now—it'll just be my aunt and my mother and me on our way to the village. But you'd better stay in here until we've come past. And watch out for Felix—he's not coming with us."

He nodded. "When you get to the church, you will know if they are looking for me?"

"Yes," I replied. If the guards had suspected his method of escape, they would want to see the truck and check that he wasn't hiding in the shed.

"What do you say if they ask questions?"

"I've already thought about that." I repeated the lines I'd rehearsed in my head. *I locked the truck, then the shed, then pushed the keys through the letterbox of the rectory. I didn't see anybody until I got back home.* "If there's any danger of them coming here, I'll find a way of letting you know," I said. "I'll pretend to be ill or something."

"Okay." The worry lines on his forehead relaxed a little. "Thank you for everything." He put his hand on his chest. "You have a sweet heart."

"I think you mean a kind heart. But that's a nice thing to hear." I smiled. I wished I could stay longer. I wanted to talk to him properly, to find out more about him and the family he had left behind in Italy. But that would have to wait. I said goodbye and headed for the door.

"Say a prayer for me in the church," he called after me.

I felt very tense when, a short while later, Mum, Aunt Ruby, Billy, and I set off for St Columba's. Billy refused to go in the pram and kept wandering off the track to examine whatever caught his eye in the hedgerow. There were scarlet berries growing in a few places, which he wanted to pick and put in his mouth.

"No, Billy!" I ran to grab his little fist. I was no expert on wildflowers, but I knew that these berries were poisonous. Not like the ones my aunt had made into jelly. I scooped Billy up and put him on my shoulders, hoping that would keep him happy on the walk to the village. As we got farther down the track, I prayed that Francesco had heeded my advice to stay inside the barn. My eyes darted everywhere, afraid of catching sight of that prison uniform.

Mum and Aunt Ruby were deep in conversation as we approached the barn. They were talking about Felix's bad stomach, and how annoying it was that no one else had been able to get into the privy that morning. Neither of them stopped talking as we passed Francesco's hiding place. Still, I couldn't relax until we reached the road.

When we walked past the rectory, I wondered if anyone from White Cross had been there, asking questions. I was desperate to talk to Dorothy, but I'd have to judge things carefully. I mustn't give any hint of what had happened last night.

When we got inside St Columba's, I looked around for her, but she wasn't there. I followed Mum and my aunt into the same pew we'd sat in last time.

"Lovely flowers, Ruby!" Mum was looking at the three silver vases on the altar. The fading chrysanthemums had been replaced with pink and white roses.

My aunt mumbled something I didn't catch. She was bending over Billy, giving him a rusk to chew on during the service. I wondered when she planned to see Carlo again, what excuse she would come up with the next time they had a secret assignation.

Dorothy didn't appear until the last minute. Humphrey was already standing in front of the altar when she took her seat in the front pew. I was on edge all through the service, half expecting armed men to burst through the doors, on the hunt for Francesco. When it came to the notices, I held my breath. Would Humphrey announce that a man had escaped from White Cross Camp? Would he give a warning to the congregation?

I had an awful feeling of history repeating itself. Three centuries ago, Robert Archer had stood in this same place, denouncing Jago Carlyon and giving a dire warning to anyone who might be harboring him. Hearing those words must have struck terror into Maria's heart. She would have been sitting here, thinking of Jago in the shepherd's hut, worrying about how long it would be before the king's men came to search the farm.

In that last vivid dream about the death of Robert Archer, I had felt as though I were seeing through Maria's eyes, that she and I were the same person. Now I had that same feeling. But this time it wasn't a dream.

Chapter 17

I sat through Humphrey's repetition of the banns of marriage for the same two couples he'd announced the previous week. Then there was a notice about a collection of Christmas gifts to send, via the Red Cross, to British troops fighting abroad.

"The next item on my list is for any member of the congregation who is a fire watch volunteer: The rota for next month will be on display in The Farmers Arms at the end of this coming week."

Each time he finished one notice and began another, my heart pumped faster.

"And finally . . ." He paused as he looked down at his notes. I held my breath. "The rota for the flowers . . ." The wave of relief was so great I didn't hear what he said after that. I was still in a daze when everyone stood to sing the next hymn.

"Silly old fool got that wrong, didn't he?" Mum whispered as I searched for the page in the hymn book. "Mrs. Jennings indeed! And after all the trouble our Ruby went to! I was going to volunteer for the flower arranging, but I shan't now."

I glanced at my aunt. She'd gone very red in the face.

During the closing prayers, I remembered Francesco's request as I'd left the barn. He wanted me to pray for him. I couldn't recall the last time I'd said a prayer that wasn't something formal, from the service book. Something already written that could be reeled off without even thinking about the words. I wasn't even sure I knew how to do it anymore.

God, if you're real, please keep him safe. And help me to help him. It wasn't the language of the prayer book, but it was the best I could do.

When the service ended, Aunt Ruby scooped Billy up and made a beeline for the door, mumbling something about having left his bottle in the pram. It looked as though she were trying to evade questions about the flowers. Mum headed out after her. I waited behind in the pew. I had to speak to Dorothy, but I needed to choose my words carefully. I mustn't say anything to arouse her suspicions.

She was still at the front of the church, talking to a man standing in the aisle, who was blocking her exit. I went and stood a couple of feet away, just in case someone else tried to corner her on the way out.

When at last the man turned away, I seized my chance. "Good morning!" I put on the bright smile I had practiced so often in the mirror back in London. "I just wanted to check that you found the keys—I was worried they might have got stuck in the letterbox."

"Oh, yes dear." She didn't return my smile. She looked distracted. "I'm so sorry—I'm needed outside: Some people from White Cross are here. Apparently, there was an escape last night and they want to search the truck."

"An escape?" I struggled to keep the panic out of my voice. I followed her as she hurried toward the door. We passed Humphrey, who was shaking hands as people filed out of church. The prison guards waited out of sight of the congregation, around the side of the building.

As she led the way, Dorothy turned to me. "Will you stay and talk to them while I go and get the keys from the rectory?"

"Er . . . yes . . . of course." My lips trembled as the words came out. The guards were looking at us. Both had guns slung over their shoulders.

Dorothy explained about the keys. "This young lady was with me at the camp yesterday evening," she said. "I'm sure she'll agree with me that there's no way a man could have hidden in the truck without us noticing."

"All the same, ma'am, we'll need to ask you both a few questions," one of the men replied.

"I'll be back in five minutes," Dorothy said. "But I'm sure Violet will be able to tell you everything you need to know."

As she turned away, my mouth went dry. No amount of rehearsing had prepared me for the fear I felt at that moment.

You're a champion liar, remember? Taslim was suddenly with me, inside my head. *Don't let them see that you're scared. Stall for time.*

"Excuse me for a moment," I said. "I just need to let my family know that I won't be walking home with them."

In the time it took for me to find Mum and Aunt Ruby and explain the situation, I fought to steady my nerves. They were shocked to hear about the escape. I had to reassure Mum that no one had been lurking in the back of the truck, waiting to pounce on me, that the visit from the guards was just a routine inquiry.

Aunt Ruby wanted to know if it was one of our workers who had escaped. I said I didn't know, which was another outright lie. But it helped me, practicing the deceit on them. It gave me a better chance of facing up to the guards. I crossed my fingers behind my back as I said I'd be back in time for lunch, then I bent over the pram to kiss Billy. I watched them start off up the hill before walking back toward the church, steeling myself for the interrogation.

The first thing the guards wanted to know was whether I'd seen anyone acting suspiciously when we were at the camp. That was easy to answer. I wouldn't have suspected Giovanni's stunt to be anything other than an accident if Francesco hadn't told me the reason for it.

"And you didn't see anyone trying to get into the truck while it was parked outside the mess hall?"

"If I had, I would have told Mrs. Frobisher," I replied. I hoped I sounded naive, slightly lacking in the brains department.

"What about when you returned here," the guard said. "Did you check the back of the truck? Unload any of the boxes?"

I shook my head. "We leave that until the day before our next visit to the camp. We get more stock delivered during the week, so there's no point sorting things out until it's arrived."

Dorothy came back with the keys then. "Here we are." She sounded out of breath. "Everything all right?" She glanced at me. I nodded.

We followed the guards, who told us to stand well clear of the shed as one unlocked it and the other stood ready with his gun aimed at the door. After a warning shout, they both went in. We heard them unlocking the truck. Then the sound of boxes thudding onto the ground. After a few minutes they emerged and told us there was no one in the truck, and no sign of anyone having broken out of the shed.

Dorothy nodded. "May I ask the name of the man who has escaped?"

"Marelli," the guard replied. "He'd been working at a farm near here."

Dorothy turned to me. She opened her mouth, looking as though she were about to say something, but then closed it again. She turned back to the guards. "Marelli." She frowned. "Why does that name sound familiar?"

Please, Dorothy . . . I willed her not to remember that he was the man the chaplain had told her about, the one who had been beaten up for helping me after my accident. I could feel the blood surging up through my neck to my face.

"We write down all the men's names when they buy something," she said. "I can check, if you like, to see if he bought anything yesterday." She went into the shed with the guards to retrieve the account book.

"That's strange," she said, leafing through the pages. "He came to the shop last week but not this time."

"What did he buy then?" One of the guards held out his hand to take the account book.

"Some writing paper and stamps," Dorothy replied.

"Hmm." The guard glanced at his colleague. "Sounds as if he could have been planning this for a while. We'll check where he was sending letters to. Meanwhile, please be careful, ladies. He might have made for somewhere he was familiar with. He could be hiding close by."

"I should think it would be difficult for him to go anywhere unnoticed in those uniforms they wear," Dorothy said.

"He might have stolen clothes," the guard replied. "From a washing line, perhaps."

Dorothy frowned. "Not on a Sunday, I don't think. But I suppose he could be lying low, waiting for tomorrow."

I could hardly breathe, petrified that they were going to ask me where I lived, and put two and two together. And I was afraid that, at any moment, Dorothy might tell them that she had left me to lock up the truck and the shed. But she didn't. She allowed them to go on believing that we had done it together.

After handing the book and the keys back, the men headed off down the road.

"Well!" Dorothy blew out a breath. "I think I need a cup of tea after that. Would you like one, dear?"

"Oh, no thank you—I'd better not. I should get home."

She nodded. "I expect they'll have lunch on the table. I'm sorry about all this. I hope it hasn't upset you." Her eyes searched my face. I wondered if she *had* remembered who the escaped prisoner was. Had she guessed that I would have helped him if I'd found him hiding in the truck?

I brushed the thought away. If that was the case, why would she have kept it to herself? Wouldn't she see it as her Christian duty to report what she suspected?

"I'm fine." I forced a smile. "Better be off, though." I hurried up the road, desperate to get back. The guards had headed in the opposite direction, presumably to scout around the village. But what if they came to the farm? I needed to warn Francesco.

I was in such a state by the time I reached the barn that I forgot to blow the hawking whistle. I got the door open and went inside, expecting to see Francesco coming down the ladder. But there was no sign or sound of him. Everything was silent. I told myself that he must be asleep. I wouldn't allow the thought that formed, like a shadow, on the edge of my mind: that he'd gone outside and Felix had spotted him.

My legs shook as I climbed up to the loft. I stopped at the top of the ladder. He wasn't there.

"Where are you?" My voice was a croaky whisper, as if I'd tried to swallow the straw that lay all around.

For a moment I stood on the ladder, paralyzed with dread. Then a small movement in the corner of the loft caught my eye. Francesco's head appeared, covered in stalks of hay.

"Violet." He smiled. "I don't hear the whistle."

My hand went to the chain around my neck. "I'm so sorry—I forgot. Something's happened."

He listened in silence as I told him about the guards from the camp coming to search the shed behind the church.

"They come here?" He turned his head, as if he were listening for the sound of approaching boots.

"I don't know. When they left, they were heading for the village. But they know that you worked at the farm. They might come. What will you do?"

"I hide under the hay. Just now, when you come up the ladder, you believe no one is here, yes?"

I nodded. "But what if they go poking around with their guns?"

"Then they catch me." His eyes searched mine. "I am not afraid of that, Violet. But I am afraid of what they do to you if they know you help me."

"Please, don't worry about that." I tried not to let the fear I felt inside show on my face. "They won't know. I'll say I had no idea that you were here, that you must have spotted the barn when you walked me home after the accident in the field."

He pursed his lips. "Okay. I think they can believe that is true."

"Listen," I said, "I must go back to the farmhouse now—they're waiting for me. But I'll be back later with some food. If you hear anything, hide. I promise to blow the whistle next time."

~

When I reached the farmyard, I found Billy asleep in his pram outside. One of the chickens had settled itself on the coverlet a few inches from his face. I lifted it off and set it back on the ground, then went into the kitchen.

Mum was alone in there, making mint sauce to go with the leg of lamb we were having for lunch. She wanted to know all about what had happened down at the church. I was halfway through the story when Aunt Ruby appeared, and I had to start all over again.

"Is it one of the men who worked here?" Mum glanced at her sister, then back at me.

"I don't know." I looked down at the table. "All they said was that he'd worked at a farm in this area. They didn't tell us which one."

"We'd better not mention it to Felix." Aunt Ruby went over to the range and lifted the roasting tin out of the oven. "He's in enough of a state as it is about the Italians."

"Won't he hear about it when he goes to the pub?" I asked.

"Not tonight." She glanced at the ceiling. "He's gone back to bed. Weak as a kitten after spending all morning in the privy." She shrugged. "With a bit of luck, they'll have caught the POW by tomorrow. I mean, where could he go in those clothes?"

I didn't repeat what the guard had said about the possibility of the prisoner stealing from a washing line, because that was what *I* was planning for tomorrow.

After lunch, I helped my aunt with the washing up while Mum went out to check on Billy. In the middle of loading plates into the soapy water, Aunt Ruby's hand suddenly flew to her mouth. "Oh my God! I hope that man hasn't gone asking Carlo for help!"

"You think he might have?" I played along, glad that her train of thought led her away from any notion that he might be hiding here, on the farm.

She nodded. "The POWs all know where Carlo's billeted. They were as jealous as hell when he told them he was going to live there."

"Would the guards think of that, though?" I asked.

"I don't know. But I'll find out soon enough."

"How?"

"I've arranged to meet him." She reached into the sink for a plate and scrubbed it hard. "The day after tomorrow. I've told your mum I've got a doctor's appointment. There's an evening clinic on Tuesdays. She's going to look after Billy."

"You're meeting him in the village? Where will you go?"

She shot me a guilty look as she passed me the plate to wipe. "Behind the church. It's not very safe, though. We might come up to the old barn."

I nearly dropped the plate. "But isn't that even more risky than the churchyard?"

She shrugged. "Not if Felix is still laid up in bed. If he's up and about, we'll just wait until he goes to the pub."

I stared at her, panicking at the thought of them climbing up into the hayloft with Francesco hiding there.

"Do you think I'm wicked?"

"I . . . it's none of my business," I faltered.

"I know what you must be thinking," she said. "And you're right. I shouldn't be carrying on with another man—especially with my husband lying ill in bed."

"No, I . . . It's not that." My mind raced. I reached for another plate, rubbing it hard as I tried to work out what to do.

"You won't say anything, will you?" The tremble in her voice made me look up. I was surprised to see tears in her eyes. She moved away from the sink, drying her hands on her apron, and fished a packet of cigarettes from the pocket. Pulling out a chair, she sank into it. "I know

I'm a terrible wife. But Felix isn't the man I thought I was marrying." She lit a cigarette and took a long drag. "You might know how that feels one day." A plume of smoke drifted across the table. "I just hope to God you don't end up trapped, like me."

~

My aunt didn't even have time to finish her cigarette before Mum came back into the kitchen with Billy squirming to escape from her arms. He didn't want anyone but his mother, and he was hungry. Mum and I finished the washing up while Aunt Ruby fed him. Then, Mum announced that she was going upstairs for a nap, and Aunt Ruby asked me if I could lay the fire. Felix would normally have done the job, but he was out of action.

Of course, I knew how to construct a pile of twisted newspaper and kindling, how to create enough ventilation beneath the logs so that the flames would catch. I hadn't done it for a long time, though. Mum didn't blame me for shying away from fire since landing up in the hospital on Black Saturday—even though she didn't know the full story. Had she not gone upstairs, she would probably have offered to do it instead of me. But as it was, I had no choice.

I told myself that I could lay the wood and paper, so long as I didn't have to strike a match and get the fire going. But when it was all ready, Aunt Ruby called from the kitchen. She wanted me to light it so that it would be nice and warm in the living room by the time she and Billy came through.

I felt my mouth go dry. There was a bundle of tapers in a tin pot on the hearth. If I put the match to one of those, I wouldn't have to get so close as the fire caught. But when I lit one, my hand shook so much that I dropped it. I had to stamp on the taper to stop it from setting the rug alight.

In the end, I lit three tapers at once and threw them into the pile like spears before jumping back. I almost lost my balance, and I grabbed the wooden beam above the fireplace for support. It was only for a split second, but I felt the strange indentations under my fingers. Those scratched letters—witch marks, according to Felix, or Marian marks, according to Dorothy.

As I retreated to the sofa, I thought of all the eyes that must have looked at them down the centuries. I don't know if it was the intense fear of the flames that licked around the logs—sending my brain into a sort of frenzy—but I suddenly felt as though the room was crowded with all those people. I was caught in a suffocating crush of bodies. I couldn't stay in there a moment longer.

"He's never going to go down after that long nap he had at lunchtime." Aunt Ruby didn't look up as I staggered into the kitchen. She was spooning mushed-up meat and potatoes into Billy's mouth. "I was hoping for a quiet five minutes before I go and do the milking."

I took a breath, trying to quell the frenzied feeling inside. "I could take him for a walk if you like."

"Would you? You don't mind going back out in the cold?"

"Not at all." I forced a smile. I felt desperate for some fresh air. And I needed to take food to Francesco. Billy gave me the perfect excuse to get out of the house.

When she went to fetch his coat and hat, I nipped into the larder and cut off a couple of hunks of what was left of the roast lamb. I took some bread to go with it and a slice of the treacle sponge cake Mum had made.

The food parcel was too big to fit into my bag, so I put it under my sweater, ran outside, and slid it under the coverlet of the pram. Billy watched this performance with interest from his high chair. Just as well he was only two years old. What better accomplice, I thought, than someone who couldn't yet string a sentence together.

As I pushed the pram toward the gate, it occurred to me that Francesco might not have any water left. He wouldn't have ventured into the farmyard in daylight—especially with the possibility of the guards from White Cross coming this way.

I dodged into the dairy and grabbed a jug from one of the shelves. A loud meow told me that I'd disturbed Kuching, who jumped down and stalked out of the open door, his tail in the air. After getting water from the outside tap, I attempted to push the pram with one hand while holding the jug in the other. It wasn't easy, going along the bumpy track, but I managed to reach the barn without spilling too much water.

Billy chuckled when I pushed the pram behind the barn. He tried to grab the spiky seedheads of the tall weeds that had sprung up in the narrow strip of ground between the wall and the hedge.

"Sorry, Billy," I said as I undid the straps that held him. "I can't leave you here—not even for a couple of minutes." There was still a chance that the guards would come to the farm. Even though the pram was well hidden, they might hear Billy if they came on foot.

I lifted him out, then retrieved the food from under the coverlet. I laid it on top of the jug, which I'd left by the barn door. This time I remembered to blow the whistle before going into the barn. Billy made a grab for it when he heard the sound. As I pried his fingers off, I caught sight of the hawk. It must have been perched in one of the trees beyond the hedge. It glided slowly over our heads, as if it were looking for the bird who had made that familiar call. Was it a male on the lookout for a female? Or the other way around? There was something sad about it searching for a mate who wasn't there.

Like chasing after a ghost.

Whose voice was that? I didn't wait to hear what else it might try to tell me. Setting Billy down, I pulled the pole out of the brackets.

Francesco was waiting when I pushed the door open. He looked surprised when he caught sight of Billy.

"I'm sorry—I had to bring him," I said. "I needed a reason to leave the farmhouse."

"It is good to see him." He bent down and scooped the child into his arms. "You come up the ladder with Uncle Francesco, yes? I make something for you."

Before I'd picked up the jug and the food, they were halfway up to the loft. Billy gazed down at me over Francesco's shoulder. He didn't look the least bit worried about being carried off up the ladder. His eyes were shining, as if this were part of some new and exciting game.

When I climbed up to join them, they were sitting side by side on a pile of hay. Francesco had found two stalks of barley with the ears of grain still on them, and he was twisting straw around them. As I watched, he fashioned a miniature person with arms and legs. He used the ears of grain for the hair. Billy watched intently.

"For you." He held it out and Billy took it, turning it over in his hands before putting it up to his mouth and chewing on one of the legs.

"I think he likes it." I smiled as I handed over the food I'd brought.

Francesco's eyes widened when he unwrapped the pieces of lamb. "Thank you. This is very good. Much better than we have at White Cross."

"Those guards haven't called at the farmhouse," I said. "You haven't heard anyone coming up the track, have you?"

He shook his head.

"Well, we might have been lucky there, but we've got to get you away in the next couple of days." I didn't want to tell him that my aunt might come sneaking in with her Italian boyfriend. Instead, I said that someone was coming on Tuesday afternoon to store machinery in the barn for the winter.

"It's okay," he said. "I know I cannot stay here. Every time you bring food to me, I am afraid you make danger for yourself." He broke off a small piece of the meat. "Hey, Billy—you want some of this? It tastes better than straw?"

I watched Francesco as he swooped the bit of lamb up and down, mimicking a plane in flight. I didn't think that Billy would be interested, having only just eaten, but he opened his mouth wide when the food came zooming in.

Francesco seemed to know just how to handle small children. Did he have a son or a daughter back in Italy? I pictured him in a sunlit garden, holding a toddler in his arms. I could only imagine how painful it must be to leave a child behind, not knowing if you would ever see them again.

"You're very good with him," I said.

He smiled. "My sister has a little boy. He is four years old now—but last time I see him, he is like Billy."

"What's his name?"

"Same as me: Francesco."

"That's nice." I offered him the jug of water, and he tipped it to his mouth. He must have been very thirsty, I thought, as I watched him drink. "What about your sister?" I asked when he set the jug down. "What's she called?"

"Sophia." He reached inside his jacket and handed me a photograph in a plastic wallet. "My three sisters, my nephew, and my mother."

The sisters were sitting on a picnic blanket, one holding a baby in her arms. There was a stretch of water and mountains behind them. Their mother stood beside them with a glass in her hand. They all had the same dark, expressive eyes as Francesco, and each woman was looking at the camera with the same shy smile I'd seen that first time I'd spoken to him, by the wagon in the sugar beet field.

"What a lovely photo," I said. "Where was it taken?"

"Lago di Como," he replied. "A lake in the north of Italy."

"It's very beautiful. Is that where you live?"

"I wish." He shook his head. "I live in the city. Milano. We go to the lake for holidays."

"You must miss them very much." I handed the photo back to him.

He nodded. "But I see them in my heart."

I don't know if it was the words themselves or the inflection in his voice as he said them. Suddenly I was welling up. Through a blur of tears, I saw him lean across the space between us. He put both arms around me, and the next thing I knew, I'd buried my face in the coarse wool of his prison jacket.

"You see him in your heart, too," he whispered. "Your Taslim. He is always there."

I drew away from him in a sort of daze. It wasn't just the realization that this man was holding me in his arms. I was astonished that he'd remembered Taslim's name.

"I hear him talking to me sometimes," I murmured. "I haven't told anyone in my family about it. My mum doesn't even know I had a boyfriend in London." I hadn't intended to tell him about my life before coming to Cornwall, but it all came tumbling out. He listened intently, only shifting his gaze when Billy tugged at his sleeve, wanting to climb onto his lap.

When I told him about the bombs falling on the warehouse, he buried his face in Billy's hair. After a moment, he looked at me and said: "You think Taslim is dead because you ask him to go to that place?"

"Yes," I murmured. "If I hadn't done that, he would still be alive."

"But you don't tell the Germans to drop those bombs."

His eyes were full of compassion. It could have been Taslim talking to me. I'd heard him say the same thing, many times.

"It is not you, Violet."

A sob rose in my chest. "I tell myself it's not my fault, but . . ." I trailed off, too choked up to finish the sentence.

"It is not enough to say it." He shook his head. "You must *believe* it. To do that, you have to forgive yourself."

I blinked away the welling tears. I'd never thought of it like that. "But I don't know how," I whispered.

"I understand." He closed his eyes. "When I am in Tobruk, I lose my friend. We are on guard, on a hill, in the dark. He says he needs a cigarette. But the pack is in our tent. He is going back but I say no, I go. I am hungry and I have candy in my kit bag. While I am away, the British attack. My friend is shot."

I tried to open my mouth. My lips wouldn't move. There were no words. I felt ashamed for the tears I'd shed, never thinking that he might be suffering, too.

Billy broke the silence. He chuckled as he poked Francesco's face, trying to make him open his eyes.

"It's okay, little man." I could hear the emotion in his voice. He stroked Billy's hair, then set him down and looked at me. "We hold great pain, in here." He brought his hand up to his chest. "But you have many beautiful memories. Some people live their whole life and never know such love."

There was such sadness in his eyes. I wondered if he was talking about himself.

Billy prevented me from putting my thoughts into words by suddenly hurling himself toward the hatch in the floor. Francesco grabbed him before he could fall.

"Thank you." I blew out a breath. "You saved him. I think we'd better go before he tries it again."

I waited at the bottom of the ladder while he carried Billy down. When he put him in my arms, he kissed my cheek. *"Dio ti benedica,"* he whispered.

I smiled. "What does that mean?"

"I ask God to bless you," he replied.

Outside, when I'd strapped Billy into the pram, I touched the place where his lips had brushed my face. My skin was tingling. And it had nothing to do with the freezing November air.

In bed that night, I lay awake for a long time, thinking about what Francesco had said. The agony of losing his friend in that twist of fate must be overwhelming. And the guilt of surviving . . . I knew exactly what that felt like.

Believing it wasn't your fault. Forgiving yourself. Was that possible? He believed that it was. And he had tried to lighten my burden by focusing on the good things. Yes, I had beautiful memories. But *was* it better to have loved someone so much and then lost them, than never to have known what real love felt like?

I tried to imagine what my life would have been like if Taslim and I hadn't met. I'd never been seriously interested in anyone else. Would I have fallen for someone? It seemed unlikely. With the coming of war, young men were in short supply. And when Dad was taken prisoner, Mum's reliance on me increased greatly.

Taslim and I carried on meeting when we could—usually only briefly. Our favorite places were parks with trees and bandstands to hide behind. That first autumn of the war, if it wasn't too cold, we'd spend evenings out on Hampstead Heath. The bombing hadn't started then. Up above the city streets, you wouldn't have known there was a war on if it hadn't been for the blackout. We'd lie on a blanket, holding each other close. I remember Taslim looking up at the sky and whispering in my ear. *No light but the stars.* And it felt as if there was no one but us in the whole world.

Hampstead Heath was on the other side of London from where we lived—far enough away that we wouldn't risk bumping into anyone we knew. But the war soon made traveling across the city more difficult. If I hadn't already been seeing him, the idea of having a boyfriend would have seemed impossible.

I thought about Maria, who had written at the beginning of her journal that she wasn't interested in having a man in her life. What was it about Jago that had made her change her mind? Was it real love, or just the thrill of forbidden fruit? I'd asked myself the same question in the early days with Taslim. Did I really love him, or was it the excitement of being in a relationship that would shock my parents?

For me, the acid test had come early in our courtship, when a policeman stopped us as we were coming out of the cinema one evening. He had asked Taslim what he thought he was doing, walking out with a white girl. He'd demanded to see my identity card and had taken a note of my name and address. He said if he ever saw me with Taslim again, he'd tell my parents.

That would have been the moment, if the love we had didn't run deep, that I could have backed out. The idea of a policeman knocking on our door and spilling out my secret was humiliating, frightening. But I'd told Taslim that night that I would do whatever it took to stay together, that having to lie and hide from public view would be a small price to pay for the time I spent with him.

Had Maria and Jago felt the same? That the strength of their feelings far outweighed the fear of the condemnation they faced? When they were parted and facing death, did each cling on to the memory of that night in the shepherd's hut? Could the power of what two people had shared light up that kind of darkness?

I couldn't fail to miss the echoes of Maria's life in my own. Both of us had known forbidden love. And now I was hiding a man on the run, just as she had done. Like her, I was terrified of the consequences of being found out. The difference was that helping Francesco was *all* I was doing. There was nothing between us, other than a mutual sympathy.

But that doesn't mean it could never go deeper.

Was that Taslim's voice? Or my own?

It was a ridiculous thought, anyway. Not because I wasn't drawn to Francesco. In another life, I would have found him very attractive. But if I'd wanted someone else—which I didn't—a prisoner of war on the run was the last kind of man to strike up a romance with.

As I mulled it over, it occurred to me that I hadn't ever considered what Taslim would want for my future, because I'd never been able to contemplate any kind of future without him. For more than a year, I'd literally lived one day at a time. But what if *I* had died and he had lived? What would I want for him?

You'd want me to be happy.

That *was* his voice. This time I was certain. And of course, I'd want him to be happy. But could I bear the thought of him loving someone else? Of marrying and having children? Was it selfish to hope that he'd be content to live his life on his own?

That night, for the first time since Black Saturday, I had a dream that wasn't a nightmare. Taslim and I were having a picnic beside a lake like the one in the photograph Francesco had shown me. When we'd finished eating, he said we should go for a swim. He dived in before I'd had the chance to take my clothes off.

When I got into the lake, he took me by surprise, swimming underwater and grabbing my legs to pull me down. We came up spluttering and laughing, wrapping ourselves around one another as we kissed.

And then he told me he wanted to swim out farther. When he reached the middle of the lake, he turned and waved to me before disappearing below the surface. I wasn't sad to see him go. I knew that he hadn't gone forever. Just that, for now, he needed to live in the water while I returned to the land.

I woke up with the strangest feeling. My whole body felt light, as though I'd shed several pounds in weight, and I was almost floating off the bed.

Don't think of me as the one you lost. I heard his voice as clearly as I had in the dream. *You didn't lose me. I just came to live in here.*

"Where's 'here'?" I whispered.

I felt something slide across my chest. The hawking whistle, on its chain, came to rest over my heart.

Chapter 18

I rose even earlier than usual on Monday morning. I didn't expect Felix to be up and about. Even if the bug had subsided, he'd probably still be feeling weak. So, that meant it would be my job to round up the cows that needed milking. It wasn't such a difficult job now that they were overwintering in the stock shed rather than grazing in the field, but it was still tricky, guiding them across the yard without being crushed against a wall in the process.

I shivered as I stepped outside. Shining my flashlight around, I saw frost glinting on the roofs of the outbuildings. I thought of Francesco, huddled in a pile of straw in the barn. If I was going to steal some clothes for him, they had better be warm ones.

Mum appeared just as I was herding the last cow through the door of the milking shed. "No sign of Felix, then?" she said.

"Not so far." I glanced toward the farmhouse.

"Ruby says he's taking full advantage of this tummy bug," she went on. "She reckons it's the strain of having to keep things going when all the paid workers left. But if that was the case, why did he let the Italians go? There was plenty more they could have done around the place, even if there was nothing to do in the fields."

I kept my head down, fetching the buckets from the far corner of the shed, listening but not offering any opinion of my own. I was afraid I'd risk giving myself away by even talking about the Italians.

"There's always so much to do on a farm." Mum groaned as she settled herself down on a stool. "I had no idea. Poor Ruby. It's never-ending. She's got all the washing to sort out as soon as she's given Billy his breakfast. And then there'll be the eggs to collect, the pigs to feed, and churning to do in the dairy."

"Well, I can help with some of that," I said. "It won't take all morning to get the cows fed and mucked out." I regretted the words as soon as they came out of my mouth. I needed time to take food to Francesco, time to go down to the village to draw money out. But I'd just volunteered for jobs that would take up most of the afternoon as well as what I'd have left of the morning.

"I'll do what I can, of course," Mum said. "But I can't wring out the washing—it's too much of a strain. And you know I can't lift those milk churns."

I told her not to worry, that I could take care of the heavy work. "We'll get it all done, between the three of us," I said, "if you can keep an eye on Billy." It had occurred to me that offering to help with the washing would make it easy to find whatever I needed for Francesco. I could take the damp clothes down to the barn to dry out overnight in the hayloft.

Later, at breakfast, a bleary-eyed Felix lumbered into the kitchen. He was still in his dressing gown and pajamas. Aunt Ruby asked him if he felt up to eating something.

"Just a bit of dry toast and a cup of tea." His voice was croaky. It made him sound even older than he was.

He stood by the range, looking pathetic, while my aunt got up from eating her bacon and eggs and went to slice some bread to put under the hot plate. I wondered why he couldn't have done such a simple task for himself. He didn't even thank her when she put the tea and toast on a tray for him to take back upstairs.

"I'd better take some hot water up for him in a minute," my aunt said as she sat down to finish her breakfast. "He needs to have a good wash and make himself presentable. He's got the slaughterman coming later."

Mum and I exchanged glances. "For the pigs?" Mum put down her fork, looking at the remains of the bacon rasher on her plate.

"Yes," Aunt Ruby replied. "The weaners from the last litter are ready now. Don't worry—you won't see anything. Might be a few squeals, though."

"I hate to think of them being killed," Mum said. "I shouldn't eat bacon, really."

"I was like that when we first came to live here," my aunt said. "You get used to it, though. Felix made me watch the first time the slaughterman came. I think he gets a kick out of seeing an animal being killed. A bit like shooting rabbits. He won't want to miss it, even if he's still feeling a bit below par."

An image of what she'd described imprinted itself on my mind's eye: Felix hovering close to the man with the knife, probably holding the animal down while its throat was slit. I imagined the look on his face—the same leering grin as when he'd caught me naked in the bath.

"Could you two get the wash on while I go and see to him?" Aunt Ruby rose from the table and gathered the plates. "Take Billy in there with you—he'll be as happy as a sandboy, jumping around in the laundry pile."

The washing was done in the sluice room off the kitchen that housed the copper. It was hard work, filling the tub with hot soapy water, agitating the clothes with wooden prongs, and then rubbing them against the washboard. Even if I could have come up with an excuse to get away, I couldn't have left Mum to cope alone. It would have been too much for her—and positively dangerous for Billy. With all that hot water around, we had to make sure he stayed in the far corner of the room, playing in the clothes pile.

"It's a miserable day for it," Mum said as she examined the grime on one of Felix's shirt collars. "We won't be able to dry this lot outside."

"No." I shrugged. A fine drizzle had set in as we'd come out of the milking shed. The washing would have to be dried indoors.

Half an hour after we'd started, we heard voices in the kitchen. There was a man's voice that I didn't recognize—the slaughterman, I supposed. My aunt was making a cup of tea for him before the work started. I couldn't hear all the conversation between him and Felix, but I caught the word "Italians." My stomach clenched as I realized the man was telling Felix all about the escape from White Cross.

I glanced at Mum. I didn't think she'd heard. She'd laid down the scrubbing brush she was using on a shirt collar and headed toward Billy, who was trying to pull a stocking over his head.

I edged closer to the door, which was slightly ajar. I heard the teapot being poured and Aunt Ruby asking the man if he took sugar.

"Did you know about this?" Felix's voice was croaky but still loud.

There was a moment of silence. "Yes, I did hear something when I came out of church yesterday." I could hear the trepidation in Aunt Ruby's voice. "I didn't say anything because you were so poorly. I didn't want to worry you."

I heard a sound that was half grunt, half chuckle. "There's a bloody Italian on the loose and she doesn't want to worry me?" I could picture him rolling his eyes, sharing the joke with the man across the table. But I knew him well enough to realize that it wasn't a joke. He would be furious with my aunt for not telling him about the escaped prisoner. No doubt there would be a blazing row when the slaughterman had left the farm.

I was relieved that she hadn't told him about the guards searching the truck I'd driven back from White Cross. No doubt he would hear about that from someone in the pub, but with luck, Francesco would be gone by then.

I heard the scraping of chairs as the men left for the pigsty. Aunt Ruby appeared a few moments later. She said that I could go and see to the cows now, and she would help Mum with the washing.

I glanced at the pile of wet clothes waiting to be wrung out. I'd have to sneak back into the sluice room when the clothes were hung up to dry.

I waited in the kitchen for a while until I heard Mum and my aunt chatting. Then I tiptoed into the larder and grabbed some food for Francesco. I glanced out of the window. It looked as though it had stopped raining. But when I went out into the farmyard, I saw that there was no chance of getting to the barn. Felix and the slaughterman were carrying out their bloody morning's work on a table they'd moved outside. They'd positioned it by the wall of the pigsty, right in front of the gate to the track.

A high-pitched shriek from one of the pigs sent me diving into the cowshed. I'd never seen an animal slaughtered. Living in a city all my life, I hadn't really thought about the animals who had been sacrificed to provide the meat we bought from the butcher. Would I eat bacon or roast pork if, to get it, I had to do what these men were doing now?

I tried to block out the harrowing sound of the pigs by shoveling muck from the floor of the cowshed. I wondered how long it would take to do what they had to do. I thought of Francesco, holed up in the barn, wondering where I was. I hoped to God he wouldn't venture outside, with Felix standing so close to the track.

~

The killing of the pigs took all morning. I hadn't expected Felix to be out there for that long—I wouldn't have thought he'd have the energy after being so ill—but the slaughtering seemed to have invigorated him.

Despite trying to keep out of the way, I almost collided with him when I went to get more water for the cows. He was carrying two buckets, the contents of which slopped over the rims as he regained his balance. To my horror, I saw that it was blood.

He smiled when he saw the look on my face. "Turns your stomach, does it? Bet you don't turn up your nose when it comes to eating it, though!"

"*Eating* it?" I shuddered.

"You're telling me you've never had black pudding?"

I stared at the thick crimson liquid in the buckets. Yes, I'd eaten slices of the fat, dark-colored sausage Mum called black pudding. But I'd had no idea that it was made from pigs' blood.

"That can be a job for you this week," he said. "Tomorrow morning, I'll show you how to make it."

I watched him cross the farmyard to the small outhouse where he hung up the rabbits he shot. The thought of being shut in there with him was as stomach-churning as the sight of the blood.

I heard Mum calling me in for lunch. I glanced toward the gate to the track. The slaughterman was still there, bundling a carcass into the back of his van. I watched him slam the door, then go over to the outside tap to wash his hands. I lingered outside, wondering if he'd drive off now or stay to eat with us. I needed to seize the chance to get to Francesco while the others were indoors. A couple of minutes later, he climbed into the driver's seat and headed off down the track.

I popped my head around the kitchen door. There was bread and cheese on the table, and Mum was ladling soup into bowls.

"I just need to go to the privy," I said. "Won't be a minute."

Before she could say anything, I was off. I glanced over to the game larder as I strode across the farmyard. The door was ajar, and I could hear the metallic scrape of buckets. Felix was still in there. Good.

I made it to the barn in less than five minutes, running all the way. I hardly had any breath left to blow the whistle. When I got the door open, I dug my hand into my jacket pocket and thrust the food at Francesco. The parcel I'd made that morning was lumpy and misshapen, but hopefully the food inside would still be edible.

"Can't stop," I panted. "Back later."

"But Violet, I—"

It felt bad, pulling the door shut in his face, but I couldn't risk staying there a moment longer. I ran back up the track, getting a sharp pain in my side as I neared the gate to the farmyard. It was only when I jogged past the tap outside the cowshed that I remembered water. I should have taken some. He was probably desperately thirsty by now. I would have to go back as soon as I could.

I made myself take a deep breath before I went into the kitchen. I mustn't give away that I'd been running.

"Oh, there you are!" Mum frowned as I walked in. "We thought you'd fallen down the hole!" She and my aunt were sitting at the table with Billy in the high chair between them.

"Sorry." I went over to the sink and washed my hands. "Where's . . . er . . ." I checked myself. I'd almost said "Felix." I didn't want to add discourtesy to my list of misdemeanors.

"Felix?" Aunt Ruby looked up from her bowl of soup. "Is he still with the slaughterman? I thought I heard the van driving off."

"It did," I said. "There were some buckets of blood, though. They needed putting away."

"Ah—he'll be in the game larder, then." She reached across the table to take away the plate covering another soup bowl. "That's yours. It should still be hot."

As I sat down at the table, I prayed that she was right about Felix. What if he'd spotted me striding purposefully across the yard when I was supposed to be having my lunch? Might he have followed me?

I told myself that he couldn't have, that I would have run into him on the way back from the barn. There was nowhere to hide along that track—not in broad daylight.

He still hadn't appeared when we'd finished eating. I was stacking the plates and bowls in the sink when I heard the creak of floorboards overhead.

"He must have worn himself out with those pigs." Aunt Ruby glanced at the ceiling, a wry look on her face. "I'd better go and see if he wants anything taken up."

I wondered why Felix had chosen to go upstairs via the dairy rather than coming through the kitchen. Perhaps he was still feeling off color and couldn't face the smell of food. That seemed unlikely, though, given that he'd just been draining the lifeblood from dead animals.

I didn't have time to dwell on why he'd avoided the kitchen. While Aunt Ruby went upstairs and Mum coaxed Billy to eat more bread and cheese, I darted into the sluice room. The clean washing was draped over a rack suspended from the ceiling. It was hoisted up and down by means of a rope.

Be careful, or she'll hear you.

I had a sudden vision of Maria, standing in this very room three centuries ago, taking a shepherd's smock and breeches to disguise her priest.

The rope creaked when I started to lower it. I froze, the rack halfway between me and the ceiling.

Be patient. I heard Maria's voice again.

The muscles in my arm began to burn from the weight. I prayed for some noise from the kitchen. The next moment, Billy started banging his fists on the tray of his high chair.

"Thank you," I whispered.

In a matter of seconds, I grabbed what I needed, rolling up the damp bundle as tightly as I could. I peered around the door. Mum had her back to me. Tiptoeing out, I grabbed one of Felix's jackets from a hook on the wall.

"Just going back to the cows," I called over my shoulder. I was out of the door before she had time to turn around.

Outside, it was raining again. Veils of drizzle drifted across the farmyard. I went into the cowshed and took an empty grain sack to carry the clothes in. Then I remembered water. I doubled back to the dairy and took a jug to fill at the outside tap. As the water sloshed into it, I thought I heard someone call my name.

I turned off the tap and looked back toward the farmhouse, expecting to see Mum standing in the doorway. But there was no one there.

"Violet!"

My heart thudded. It was Francesco.

"Over here." A hand appeared around the side of the privy wall.

I put down the jug. *Walk, don't run.* Maria was still there, inside my head. When I reached the privy, I pushed the door open, as if I needed to go inside. Glancing over my shoulder, I checked that no one had come out into the farmyard. Then I dodged around the corner.

Francesco was crouched down on the ground. If he'd stood, his head would have been visible above the top of the wall.

"What are you doing?" I gasped. "Are you thirsty? I'm sorry I forgot the water."

He shook his head. "It is not that. I hear something come past the barn. Sounds like a truck. I think the guards come and you are in danger. That is why you run away from me, yes?"

"No, it wasn't the guards," I said. "Just a man coming here to kill pigs. I should have told you when I brought the food." I bit my lip, cross with myself for not thinking of the worry the slaughterman's truck would have caused him. "Go back to the barn. I'll follow in a minute or two."

"But I must speak with you now—before you do more things to bring trouble."

"It's okay," I said. "I've got clothes for you—they're still wet from being washed, but we can dry them in the barn tonight. If I'm quick, I can get down to the village this afternoon and get money. And the bicycle . . ."

"No!" He held up his hand. "I cannot take these things. Last night, when I think about it, I see that it is impossible."

"Impossible?" I searched his face. "Why?"

"Because they might catch me. Not here, perhaps, but somewhere I go when I leave. The clothes, the bicycle—everything leads them back to you. This I cannot do."

I stared at him, uncomprehending. "But what else *can* you do?"

"Go back to the camp."

"What? You're going to give yourself up? With that man waiting to kill you?"

He looked down at the muddy ground between us. "I have no choice."

"Please, Francesco, let's just think about this." I reached for his hand, grasping it in both of mine. "I can't bear to think of you going back to that place and being . . ." I faltered, horrible images forming in my mind's eye. "Just give me one more night, will you? Don't do anything yet." There had to be some other solution. I couldn't let him go back to White Cross.

Chapter 19

I returned to the cowshed and waited a good half hour before following Francesco back to the barn. Despite what he'd said about the chance of Felix's clothes giving away my involvement in any escape plan, I'd decided to take them to him anyway. I cut out the labels with the knife I used to sever the twine on the hay bales for the cows. Without the labels, I didn't see how anyone could prove whom they'd once belonged to.

As I bundled the clothes back into the sack, it occurred to me that if Francesco was caught, he could simply say that he'd stolen the clothes himself. He could say that when he'd walked me back after my accident, he'd formed a plan to hide in the barn and sneak into the farmhouse to get what he needed.

I left the shed with the sack slung over my shoulder, then went over to the tap and picked up the jug I'd filled earlier. If anyone saw me, they wouldn't have suspected what I was up to. Now that I was looking after the cows, I was constantly going back and forth with sacks of feed and water to top up the trough.

I had no good reason to take the sack and jug through the gate, though. The only way to get them safely out of the farmyard was via the pigsty, where I'd be out of sight. Once in there, I could lift the supplies over the wall and climb out onto the track the same way.

The pigs started to squeal when I went in. The poor things probably thought it was the slaughterman coming back. I dodged around them, trying to get to the far wall before one of them nipped my legs. From my experience of mucking them out, I knew they could bite when they felt like it.

It was difficult to get the jug over the wall without spilling the water. I had to lie across the top to make sure I put it down on a level patch of ground. The sack was easier. When I tried to follow, a pig got hold of the boot on my right foot, and I almost lost my balance. I tugged with all my strength to free my foot from its grip, and when I succeeded, I fell to the ground with such force it winded me. Luckily, I landed on the sack of clothes. I picked myself up, sucking air back into my lungs, and started down the track, keeping close to the hedge.

The hawk appeared before I reached the barn. It swooped down and landed on the track, right in front of me. I paused, mesmerized. I'd never seen it on the ground before. It stayed there, preening itself, until I took a step forward. Then it rose up and flew toward the woodland. I saw that it had left something behind: a single feather, just like the one I'd found in my room.

I put down the sack and picked it up. Tucking it in my pocket, I felt that the bird had given me a sort of talisman. Was this Maria, wishing me the luck that had evaded her and Jago? Or was it Taslim, urging me on when the odds against Francesco were so great?

When I opened the door to the barn, I saw Francesco climbing down the ladder. He jumped down the last few rungs, turning in midair, as nimble as a cat. There was no smile of greeting. His face was set.

"I've got a plan," I said, handing him the jug. "Have a drink first, then I'll tell you about it."

Up in the loft, I emptied out the clothes and explained how he could take them without implicating me. "You could say you did it all on your own," I said. "That you spotted the barn as a potential hiding place when you brought me back that time and realised you could take clothes and a bicycle from the farmhouse."

He thought about it for a moment. "It is possible they believe that."

I nodded. "And I've thought of something else. Money. I didn't know how on earth I was going to get down to the village today to get some out. But I don't need to: I can take some from the tin in the kitchen. You can say you stole that, too."

The worry lines on his forehead deepened.

"I plan to replace whatever I take," I said. "Hopefully I can do that before they even notice it's gone. But that's your story—just in case."

"You think you can do this? They don't catch you?"

"Yes, I can." I made myself sound convincing. I didn't want to give him any reason to revert to the decision to give himself up. "Have you decided where you'll go, when you get away from here?"

He shook his head. "I don't know. I try to get on a ship. But not here. A bigger place."

"Falmouth is a big port. It's south of here. It's not very far: only about thirty miles. And there are lots of foreign people there, refugees from France and Belgium. You wouldn't be so noticeable in a place like that."

"Falmouth." He repeated the name slowly, as if trying to commit it to memory. I wondered how he would find his way. There were no signs on the roads. But he'd said he could tell where north was from the stars. Please, God, let it be clear tonight, I thought.

"I'll bring the bicycle once it gets dark," I said. "I'll put money and some food in the basket. It might be late, though. I don't know if Felix is going to the pub. If he is, I'll have to wait until he gets back."

"Yes, I understand," he said.

"In the meantime, try to get some sleep."

"Thank you, Violet." He took my hands in his. "You do all this for me. I give nothing back to you."

"That's not true," I said. "You've helped me, Francesco—just by listening and talking. You know what agony it is to lose someone close to you and to blame yourself for what happened to them. And hearing what you went through changed something inside me. I feel . . ." I faltered, searching for the right word. "A sort of peace."

"Then I am happy." He smiled. He looked so different, then, from the troubled, guilt-ridden person he had been just minutes earlier. I had a vision of him standing beside the lake in the photograph he'd shown me, wearing this same smile as he captured the lovely image of his family at the picnic. And for some inexplicable reason, I imagined myself standing beside him, taking the camera from him to frame his face with the lake and the mountains behind him. The way he looked now, his dark, soulful eyes lit up with pleasure, would stay with me always.

"I wish there was some way you could let me know how you get on, when you leave here," I said. I didn't say what was in my mind—that if he was caught, it would be headline news. I had to cling to the hope that he would find a ship, and that somehow, he could make his way across war-torn Europe to his home in Milan. Was that even possible?

"I can write a letter," he said. "But that make trouble for you, no?"

I nodded. A letter with foreign stamps, addressed to me, could never go unnoticed. "You could send it to Dorothy," I said. "Make it sound like you're saying sorry for hiding in the truck. Say you sneaked out of the shed before I'd had a chance to lock it up—something like that. And tell her the reason why you had to escape from the camp."

"And she tells you if she gets this?"

"Absolutely." I told him how concerned she'd been after the visit from the chaplain, how unfair she'd thought the punishment was.

He made me repeat her name and address twice, so he could commit it to memory.

When I left him, he said he hoped that one day, he might see me again. Then he asked if he could kiss me.

I hesitated for a split second. Was I betraying Taslim? A kiss on the lips would be crossing a line. But I knew that after tonight, I would probably never set eyes on this man again. That he might be shot if he was caught on the run or die on the long road back to the family he loved. How could I refuse him one kiss?

I wasn't prepared for the effect it would have on me. The touch of his lips on mine unleashed a storm of emotions. Part of me wanted it to go on forever. Another part wanted to pull away and run. For once, there were no voices inside my head, telling me what to do.

Chapter 20

I didn't go straight back to the farmhouse when I left Francesco. I went into the cowshed and stayed there for a while. The munching and lowing of the animals comforted me. I sat down on a hay bale and took in a long breath. On most days, the smell of the cows was something to be endured, but now it seemed earthy and reassuring—something steadfast in a world full of doubts and hazy possibilities.

In a few hours Francesco would be gone. Unless he was captured and taken back to White Cross, I would never see him again. I tried to imagine what it would be like, catching sight of him as I drove the mobile shop into the camp. No doubt he would be banned from buying anything or coming anywhere near us.

I didn't know what the punishment for escaping from such a place would be. A long spell in solitary confinement, at the very least. And he would live in constant fear of being killed by the man who had attacked him.

I told myself that wouldn't happen. That with the clothes, the bicycle, and the money, he had every chance of making it to Falmouth without getting caught. If he managed to find his way without getting lost, he could be there by daylight. This time tomorrow, he could be on a ship bound for Europe.

The rattle of wheels on the cobblestones outside interrupted my thoughts. Through a gap in the shed door, I saw that it was Mum taking

Billy for a walk in the pram. With a bit of luck, there would be no one in the kitchen. It was my chance to get the money for Francesco.

I waited until Mum was a few yards down the track before going into the house. The kitchen was deserted. The tin sat on the top shelf of the dresser, a few inches from Felix's gun. I listened for sounds from upstairs before I lifted it down. There was nothing to suggest that anyone was moving about up there. Perhaps Felix was asleep. But where was my aunt?

I wondered if they'd had a row over her failure to tell him about the escape from White Cross. Was that why Mum had gone out? To remove herself and Billy from an uncomfortable situation?

I needed to act quickly, just in case she suddenly walked in. Opening the tin, I found a wad of paper money as well as a pile of coins. A couple of pounds should be enough, I thought. That was the amount Mum used to pay me as a weekly wage out of the takings from the shop.

I took two five-shilling notes, two half crowns and an assortment of other coins. I left enough money to prevent anyone noticing that some was missing. And it was unlikely that Felix or Aunt Ruby would check it before tomorrow morning.

I'd only just replaced the tin when I heard the creak of the treads on the stairs. By the time the kitchen door opened, I was standing at the sink, filling the kettle.

"Making a cup of tea?" Aunt Ruby was smiling. Perhaps Felix hadn't had the energy for a row.

I put the kettle on the range and emptied the soggy leaves from the teapot. "How's the patient?" I glanced at the ceiling.

"Having a nap to build himself up for a trip to the pub tonight." She rolled her eyes. "You'd think he'd want to avoid beer, wouldn't you? He's been as sick as a dog these past couple of days. But no. He must go. Says he needs to check the fire watch rota to find out when it's his turn."

"Well, rather him than me," I said. "It's not very nice out there. Looks like it might rain again." It was frustrating that Felix was going to the pub. If he'd stayed at home, I could have taken the bicycle to Francesco as soon as it got dark.

As I reached for the tea caddy, the stolen coins shifted in my jacket pocket. I was a bag of nerves. When the kettle boiled, it was hard to keep my hand steady as I poured the water into the teapot.

"Are you okay?" My aunt looked me up and down as I set the teacups on the table. "You look a bit pale. Not coming down with something, are you?"

Now I felt even more jumpy. "Just a bit tired, that's all," I said. "The cows are quite a handful, aren't they?"

"I'll say. I was terrified of them when we first came to live here." She took out her cigarettes and put one in her mouth. When she flicked up the lid of her lighter, instinctively I looked away from the naked flame. I heard her inhale. A curl of smoke drifted past me. "I keep telling Felix we need more help, not less," she said. "It's too much for you, looking after those cows all on your own. But he won't hear of getting the Italians back. Especially not now that he knows one of them is on the run."

I picked up my cup. The tea burned my lips. But it allowed me to stay silent. I didn't trust myself to join in a conversation about the escape.

"I'm dying to know if you-know-who has heard anything." She lowered her voice. "I just hope it doesn't make them tighten up on the other prisoners. I couldn't bear it if Carlo was sent back to live at White Cross."

"Are you still going to meet him tomorrow?" It occurred to me that the risk involved had increased dramatically. People in the village were going to be more watchful than ever for any stranger passing through.

She put her finger to her lips, glancing upward. "It'll be dark by the time he comes," she whispered. "He'll kill the lights on his bike before he gets to the village and push it to the church. He won't be spotted."

I made a mental note to pass this on to Francesco, to switch off the lights in any town or village he passed through. Anything to reduce the risk of him getting caught.

A sound from the room above made us both look up. Aunt Ruby stubbed out her cigarette. "He's awake. I'd better take him a cup of tea."

She glanced at her watch. "I need to make a casserole with that leftover lamb. Will you make a start on the potatoes?"

When Felix came downstairs, I was hard at work with the paring knife, surrounded by peelings. He put his cup and saucer in the sink and announced that he was off to do the milking.

"I'll be with you in a minute." Aunt Ruby began untying her apron.

"You stay here," he said. "I can manage on my own."

He headed for the door. My heart raced. Would he notice that his jacket was missing? To my relief, he didn't even look at the coat hooks. He went outside in what he was already wearing.

"Well, that's a surprise." Aunt Ruby sliced into a turnip, pressing down hard to cut it in half. "He must be feeling guilty about us running the place without him for the past two days."

I nodded. In the fading light, I could just about see Felix through the window. He was heading toward the cowshed. I had another surge of panic. What had I done with the labels I'd cut from his clothes? Had I left them in there?

In my agitated state, I cut myself with the paring knife. It was only a nick, but blood dripped onto the potatoes as I brought my finger up to my mouth.

"Here, stick it under the tap." Aunt Ruby grabbed my hand and marched me over to the sink. "Have you got a hankie to wrap round it?"

As I dug my uninjured hand into my trouser pocket, I felt the labels, scrunched up alongside my handkerchief. I offered up a silent prayer of thanks to whoever was watching over me.

~

Supper was on the table when Felix returned from milking the cows. He said he didn't feel like eating and was going straight to the pub. He reached up to the hooks by the door for an overcoat. I held my breath, thinking he might realize that the tweed jacket I'd taken for Francesco was missing, but he didn't seem to notice.

"I'm sorry there's not more meat in this casserole," Aunt Ruby said as we started on the meal. "There wasn't as much left over from yesterday's lunch as I thought. I think Felix must be fibbing about not being hungry—I reckon he's been helping himself to that leg of lamb on the quiet."

I couldn't look at her. I was afraid she'd see the guilt on my face. I kept my head down, willing Mum to steer the conversation in a different direction. She obliged by saying how much Billy's eating had improved since we'd arrived at the farm, that he hardly took any coaxing now when it came to mealtime.

An image of Francesco flashed into my mind. I remembered how he'd fed Billy chunks of the meat I'd taken him, whirling them in the air like a plane doing loop the loops. I wondered what he was doing at this moment. I hoped that he'd taken my advice and was getting some sleep before the long night ahead.

When we finished supper, I told Mum and Aunt Ruby that I had to go out to the privy. I didn't really need to go—I wanted to see what the weather was like. I'd been praying for the blanket of cloud that had hung over the farm all day to lift, so that Francesco could navigate by the stars.

I shivered as I walked across the farmyard. The temperature had dropped a few degrees. When I reached the privy, I switched off my flashlight and looked up at the sky. At first, it looked as though the clouds hadn't shifted. But as I gazed upward, I caught a glimmer of something. I didn't know if it was a planet or a very bright star. Over the next couple of minutes, more pinpricks of light appeared. I could see the shapes made by groups of them. I looked to where I thought north was and saw the pattern of the only constellation I knew. The polestar was there, at the top of it, shining more brightly than all the others.

I tried to work out which direction I'd need to take if I tried to go south from here. I pictured the points of the compass. I'd need to keep that star right behind me.

I shivered and dug my hands into the pockets of my jacket. I felt something soft in one of them. The feather that the hawk had left on the track. I rubbed it between my finger and thumb, willing it to bring Francesco all the luck he was going to need to make it to Falmouth.

In my room, I prepared for the long wait for Felix to return from the pub. I'd asked if I could take the newspaper up to bed, promising to return it to the kitchen table first thing in the morning. Felix regarded the weekly paper as his—he didn't like anyone else taking it.

The stories were so dull I almost fell asleep reading them. A farmer had appeared in court for failing to cut down weeds in a wheat field, half a dozen people had been fined for failing to obscure lights in their homes at night, and three men had been made to pay five shillings each for riding a bicycle with no lights during the blackout.

The article about the cyclists was worrying, though. What would happen if Francesco was caught riding without lights? I'd better tell him to keep them on, rather than trying to ride through towns and villages unnoticed.

I was still reading the newspaper when I heard something outside my bedroom window. It sounded like someone tapping on the glass. But that was impossible. I turned off the flashlight and opened the curtains. The tapping stopped for a moment, then began again. As my eyes adapted to the darkness, I could see a moving shape, almost covering one half of the window. It was a bird. A big bird. And the noise was its beak pecking at the glass.

I had a sudden, overwhelming conviction that it was the hawk, that it was trying to tell me something. But I was afraid to open the window in case it flew in. I watched, mesmerized, as its head bobbed back and forth. Then I caught sight of something else. Behind the bird, in the starlit sky, there was a tall, vertical cloud. But it wasn't floating—it seemed to be rising from somewhere along the track that led out from the farmyard. Like smoke. I froze.

Please, God—not the barn.

Chapter 21

The hawk stopped rapping on the glass. A moment later it flew away. I fumbled for the catch on the window and wrenched it open. The breeze brought the smell of smoke. A sick feeling welled in my stomach. I gagged as I jumped off the bed. The horrible, familiar panic was magnified a hundred times at the thought of where the fire was and who was in there.

I grabbed my flashlight and switched it back on, pacing the room. Mum and Aunt Ruby were downstairs. But I couldn't send them out to the barn. If I did, I'd have to tell them about Francesco.

You must go to him. Don't be afraid. I had a vision of Maria standing by the bed. Her hands were clasped together, as if she were praying.

"Will you help me?" At that moment I thought I must truly be losing my mind, asking the long-dead inhabitant of this room to come to the rescue. But as I stood there, I had the same experience as in the dream of Robert Archer's death. I felt as though I'd suddenly switched my body for hers.

Moments later I was hurtling down the stairs and through the dairy. I didn't stop running until the barn was in sight. I could see flames of gold and scarlet licking along the thatch. The terrible stench of the fire filled my lungs as I panted for breath. The door was ablaze. There was no way in. Then I remembered the hole Francesco had made in the wall. Could he have got out?

I tried to shout his name, but I had no voice. I didn't even have the breath to blow the hawking whistle. I retched as I cast around with my flashlight, frantically searching the track and the hedgerows. Was he still in there, fast asleep, oblivious to the inferno around him?

I darted around the back of the barn and shone the beam along the wall. When I found the opening, I had to kick away the hay bales that blocked it. Smoke billowed out as I climbed inside. It was like stepping right back into the horror of Black Saturday. I heard the crash of the rafters near the door falling to the ground, raining fire as they collapsed.

The panic surged inside me. I felt Maria slipping away.

"Don't leave me!" I croaked as I waved my arms in front of my face, trying to see through the smoke.

I'm still here. Her voice rang out inside my head. *He's in the hayloft.*

Could he be up there? I could see the ladder, still intact. I grasped the whistle and tried blowing it again. By some miracle I managed to produce a sound. I strained my ears for an answering shout—but I could hear nothing but the crackle of the flames.

Go up there. Be quick.

"I . . . I can't!" My throat tightened. I felt as if I were suffocating.

You can. Just take one step. Now it was Taslim's voice urging me on.

Somehow, I moved forward. My legs felt stiff and heavy. How I ran to the ladder and climbed up it, I'll never know. I saw the shape of Francesco's body, lying on straw that, mercifully, was not yet alight.

"Francesco!" I shook him, but he didn't stir. "Please! Wake up!" For a terrible moment I thought that he was dead. I cradled his head in my arms, my face next to his, desperate to feel his breath. I heard the faintest sound above the hiss of the fire: a murmur from somewhere deep inside his chest. How could I wake him? I couldn't carry him down the ladder. But if we didn't get down fast, the whole roof would come down on us.

Something flashed in the corner of my eye: the metal jug from the dairy, glinting in the orange light of the flames. I made a grab for it.

The handle was warm, but not too hot to hold. I splashed what water was left in it over Francesco's face.

He opened his eyes. It took a few precious seconds for him to recognize me and remember where he was.

"The barn's on fire! We've got to get out!" I tried lifting his shoulders. It took all my strength just to get him into a sitting position. Now he could see the fire. It was spreading along the roof, just a few feet away from where the ladder rested against the hatch. "Can you make it to the hatch?" I pulled his arms. "You don't have to stand up—just crawl along the floor."

He looked how I had felt, waking up in the hospital after being found, unconscious, in the street outside the burning warehouse. They'd told me that I was suffering from the effects of breathing in too much smoke, that I needed to rest because it would take a day or two before my lungs were back to normal. But we didn't have a day or two. A couple of minutes, if we were lucky.

"Come on—you can do it." I tugged desperately. There was a crash as more rafters collapsed and plummeted to the ground. I got behind him and tried pushing him. But I was afraid that if he went headfirst down the ladder, he might break his neck.

Suddenly he began to move on his own. He stretched his arms toward the hole in the floor and inched forward on his elbows, dragging his legs behind him. He grunted with the effort. When he reached the ladder, he looked back over his shoulder at me and pointed down. He couldn't speak—but he was telling me I should go first.

There was no time to argue. I wanted to see him get safely down before I followed. But if I went first, at least I could break his fall if he lost his footing.

The wood felt hot as I grasped the sides of the ladder. I could barely see the floor below—the smoke was so thick. I got halfway down, then looked up to make sure he was following me.

"Francesco!" A feeling of dread squeezed my heart, that he knew he couldn't make it and had urged me to go ahead of him to save myself.

Then I saw one foot coming through the hatch. For a second it hovered perilously, searching for the rung of the ladder. I braced myself. If he fell, I wouldn't have the strength to catch him.

Sparks flew around me, catching the sleeve of my jacket. I didn't dare to snuff them out in case I made the ladder wobble. He had both legs on the top rung now. As I watched, he came toward me, sliding down. To get out of his way, I jumped down the last few feet. I lost my balance as I hit the ground. When I got up, I ripped off my smoldering jacket and stamped on it.

Francesco was lying at the bottom of the ladder.

"This way!" I grabbed his arm and heaved. By gripping the ladder with the other hand, he managed to stand up. It seemed to take an eternity to reach the hole in the wall. I was coughing with each step, and my eyes were streaming. It was a struggle to breathe. Mercifully, the hay bales stacked beside the hole hadn't yet caught fire. I pushed him through the gap, then scrambled after him.

For a moment, we lay there among the weeds, exhausted by the effort. Then I dragged myself up, onto my knees. I opened my mouth to urge him on, away from the burning building, but all that came out was a croak. I tugged hard at his jacket and pointed. We crawled away from the barn. I could feel the wet grass seeping through the knees of my trousers, then the sharp stones at the edge of the track.

I don't know how long we lay there. My head felt as if it would explode. I couldn't believe what I'd done.

Phantom will set you free.

Maria's words came back to me as I stared up at the stars. It was true. If the bird hadn't come tapping on my window, I would never have known about the fire, would never have had to conquer my crippling phobia. Could I have done it without the conviction that it was Maria, not myself, entering that blazing building?

Taslim had been there, too. I was certain of that. The spirits of two people, separated in time by more than three centuries, had given me the strength I needed. To anyone else, that would sound fanciful, bordering on insanity. But I *had* done it. That was all that mattered.

Suddenly, I heard voices in the distance. Men shouting. I raised myself up on my elbows. They were coming from the village. The fire watch patrol. They must have seen the flames.

I gagged as I tried to speak. "We need . . ." I coughed, fighting to get the words out. "You need to hide!"

He turned his face to me. In the light from the flames, I could just about see it, though my eyes were still streaming from the acrid smoke. He was shaking his head. He opened his mouth, fighting for breath.

"You go." His voice was the faintest whisper, but there was no mistaking the vehemence of what he was telling me to do. He raised both arms, palms up, pushing the air, as if to shoo me away.

The voices were getting louder. I couldn't make Francesco crawl across the track to hide under the hedge. He wasn't thinking of himself. All he cared about was them not seeing me. They would find him. But at least he was alive.

~

I staggered across the track. I couldn't see properly, and I scratched my hands as I blundered into the hedge. I crouched down, then crawled along, twigs and thorns catching in my hair. I was trying desperately not to cough.

When I rounded the bend in the track, I attempted to stand up. But my knees buckled under me. I felt for a thick branch and grasped onto it to pull myself up. I made my way back to the farmhouse at a snail's pace, never letting go of the hedge. When at last I reached the gate, I dropped to my knees again and crossed the farmyard on all fours. My hands slithered on what the cows and chickens had deposited on the cobbles. I almost fell again as I heaved myself up on the handle of the dairy door.

Some superhuman strength got me up the stairs to my room. I slumped on the floor and lay there for a moment, overwhelmed with exhaustion. Francesco's face floated in front of my closed eyes. What was happening to him? Would they realize who he was? If he spoke, they would know he was a foreigner. But if he kept silent, they might think that he was some local man. Would they take him to the hospital?

A sense of despair overtook me as I realized that whatever happened, they would find out sooner or later. He would end up back at White Cross. Saved from death only to be delivered up to the man who wanted to kill him.

I lay there in the darkness, longing for oblivion. But I couldn't allow myself to fall asleep. I needed to get out of my filthy, singed clothes and clean myself up while I still had time. The fire watchers were bound to come to the farmhouse to raise the alarm. And when that happened, Mum would be up here like a shot.

I fumbled in the pocket of my dungarees for my flashlight. Miraculously it hadn't fallen out in the struggle to escape the fire. I eased myself up by holding on to the side of the bed. As I shrugged off my clothes, I caught sight of myself in the mirror. My face was covered in soot, and my hair was gray, as if I'd aged decades in the time I'd been away.

I stuffed my shirt, dungarees, and underwear beneath the bed, then reached across to the dressing table for the bowl and the jug of water. I felt so weak I could only lift them one at a time. I set the bowl on the floor. When I tried to pour the water, my hand shook, and I spilled some of it. I knelt over the bowl and dunked my head in. The shock took my breath away. It was freezing.

I grabbed my towel and rubbed at my face and hair. The water in the bowl was pitch black. It rippled as a movement outside sent vibrations along the wooden floor. Instinctively I shifted the towel to cover my naked body. In my haste, I'd forgotten to lock the door. I pictured Felix, back from the pub, with news of the fire as an excuse to come into my room.

"Violet—can I come in?" It was Mum's voice. The hammering in my chest eased a little.

"Hang on a second!" I fumbled under the pillow for my nightdress and pulled it on. Then I wrapped the towel, turban style, around my hair before opening the door.

"You'll never guess what's happened!" Mum couldn't conceal her excitement. "There's been a fire—in the old barn—and that Italian prisoner was hiding there! He's in our kitchen and Ruby's giving him brandy!" She paused for breath, looking me up and down. "You've been washing your hair? On a Monday?" She frowned. "What's that on your . . ."

Before I could back away, her hand was on my cheek. My blood surged as she examined her fingers. "Looks like soot," she murmured. "If I didn't know you better, I'd think you'd had your head up the chimney."

I went to tug the towel further down the side of my face, desperate to hide anything else I'd missed in my perfunctory wash. But I pulled too hard, and it slipped off, onto the floor. The pink fabric was streaked with black. Mum's eyes went from that to the bowl of water.

"What on earth have you been doing? Not dyeing your lovely hair, surely?"

I stood there, staring at the floor, unable to reply. I could feel the pulse in my left temple. I felt as if my head were about to explode. Hot tears prickled the backs of my eyes. Suddenly the wooden boards seemed to melt and move toward me. Then everything went dark.

Chapter 22

I didn't know it when I woke up, but Mum had been with me all through the night. For a moment, when I opened my eyes, I thought I was back on the underground platform at King's Cross station.

"Is it time to go to the shop?" My voice sounded strange—not like me at all. And my throat felt dry and sore.

Mum's face was inches from mine. "Not today, love. We're at the farm. Do you remember? We came here on the train." She had a glass of water in her hand. "Can you try sitting up? Are you thirsty?"

At first it was hard to swallow, but when I got some down, the cold liquid soothed my parched throat. I looked around at the walls, the dressing table, the curtains, my brain slowly fitting the images together, like pieces of a jigsaw.

"Is that better?" Mum took the empty glass from me. "You've got some colour in your cheeks now. The ambulance crew said you just needed to rest."

"Ambulance crew?" I stared at her, uncomprehending.

"The ones who came to take the Italian to the hospital. They looked you over before they left."

"Francesco!" I blurted out his name as his soot-smeared face swam before my eyes. I clapped my hand to my mouth, realizing I'd given myself away.

Mum got up and walked across the room with my glass. "He's going to be okay. They just took him to the hospital for observation."

I heard the creak of wood as she leaned against the dressing table. She was looking not at me, but at the room reflected in the mirror. "I know that you rescued him."

"You *know*?"

"You were talking in your sleep. You said his name. You were calling him, saying he had to wake up because the barn was on fire."

"I . . . saw the smoke out of the window," I mumbled.

"That's what I don't understand." Mum's voice had an edge now. "You're terrified of fire. But you went out there to save him. An *Italian*."

In the silence, I could hear a whisper inside my head. Taslim. *Don't be afraid. She has to understand. You have to make her.*

I took a breath. Felt the rasp in my chest. I didn't know if I could get the words out. "He's a good man, Mum. He was the one who walked me home after the accident." I swallowed hard to stem the cough rising from my lungs. "He escaped from White Cross because another prisoner threatened to kill him, just for being kind—said Francesco should have murdered me while he had the chance, as revenge for the Italians who've died in the war."

"Oh my God!" She spun around.

"Don't you see, Mum? There are good people and bad people. In all countries. And this war isn't Francesco's fault."

She dropped her head. "He was able to speak a little after Ruby gave him the brandy. He apologized for stealing food and clothes while he was hiding in the barn. He sounded a decent sort of man, but I didn't want to believe it."

"Let me tell you what I know about him." I tried to ease myself into a sitting position against the pillows. Every bone in my body ached. "Before the war, he worked as a waiter in a hotel. He has three sisters and a little nephew. He idolizes Billy because his nephew was the same age when he last saw him." My voice wavered and I struggled to clear my throat. "I've been taking him food and water, but he was so worried about the risk to me that he wanted to give himself up and go back to the camp, even though that man was waiting to kill him." I searched her face. "He *is* a decent man, Mum. Will you believe it now?"

She held my gaze for a long moment. "I know I've gone on about the Italians," she said. "Perhaps I shouldn't have said those things. I'm not going to ask how you knew that he was in the barn. But after what you've told me, I don't blame you for helping him."

I don't know whether it was what she said or the way she said it that made me well up. She sounded so gentle, so compassionate now—so unlike the brittle, judgmental person I'd shied away from confiding in since the day I fell for Taslim.

"Oh, love—don't cry!" She held out her arms and hugged me to her.

My tears gave way to racking sobs. I wasn't just crying for what I'd hidden from her since we came to Cornwall. It was like a dam had burst, and I was weeping for all the lies and all the heartache of the past two years.

"My brave girl," she whispered. "I wish you could have told me about him. But I understand why you felt you couldn't. Please forgive me."

~

Part of me wanted to tell her everything. But another part was afraid of shattering the fragile bond her change of heart had forged. Would the softening toward Francesco and his compatriots extend to acceptance of someone with a different skin color?

Before I could say anything, she made me lie down again while she went to fetch me some breakfast.

"Soft-boiled eggs with bread and butter," she said as she came back into the bedroom, balancing a tray. "Nice and gentle on your throat. And a cup of tea with two sugars, to pep you up."

When I'd finished it all, she took the tray, then sat down beside me. "You said something else in your sleep," she said. "You mentioned the wharf down by the docks, where they found you when the Blitz started.

And you kept saying a name. I couldn't make it out at first, because it was foreign. Then it dawned on me: It was the boy from the Indian shop—the one who died that same night."

"Taslim." I held her gaze. Perhaps I wouldn't need to tell her. Perhaps my unconscious mind had already given enough away for her to guess the rest.

"I always thought it was a coincidence, that you and he were in the same part of London when the bombs fell. But I was afraid to ask you about it—you were in such a state when I brought you back from the hospital. I was trying to cope with everything, without your dad, and I just pushed it to the back of my mind." She turned away from me, gazing at the patch of blue sky outside the window. "I should have gone over to the Indian shop. If they'd been English, I would've taken a card and flowers. But I told myself they wouldn't understand me. I think, deep down, I was scared they'd tell me what I didn't want to know."

"I wanted to tell you." I reached across and squeezed her hand. "But *I* was scared, too. Growing up, I just wanted you and Dad to be proud of me. But when I fell for Taslim, I knew you wouldn't approve."

"I should have realised." There was a faraway look on her face. "What kind of mother wouldn't sense that her only child was in love?" She pressed her lips together, as if she were willing herself not to break down. "I think I was afraid of his family because they were different. But war changes things, doesn't it? I used to see them out of the window sometimes when I was in the shop. They looked so happy in their work—always smiling. But after they lost their boy, that changed. There was a weariness about them, as if they were carrying huge, invisible burdens on their shoulders." She closed her eyes. "Remembering that now, I see that it doesn't matter who you are, what colour your skin is, what language you speak. You hurt. You cry. You love."

My throat tightened. How I wished she could have said those things months ago, years ago.

She turned to me. "How long were you together?"

"It started in the spring before the war broke out." I told her about our plan to run away to Scotland to get married, and how that had been shelved when Dad had joined up and been sent to France. "We just had to go on meeting in secret, whenever we got the chance," I went on. "And that's why we were together, in the place where he bought supplies for their shop, when the Blitz started."

"You could have been killed. And he *was* killed." Her eyes were glassy with tears. "If I hadn't been so . . ." She doubled over, her head in her hands.

I gathered her up in my arms and rocked her against me, as if I were the mother and she the child. In that moment I saw Taslim's face hovering over Mum's shoulder. He was looking down at us. And he was smiling.

Chapter 23

I wanted to get up and dressed, but Mum urged me to try to get some more sleep. I think she wanted me to stay out of Felix's way. She said that he'd come back from the pub in a terrible temper, furious that an Italian had been hiding in his barn and that the building had been reduced to ashes.

I gripped the sides of the bed. "Does Felix know that I rescued Francesco?" Dread swept over me. If *he* knew what I'd done, he'd surely throw me out—and Mum with me.

She shook her head. "The ambulance crew are the only ones who know you were anywhere near the barn—and they won't say anything: They're not allowed to. Ruby was there, of course, when I asked them to check you over. But she knows better than to say anything to Felix."

"I hope so."

"He asked why you weren't there for the milking this morning, but I told him that you were ill in bed with the same tummy bug he'd had." She huffed out a breath. "I can't believe I got him so wrong. When we first arrived, I thought he was lovely, that Ruby was so lucky to have him. But it was all a front—and he couldn't keep it up, could he? When he comes into a room, it's like a black cloud follows him."

After she'd gone, I lay down and closed my eyes, but I couldn't sleep. Images of the blazing barn crowded my mind. Francesco in the loft, lying so still I thought he was already dead, while tongues of flame licked the rafters and sent showers of sparks onto the dry straw. I could hardly believe we'd made it out of there alive. I remembered the sleeve of my jacket catching fire, and the panic as I ripped it off and stamped on it. Then the sound of voices as I cradled Francesco in my arms, willing him to stay alive.

He's going to be okay. They just took him to the hospital for observation. Mum's words came back to me. I clung on to them. In a day or two, he would be going back to the camp. Would he tell the guards what he'd told me? Would they do something to protect him from the man who wanted to kill him?

Say a prayer for me. I pictured him calling after me when I'd dashed off to get ready for church. He'd been sitting on his makeshift bed in the hayloft with the food and water I'd brought him. And the paraffin lamp—the one I'd stolen from the milking parlor—was just a few inches away. A shard of ice formed in my belly as I realized that was the only way the fire could have started. He must have fallen asleep while it was still burning, knocked it over somehow, and sent it tumbling down the hatch to the floor below.

I don't know what made me get out of bed and reach beneath it for the Jacobean box. Perhaps it was the memory of what had given me the strength to conquer my fear and go into that burning building. I felt the need to hold Maria's book in my hands, to connect with her, and whisper words of thanks.

I lifted the journal out and climbed back into bed. I opened it to the first page and ran my fingers over the handwriting. Was it possible that a woman who had lived in this house more than three centuries ago could communicate with someone in the here and now? And if it was, why had she chosen me?

Because she wanted you to do what she was unable to.

As Taslim's voice whispered inside my head, something slipped from between the pages of the journal. It was the playing card. The ace of hearts, with the portrait of Jago Carlyon on the back. I turned it over and gazed into the dark, soulful eyes of the priest. In that moment I felt Maria's agony, painting those flames, knowing that her lover was going to be put to death, that fire would consume some, if not all, of his precious body—and that there was nothing she could do to save him.

Suddenly I heard the creak of the floorboards outside my room. I bundled the book and the portrait back inside the box and pushed it under the bed just as the door opened.

"Sorry, love." Mum's face appeared around the door. "I should have knocked." She must have thought it was the chamber pot I was pushing under the bed. "I just came to tell you that the rector's wife is here. She came to see how we all were after the fire. She asked after you, but I told her you weren't well."

"Could I see her?" I could only imagine what must be going through Dorothy's mind. No doubt she'd have put two and two together when she heard that Francesco had been hiding in our barn. She would be bursting with questions, and I owed her the truth.

"Well, if you want to," Mum said. "I could bring her up if you don't mind her seeing you in your nightclothes."

In the few minutes it took for Mum to fetch her, I tried to make myself look more respectable. But I had scarecrow hair and dark circles under my eyes. I fashioned an untidy bun, put my dressing gown on over my nightdress, and got back into bed.

If Dorothy was alarmed by the sight of me, she hid it well. "Oh, Violet, I didn't want to disturb you. How are you feeling?" She came across the room and took my hand.

"I'm all right—really I am." I felt my lip tremble. "I'm so sorry—I owe you an apology."

"Whatever for?"

"Please, come and sit down." I motioned to the chair in front of the dressing table. "I didn't tell you what really happened the night we went to the camp. I found the escaped prisoner—Francesco—in the back of the truck, and I hid him in the barn. I should have told you after the guards came to the church, but I was afraid to."

"I had a feeling you were keeping something back," she nodded. "When they said his name, I remembered the chaplain telling us about the man who'd been beaten up for helping you. It was the same man. It made perfect sense that if you'd known he was hiding in the truck, you would have wanted to help him."

"I knew it was wrong," I said. "But I felt so guilty about what had happened to him because of me."

"Well, no one needs to know." She let out a long breath. "I'm sure I would have felt just the same in your shoes. It's not always easy to know the right thing to do—not in a situation like that."

I told her how I'd sneaked past her house with Francesco after dropping the keys through the letterbox, how I'd stolen food and clothes for him while he hid in the barn, and how I'd helped him plan an escape from Britain via Falmouth.

"He was supposed to leave last night," I said. "I was going to steal a bicycle for him. But when I looked out of the window to check that no one was about, I saw the smoke." I wanted to tell her about the hawk rapping on my window, but I was afraid she'd think I'd lost my mind. Instead, I described finding Francesco, and the struggle to get him out of the barn before the whole building collapsed.

"I can't even remember how I did it," I said. "It's all a blur. You see, I'm terrified of fire. I've had a phobia ever since the night I told you about, when my boyfriend . . ." My voice fractured as that word came out. I couldn't finish the sentence.

"I'm not surprised." Dorothy put her hand on my arm. "It was incredibly brave of you to go in there and rescue Francesco. You know, dear, I've been praying for you ever since you told me about what happened to you in London."

Her worried smile triggered a prickle of tears. "I prayed, too, once," I murmured. "In church last Sunday, I asked God to keep Francesco safe. But he didn't. He could have died in that fire."

"But God *did* save him," she replied. "Through you."

"Did he?" I looked away. I was thinking about Maria, of the vision I'd had of her in this very room, taking over my body and propelling me down the stairs and along the track to the barn. Was that how God, if such a being existed, answered people's prayers?

"Can I show you something?" I slid out of bed and retrieved the box from underneath it. "This is the journal I was telling you about. Maria Wolveden's confessional. And inside is a portrait of Jago Carlyon." I put the book in her hands. "I know you'll think it's mumbo jumbo, but I really felt her presence when I was standing here, smelling the smoke coming through the window, trying to conquer my terror of going out there. It was as if she was giving me her strength, her courage, and . . ." I trailed off. I couldn't tell Dorothy what I'd truly felt: that Maria's spirit had possessed me for the time it had taken to get Francesco out of danger.

An expression of wonder spread over her face as she opened the book and began reading. Perhaps she hadn't heard what I'd said. "What an amazing thing!" She ran her fingers over the stiff leather binding, as if she were caressing someone she loved. Then she slid the playing card out from between the pages and examined it, front and back. "Jago Carlyon," she whispered. "What a handsome fellow. No wonder she fell for him. But these flames behind him . . . It's so tragic . . ." She looked up. "I heard what you said, dear—about you feeling that she was giving you strength in your hour of need. Who knows if or why that could be true? But God moves in mysterious ways. What matters is that whatever happened to you last night was a force for good. A man's life was saved because of what you experienced. And it was a direct result of you finding this book."

"I hadn't thought of it like that," I said. "But what'll happen to him now? As soon as he's better, they'll take him back to White Cross, and that man will be waiting for him."

"Try not to worry," she replied. "Humphrey's been on the phone to Lieutenant Colonel Graves. He's told him exactly what happened: the reason why Francesco had no choice but to escape. The man who threatened him is going to be moved to a different camp in another part of the country."

I cried when she told me that. But this time they were tears of utter relief. We sat hugging each other until Mum came up with a tray of tea.

"She's very good, your mum," Dorothy said as the door closed again.

"I know," I murmured. "And in case you're wondering, I've told her all about what happened with Francesco. She knows about Taslim now, too."

"Well, that's good news. It must have been such a strain for you, bottling it up."

I nodded. "The strange thing is that telling her about the fire helped me let go of everything else. I was always so afraid to tell her about Taslim. But she's changed—and I think Francesco had something to do with that."

Dorothy smiled over the rim of her teacup. "As I said, dear, God moves in mysterious ways."

I must have fallen asleep soon after she left. There were no nightmares, no dreadful images of blazing buildings and melting faces. Just peaceful darkness.

It was just after four o'clock when Mum came to tell me she was going to take Billy for a walk in his pram. "Ruby has a doctor's appointment," she said. "So I said I'd look after him while she's out."

My stomach turned over. I'd forgotten all about my aunt's assignation with Carlo. I couldn't believe she was still going ahead with it. Surely it was madness, with all the furor over Francesco. I swung my legs out of bed and stood up. "I'll come with you," I said. "I feel absolutely fine now."

"I don't want you to overdo it, love," she replied. "Why don't you go and sit in the kitchen—you could make a start on peeling the potatoes if you feel up to it, then when I get back, we'll make supper together."

When she'd gone, I pulled on some clothes. I needed to go to the privy. As I opened the door of my room, I heard raised voices coming from the bedroom across the landing. I paused to listen.

"You're wearing lipstick? To go to the doctor's?" Felix bellowed the accusation. He sounded as if he were standing right next to me.

Aunt Ruby said something I couldn't make out.

"Are you sure you're not jumping on the Bodmin bus to visit that Eye-tie bastard in hospital?" The venom in his voice was chilling. "I should have finished him off when I had the chance!"

"What are you talking about?" This time my aunt's voice rang out loud and clear.

"I saw him—sniffing around the farmyard, like a dog after a bitch on heat!"

"What?"

"I followed him all the way back to his hiding place. Should've taken the bloody gun. Shouldn't have waited."

"You *knew* he was in the barn? Felix! You didn't . . . ?"

"You'll never know that, will you? Nobody will."

I stood, paralyzed, unable to take in what I'd just heard. There was a shout and a thud, then the sound of footsteps running down the stairs on the other side of the house.

"You come back here, Ruby! I swear I'll kill you if you don't!"

I heard him curse, and the creak of the floorboards, as if he were pacing up and down the room. I crept down the stairs. I was terrified that he'd hear me and realize I'd been listening. But I was more afraid for my aunt. When I opened the door of the dairy, I caught sight of her. She was through the gate and running along the track.

I had a sudden, horrifying premonition of Felix going after her with his gun. I raced back through the house to the kitchen. If I could get there before him, I could hide it. But I was too late. I saw him through the window, striding across the farmyard with the gun down by his side.

He was through the gate when I got within hailing distance. "Wait!" I panted for breath as I yelled at him.

"You!" He turned as I caught up with him. "What the hell do you want?"

"Please," I gasped. "Don't go after her!"

He looked at me as though I were something on the bottom of his boot.

He raised the gun to shoulder height and pointed it straight at me. "Get back in the house! *Now!*"

I thought my legs would buckle under me, but I stood my ground. My throat was so tight I wasn't sure I could speak. But I had to. It was the only way to stop him. "You've got it all wrong! It wasn't *her* the Italian was looking for—it was me!"

"What?" He lowered the gun.

"I hid him in the barn when he escaped from the camp. Aunt Ruby had nothing to do with it."

"You little whore!" In one quick movement he was through the gate, pushing me back against the wall of the farmyard, pressing the barrel of the gun against my neck, choking me. I clawed at him, trying to catch his face, but I couldn't reach. I could hear him breathing—that vile rasping—and I could feel his fingers on my belly, yanking at the waistband of my trousers. I tried to scream, but he'd jammed the gun against my windpipe.

Suddenly, the sky went dark. I couldn't see. But I could still hear. An almighty screech—as if the gates of hell had opened and the devil himself had flown out. Then a human sound: Felix cursing, crying out. I fell sideways as the gun came away from my neck. I was on the ground when the air above my head exploded.

For a moment I lay there, stunned, my ears ringing. I thought he'd shot me. But I felt no pain. Slowly I eased myself up on my elbows. And then I saw him. He was flat on his back, blood pooling in the dirt beneath his head. And perched on the gate, gazing down at him, was the hawk.

Chapter 24

The sudden rumble of wheels sent the bird flying off out of sight. It was Mum, bringing Billy back along the track in the pram.

I thought she would go to pieces at the sight that met her eyes as she came through the gate. But it seemed to ignite an inner strength I didn't know she possessed.

By some miracle Billy had slept through the noise of the gunfire. Once Mum had helped me inside and sat me down with a cup of tea, she told me what she'd seen: the hawk, swooping down on Felix, raking his head with its talons, knocking him off-balance. She hadn't realized that I was there, too. My head had been below the top of the wall.

I told her that I'd come out of the privy to find him taking aim at the hawk, and when I'd challenged him, he'd turned on me. I could have told her what he'd planned to do to me, but I didn't. Explaining it would have meant telling her the real reason he'd been out in the farmyard with the gun. And I couldn't do that, because Aunt Ruby was going to need Mum's support more than ever now.

What I'd learned was that sometimes it wasn't wise to tell the whole truth. You had to wait for the right time. And in my aunt's case, that might be never. If she chose to tell Mum about Carlo, that had to be her decision, not mine.

I said I'd go down to the rectory and ask if I could use their phone. But Mum insisted on going herself. While I waited for the police to arrive, I went to check on Billy, who was still lying asleep in the pram outside the kitchen door, blissfully unaware that his father's dead body was lying just yards away.

It hit me that it had happened again, that tragedy seemed to follow wherever I went. This little boy was going to grow up without a father. And that wouldn't have happened if I hadn't gone running after Felix.

He had it coming. He was the author of his own destruction. Taslim's voice had an edge I hadn't heard before. *And your aunt was seeing Carlo before you came on the scene. It was bound to end in violence. He might have killed her if you hadn't stopped him.*

"I know it wasn't my fault that the gun went off," I whispered. "And you know how mean he was to me. But I feel as bad as if I'd shot him myself."

Mean? That's putting it mildly. He would have raped you, Violet. And he would have shut you up by threatening to throw you and your mum out if you said anything.

Billy stirred in his sleep, his dark eyelashes fluttering like butterflies as some dream unfolded. As I watched him, an image flashed across my mind's eye. I saw Maria, pinioned against the rowan tree in the woods, Robert Archer leering at her. The dream played out in slow motion. I saw Phantom's talons extend as the bird hurtled through the branches, saw the flesh open on Archer's bald head, heard the crack of bone as he fell against the tangled roots of the tree.

History repeats itself. There was no mistaking the vindication in Taslim's voice.

~

Dorothy was a great support to us all in the weeks after Felix's death. She petitioned Lieutenant Colonel Graves to allow men from the camp to provide the help we needed to keep the farm running. He agreed on the condition that the prisoners lodged in the village, not at the farm itself, because we were three women without a man. Dorothy kindly offered to put them up at the rectory.

We were allowed to choose two prisoners from the gang I'd worked with in the fields. I asked for Francesco, but I thought it unlikely he'd be allowed to leave the camp after what had happened. To my surprise, the request was approved. Dorothy said the chaplain at White Cross had supported his case because Francesco had worked so hard to build the Catholic chapel at the camp.

He brought Giovanni, the doctor, with him. As well as lifting the almost impossible burden of keeping the farm going, their presence brought a lightness to the place. The sense of dread I'd felt when Felix was alive vanished. Waking up on those dark winter mornings, I didn't mind going off to the milking shed, knowing that Francesco would be waiting for me there. Dorothy and her husband were very relaxed about their lodgers' comings and goings, so we often spent our evenings together as well.

Sometimes we looked after Billy when my aunt went out on a date with Carlo. She couldn't bring herself to admit to Mum what had been going on while Felix was still alive—so her story was that she was going to the cinema with a friend. I was still afraid for her, breaking the law to see the man she was in love with, but I could see how happy it made her.

The week after Christmas, when I went to take the mobile shop to White Cross, Dorothy greeted me with great excitement. She said she'd received a letter from the friend who worked in the Bodleian Library in Oxford.

"She's found a book published in 1621 by a man called James Lyon. It describes his escape from the Tower of London in 1606. At the end of April that year, a Spanish envoy was sent to England to congratulate King James on his deliverance from the Gunpowder Plot. Lyon said he escaped the Tower of London by pretending to be part of the envoy's retinue. The livery was smuggled into his cell, in advance of a request by the Spanish delegation to visit the famous fortress. Lyon passed for one of the attendants and slipped away unnoticed. He sailed to Spain with them a few hours later."

I stared at her, bewildered. "James Lyon?"

She nodded. "I know—it took a while for the penny to drop when I read it. Jago is the Cornish version of James, and Lyon could be a shortened version of Carlyon. But there's something else that absolutely nails it." She smiled. "Look at this." She passed me a sheet of paper. The typescript at the top said "Transcript Folio 113B, Page 67, Bodleian Library." As I read it, my heart soared.

> *I was joined on the ship by the lady who concealed me from my pursuers when I was a fugitive in Cornwall. Whilst I was held prisoner in the Tower of London, awaiting execution, she was arrested for the crimes of witchcraft and murder. These were baseless accusations, but she, too, faced execution. By God's good grace, she escaped from Launceston Gaol thanks to the same friends who had conveyed me to her farm. They had learned of her fate when attempting to deliver a secret letter from me.*
>
> *They were able to free her by means of a hawk, which flew to the window of her cell with a key attached to its leg. Under cover of darkness, she rode across country until she reached a safe house in London. After hiding there for several weeks, she took her leave in the same manner as me, dressed in the livery of the Spanish envoy.*
>
> *We were married in Santiago de Compostela in September of the same year, following my departure from the priesthood. We rejoice in a son and a daughter from our union.*

I had tears in my eyes as I passed the paper back to Dorothy. Maria had escaped. She hadn't met a miserable death in a grim prison cell. She had reunited with the man she loved. And he had kept his promise to her.

~

I told Francesco all about it as we sat by the fire that evening. I showed him the journal, with the painting inside, and explained how I'd found it, along with the hawking whistle, under the floor in my room. I told him about the persecution of Catholics in Britain at the time Maria lived at the farmhouse and pointed out the marks scratched into the wooden beam.

He went across to the fireplace and ran his fingers over the letters. I could see his lips moving, puzzling out their meaning. When he turned to me, with the flames behind him, I had the strangest feeling, as if the image on the back of the ace of hearts had suddenly come to life.

I moved toward him. The spitting logs and the curls of smoke no longer had the power to frighten me. I think I knew in that moment that, just as I had overcome my fear of fire, I could rekindle the ability to love. I wanted to put my hand over his, feel the warmth of his skin. But I hesitated. In the weeks since he'd come to live in the village, he'd never tried to repeat that kiss we'd had in the barn. We both knew the risk of stepping across that line. He was forbidden to me, just as Taslim had been.

This war stole your first love. It was Maria's voice, whispering in my ear. *Wars don't last forever. Don't let your hearts grow cold.*

I took a step closer to the fire. Reaching out, I traced the marks on the wooden beam, until my fingers met Francesco's.

"She protected you," he whispered.

"Maria?" Was *he* hearing her, too?

He nodded. "The letters—the double *V*, the *A*, and the *M*. We have the same in my country: We call her the Virgin of Virgins. And when we ask for her help, we sing 'Ave Maria.'"

I smiled. A different Maria. But no doubt Dorothy would agree with him—that the source of the strength I'd found was the higher power they both believed in.

I would never know how what I'd experienced was possible. But as I stood there by the fireplace, I felt a warmth inside that had nothing to do with the heat from the burning logs.

Thank you. I didn't say the words aloud. I didn't need to. Because wherever she was now, I was sure she would hear me.

ACKNOWLEDGMENTS

I have my brother-in-law Graham Lawrence to thank for pointing out the "witch marks" etched into the wooden beams of our house by people who lived in it more than four centuries ago. Graham is a conservation planning officer and spends his working life inspecting ancient buildings. Without his expert eye, I would never have spotted the marks nor understood their significance.

Thanks also to Nicola and David Craddock, whose lovely Cornish home I stayed in while researching the nearby village of St Columb Minor.

I'm grateful to the Penybont History Group—it was on their tour of Radnorshire Museum that my attention was drawn to the silver hawking whistle from the Tudor period.

Thank you to my agent, Danielle Marshall, and to Marilyn Brigham and the team at Lake Union for the great job they do. I'm also grateful to Jodi Warshaw for her invaluable input in the editing process.

My friend Janet Thomas remains a constant source of advice and encouragement. Many thanks to her and to my family, as always, for their love and support. I have dedicated this book to the youngest member, Ivy—she's only two years old, but I hope that she'll enjoy reading it when she'd old enough.

AUTHOR'S NOTE

Although fictional, Lowartha was inspired by a real place—the late medieval farmhouse that I have been lucky enough to call home for the past two years. It's located in Wales, not Cornwall, but the architecture and interior are the same—including the "witch marks." The only concessions to the modern era are electricity and indoor bathrooms.

The idea that the house might once have been occupied by a young woman who hunted with a falcon came from the discovery, in the local museum, of the Tudor hawking whistle. The haunting cries of kites and buzzards are a regular feature of life at the farmhouse today.

Maria's forbidden lover, Jago Carlyon, was inspired by a portrait painted by the celebrated Elizabethan miniaturist Nicholas Hilliard. The name of the subject has been lost over the centuries, but to my eyes, the man with the cross-shaped earring looking out from a background of flames was a Catholic priest who risked death by fire for his faith.

History records that one such priest, John Gerard, escaped imprisonment in the Tower of London after being tortured. Suspected of involvement in the Gunpowder Plot, he boarded a ship disguised as a footman in the retinue of the Spanish ambassador. He wrote a book titled *The Autobiography of a Hunted Priest* and lived to be seventy-two years old.

Taslim is a fictional character, but the Taj Stores really existed, being one of the first grocery shops set up in London by migrants from India in the 1930s.

St Columb Minor is a village near the sea in West Cornwall, and in the 1940s nearby White Cross Camp held Italian and German prisoners. After the war, more than a thousand Italian POWs remained in Britain as civilian rural workers. The law against them fraternizing with British women was lifted in 1946.

ABOUT THE AUTHOR

Photo © 2017 Isabella Ashford

Lindsay Jayne Ashford is the bestselling author of the historical novels *Through the Mist*, *A Feather on the Water*, *The House at Mermaid's Cove*, *The Snow Gypsy*, *Whisper of the Moon Moth*, *The Woman on the Orient Express*, and *The Color of Secrets*, as well as the Megan Rhys contemporary crime series. The first woman to graduate from Queens' College, Cambridge, Lindsay earned a degree in criminology and was a reporter for the BBC before becoming a freelance journalist, writing for a number of national magazines and newspapers. She lives in a late-medieval farmhouse in Wales with her husband, Steve, and their dog, Pablo, and has a writing cabin among the trees that she shares with a pair of tawny owls. When she's not writing, she enjoys dancing and gardening. For more information, visit www.lindsay-jayne-ashford.com.